Whole Lot of Hullabaloo

Whole Lot of Hullabaloo

A Twenty-First Century Campus Phantasmagoria

Christopher Fried

Retro 85

Richmond, Va

Christopher Fried/Retro 85
www.christopherfried.com

Publisher's Note: This is a work of fiction. Names, characters, places, and incidents are a product of the author's imagination. Locales and public names are sometimes used for atmospheric purposes. Any resemblance to actual people, living or dead, or to businesses, companies, events, institutions, or locales is completely coincidental.

Whole Lot of Hullabaloo/ Christopher Fried. -- 1st ed.
ISBN 978-1-7357113-1-7

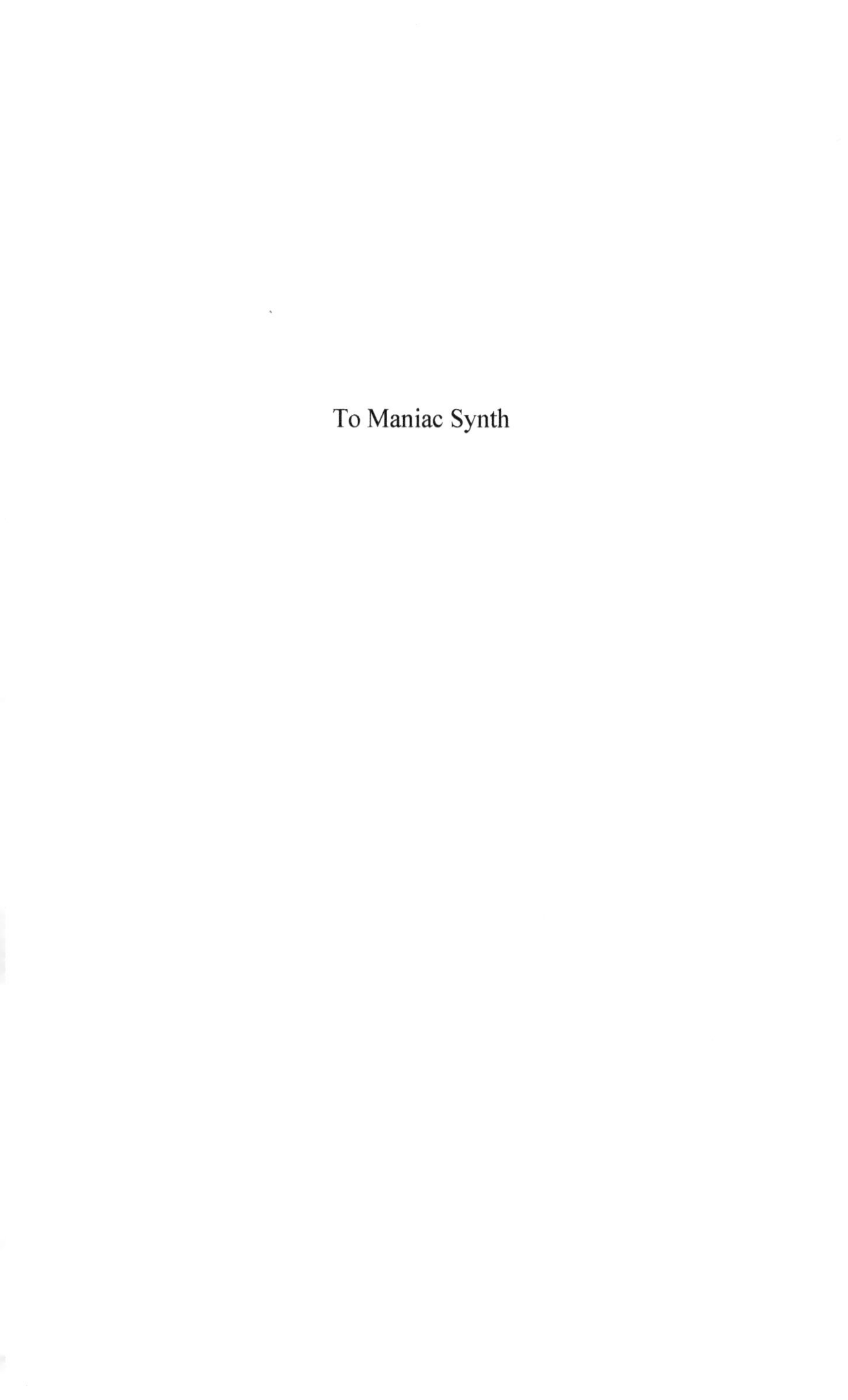

To Maniac Synth

Chapter 1

Sam stared out the open window, observing some commotion below. The late summer breeze swept into the room, blowing a few papers off the desk. Turning around, he gathered them up, placing them back on the corner of the desk under a paperweight. He then resumed his position before the window, letting out a loud sigh. One could see his belly rise and fall like a small wave. He sloppily wore a sport coat and khaki pant combo. Just missing his navy sport coat, a seminoticeable smudge of mustard stained his shirt. His blue and white tie of a traditional pattern was lightly worn. His glasses of medium thickness fit his face perfectly and said that he was a professional in the service of humankind. As he lifted his head upward, another short exhalation shot out of his tight, thin lips.

"Sam, anything wrong?" said the secretary sitting in the corner of the room. She looked away from her computer monitor, still typing away furiously.

"No, Jane. I'm just thinking as I look on this." He raised his arm and thrust it out the window as if a leader showing a group the way to a promised land or at least the way to the newest Asian fusion joint a couple blocks down the street.

"Well, it's a beautiful day. Rather cool for this time of the year. Before I came into work, I thought it was going to be very torrid, but it's been very pleasant today. I probably should've looked up the weather. You know, I normally do. But because you had me working on those files at home, I didn't have time.

But now, with you having that window wide open, I think that I'm going to have to get my jacket on." She started to get up to retrieve it but then stopped herself.

"My thoughts are less on the weather and more on all that activity. Can you hear it?" Sam cupped his ear and positioned his head outside the window.

For a brief moment, Jane had the image of Sam slipping and falling to the ground below. "You mean the students?"

He turned around and stared at Jane. "Of course I mean the students. If you were where I am, you could see the frenzy of activity, the rushing to class, the earnestness on their faces as they discuss things. It's a wonderful thing."

"I'm sure it is." Her face had dropped down to a number of papers she had collated for the day.

"You see, I don't believe that you understand. I was born for this moment. I mean, not this specific moment, but for this position. I remember when I was a little boy, say when I was around seven or eight, I dreamed of running an empire just like Napoleon. Not to say I wanted to become a tyrant. Even by the time I became a teen, I found the military life distasteful from reading books. No, I knew that I was destined to run whatever I did as a well-oiled machine. All different parts coming together. That's what I see when I observe these bright, earnest youths swarming around like bees in spring."

"I always enjoy the students when they come and see me," Jane said. "You never know what some of them are going to say. Such personalities."

"Oh yes. That's why I plan for this school year to be the best ever. Sound ambitious?"

"A little." The secretary had a puzzled look on her face that was juxtaposed with the trust that she usually had for him. He had led the last two years at Central Ohio University decently.

"We've got excellent programs, hardworking professors, and outstanding, exciting upcoming events," he said. He beamed a wide smile while turning his head back to a scene below. "And programs of inclusion. We mustn't forget that."

"I agree." She nodded, although one wouldn't know whether weariness also contributed to the head movement.

"We're embarking on new endeavors. I want this to become the finest university in the Midwest. Perhaps the finest research institution in the region. We can make it happen. I have faith." He scratched his moustache and then shut the window.

She was glad as the chill of the breeze was beginning to sink into her bones. She was also getting a bit tired of her boss's rhetoric, although she wouldn't complain to his face. He was president, and she was just a secretary. He always had much on his mind. Perhaps too much. However, he was Mr. Castle. He needed to have much on his mind. It's required, or else all would go to pot.

"Listen here…" Sam began. The phone began to ring, and Jane picked it up.

"The office of President Castle; Ms. Jane Stewart speaking. How may I help you?"

A moment of silence passed on the phone, then the sound of heavy breathing began.

"Hello?" she said.

"Ah, yes—this is the dean of students. I hoped to speak to Sam if he's available. I know that they dropped a heavy workload on his desk."

"Who is it?" Sam said. He walked away from the window, almost appearing to glide to Jane's desk. He leaned forward, hanging over the desk.

She turned the phone away from her and said, "It's Tom. He says that he wants to speak with you. I'm not sure, but it sounds urgent. He sounded out of breath over the phone." She handed the phone to him.

"Hey!" Sam said. "How are you feeling? I heard that you came down with a cold. I hope you're resting."

"I'm feeling a bit better. My wife has been giving me so much hot tea that I feel like I have to go piss every couple of hours these past days. However, I guess I'm getting out whatever I have in me. You know that normally I'm never missing at work. I feel like I'm letting the students and staff down when I'm absent." A slight cough sputtered at the end of the line.

"Ha! I know that you're not slacking off. I don't think you missed more than two days last spring term." Sam paused as if hesitating to ask a serious question then continued, "Well, what's it you want to ask me? You know that I'm a busy man." He chuckled.

"You're always a kidder. However, it's nothing urgent. Has the mail arrived at the office?"

"I believe so. Let me check." Removing the phone from his ear, he said, "Jane, has anything come in today?"

"Yeah, the mail carrier arrived about forty-five minutes ago. I believe you received something."

"Hey!" Sam spoke back into the phone.

"Sam?"

"Yeah, the mail was just delivered. I don't know if you personally received anything, but I can check your box. If you want, I can swing by your house this evening and drop it off if you have something. I want to talk to you anyways about some plans I have for this term and the spring. Is that okay?"

"Sounds fine. My wife is preparing lasagna. I know how you love it."

"Great, I'll see you then." Sam hung up the phone and turned to Jane.

"Was anything the matter?" she said. "His voice sounded rough."

"Just a bit of a cold, but I believe that his mail has started to pile up. I'll bring it by this evening. He should be returning to work in a few days, but I want to check up on him. You never know how this thing is going to go because he's rarely sick."

"That would be nice of you," she said. She thought, *What a kind man. All colleges could benefit from such an attitude.*

Little did she know that although Sam cared for the health of his staff, more than altruism had compelled him to make a home visit. Plans existed. Grand plans that had to be discussed if they wanted another successful school year. Sam smiled to his secretary as he gathered some papers that she had set on the other corner of his desk. He then left the room, waving goodbye without looking behind. Jane dreamily watched him before she returned to arranging the papers in front of her.

* * *

"Troy!" a voice yelled. Troy recognized that sound. He looked around the campus gardens for his friend Ian. To his left the ultimate frisbee fiends dashed and crashed. Someone had missed the thrown disk and fallen to the ground. The player quickly rose and resumed playing. To Troy's right a trio of foxes sunbathed while they alternated between studying and conversing. *Thank God that the weather warmed up*, he thought. *Have to love the views.* He stared a bit before turning his head, catching sight of Ian. Good old Ian. What a character.

"Just coming from class?" Troy said. He gave a slight salute. He didn't know why he had done it. He never gave this greeting to his other friends.

"No. Biology ended about forty-five minutes ago. I stopped at the cafeteria. See the bagel?" He took a giant bite out of the cream cheese–slathered monstrosity.

"It's almost dinnertime. Don't you want something more substantial? I thought we were going to go work out around five." Troy pulled out his cell phone and tapped it.

"Who says that bagels only have to be eaten at a certain time? Anyways, they give me a decent energy boost." Ian waved the bagel after taking another big bite.

Boy, he's demolishing that thing, Troy thought. By the time they finished talking, he would likely devour the whole thing. As he shook his head, he turned his attention back to the trio of girls. He wondered if they saw him sneaking a peek at them. That was always a dilemma a young man had to face when looking at the ladies. Turning his attention back to Ian, he said, "I'm kidding with you, man. It's not the first time I've seen you chow down on those things in the afternoon. Anyways, how about going to the gym?"

"I'll head over there after I grab my bag back at the dorm. What time is it? I left my phone back in my room."

"It's almost five, man." Troy slightly raised his voice. His hands rose too. "Literally, it's ten till. You see my bag."

Ian glanced down at it and smiled. "I better hurry. The gym gets crowded quickly on Fridays."

"That's cool. I'll meet you there." Troy shrugged his shoulders and picked up his bag. "See you soon."

Ian ran over to a trash can by the gardens and threw the bagel remains away. He then pushed through a crowd of students as he sprinted to the WHH dorm.

Troy shook his head. *Ian—the guy's crazy, but you got to love him.* He began walking to the gym, but not before he took another glance at the sunbathing beauties. He then jetted off.

* * *

A frenzy of activity exploded in the gym. Legs treading, pumping, climbing, cycling, stretching, walking, jogging, and running. Arms pushing, pumping, climbing, pulling, stretching, bending, and rowing. Silences simmered, and then grunts and groans flooded out. First, there was strain, then the relaxation of completed exhaustion. All this on a Friday evening before the onset of the weekend pleasure journey.

Troy exerted himself on one of the cycle machines. He had a fierce look of determination on his face, as if his pedaling would eventually unhinge the cycle from the floor and propel it to freedom outdoors. He wiped away the sweat dripping into his eyes. He looked back to the entrance as he had ten minutes earlier. *Where is that crazy fool?* he thought. *He's not going to get any playing time this year if he doesn't take his exercise regimen seriously. Anyways, why should I worry? He knows what's necessary.*

As Troy contemplated, the heavy doors of the gym swung open and shut with a bang. Ian jogged over to his friend with his earbuds blasting some party/exercise anthem. He removed them before speaking.

"Sorry that I'm late. Eric was waiting by my room. He had some papers from Coach Leonard that I needed to review. I didn't have time to look over them in detail, but I wanted to have a cursory glance through."

"What are they about?"

"I think it concerns practice rescheduling. That's all I really looked at. When I get back to the dorm, I'll take a closer look. I bet that it's nothing really important." He put down his bag and hopped onto the cycle beside Troy.

"Before you came in, I was thinking about that. You told me that Coach Leonard wanted a perfect season this spring. No screwups. You slacking on your workouts won't cut it." Troy gave Ian a knowing look then restarted his cycling.

"I got everything covered. I know that Coach Leonard is a pain. I know more than you do. Why do you even care? You don't even play lacrosse."

"I played in high school. Moreover, I'm your friend. And I hate people getting on the case of my friends even if those people have a point."

"Hey man, I'm going to do great this year. I didn't get a lot of playing time last year, but it wasn't my fault. Anyways, the coach needs me this season. We lost too many seniors last year to graduation. I'm sure that I'm going to start; I'm not going to warm any benches."

"You better start getting serious. You want to lose that

scholarship?"

"Don't worry. Everything is under control. It's why I'm here busting a sweat beside you." Ian shot out a slight smile, pedaling as hard as ever.

Troy shook his head. "You're one crazy dude. But I guess I wouldn't have it any other way."

"You know what?"

"What?" Troy said, curious as Ian had had that transformation of his face when he went from joking to serious in an instant.

"Seen any nice girls lately?"

Troy turned on his cheesy grin face. "Just look around you. We're surrounded by all these workout bunnies."

"I'm not kidding around." Ian went from serious to serious overdrive.

"Why are you asking me?"

"I just wondered…" Ian said. He looked up and then turned to his friend. "It's just that there's this girl in my class."

"Have you asked her out yet?"

"Quit jumping the gun, Troy. I said that I just saw her."

"No you didn't, but continue."

"She's kind of cute. Almost hot.

"What's her name?"

"Milly."

Troy laughed. "As in Milli Vanilli?

"Your such a douche, man!" Ian retorted. "Her full name is Milly Kwon."

"I know that girl!" Troy's voice rose, and a few gym rats looked askance at him. Troy paid them no mind.

"You do?" Ian's facial expression switched from seriousness

to bewilderment.

"I don't know much about her. I only spoke with her a few times. She attended my freshman drama class last year. It was a good class. Pretty chill and slack. Milly got really into it. During one of the few times we spoke, she said that she wanted to become an actor. Said that her parents weren't cool about it. I told her to go for it. She's pretty talented. Although I'm not much of a theater person, I saw her in a play last year. It was all right."

"I don't know what to do. I don't even know if I'm her type."

"Ian! For a person whom some people on campus say is outrageous, you can be so timid at times. You don't even have to ask her out on an official date. Just say you want to go to the movies. Even invite her to a party. Isn't there one coming up soon?"

"Jay's having something on September seventeenth. Did you hear about it? He always throws good parties. Probably plenty of shennanigans. Before his graduation he wants to go out in style."

"Afterward we could go the movies. I don't mind playing third wheel, although I bet that I could pick up some chick from the party. How's that sound?"

"Seems like a plan, brother." With things optimistically a go, renewed determination appeared on Ian's face. He put that determination into his pedaling, and in a few minutes, he reglistened from his exertion.

For the next ten minutes Troy pedaled in silence. He thought about the upcoming school year. The classes, the parties, the chicks. If only he were sure what he wanted to major in, life would be a slam dunk. However, he still had until spring semester for that decision. Now was the time to grab life by the bollocks, as they say. Life here seemed dull, but it could also be interesting if the people were interesting. And yes, Central Ohio had some interesting characters, especially his friend Ian. Troy then moved from the cycle machine over to the leg lift machine.

* * *

The drive over to Tom's house from the university was pleasant. Sam expected heavy rush hour traffic, but the traffic flow was steady, and there were none of the jams that there usually were at the start of the weekend. It was a relaxing half-hour drive, especially since Sam had one of his favorite CDs playing. Sam sang along, looking from side to side to make sure that other drivers didn't notice. He tapped his fingers on the roof of the car and the steering wheel and thought of what he wanted to mention to Tom.

Pulling up to the house, he gathered together his papers and Tom's mail. He sauntered up to the side door and gave a resounding knock. After a slight delay, the door opened.

"Sam!" Tom showed up at the door, pressing a handful of tissues to his bright red face. With him being a ginger and suffering from a cold and his constant nose blowing, his head looked like a firecracker at explosion point. He didn't look well.

"I'm sorry that you've felt sick. I know that you're worried about your paperwork piling up." Sam stepped through the doorway, nodding to Tom's wife, who was shifting various dishes from the stovetop to the table in the dining room. "Hello, Lisa. Slaving away in the kitchen again? Smells very good. What is it? Garlic bread?"

She turned around and said, "Yes, along with the lasagna. I also made some salad, although I know that it's a struggle for you to eat your greens. You should try to eat some. You can't survive on carbs alone."

"I know." Sam rubbed his belly. "I probably should cut back on them anyway. I've gained some weight this past month. Always seems to happen at the beginning of fall term. It's probably nervousness." He stopped rubbing, moved over to the dining room table, and sat down.

"What about Valerie? Has she noticed?" Lisa's hands rested on her hips in a motherly manner.

"Didn't Tom tell you that she left for Tokyo?"

"No."

"Yes, I did." With a hoarse voice, Tom spoke up. "You probably forgot." He moved to sit across from Sam.

"When did she leave then?" she asked. Although Lisa wasn't close with Valerie, she usually knew whether she was in Columbus or not.

"Just after opening convocation, on the twenty-seventh. You know how she's devoted to her artwork. She has a showing this month." Sam looked at the tablecloth and saw a smudge of a stain. He took his index fingernail and tried to remove it. It wouldn't come off, even with brute irritation. He looked up at Lisa. "Don't misunderstand me. I support my wife's career. She's a brilliant painter, and I can't wait to hear about the success of her exhibition." He paused as a downcast demeanor hovered over his face. "But it seems like she's always on the go. Sometimes it seems like I don't even know where she's going, or at least where I'm going with her." A tear appeared at the corner of his eye. He turned his face away in embarrassment.

"Listen, Sam, has distance grown between you two?" Tom

said.

"No, nothing like that." He paused. "At least I don't think so. It's hard to explain. You see, Valerie would hardly ever make an effort to make a meal like this. Even if she didn't have to cook, she wouldn't go out of the way to host. It's not in her. But I shouldn't complain. I knew this when I married her eight years ago. I don't know." Sam shook his head and turned his attention back to his hosts. "At times, I feel that there is this black hole in what ostensibly appears to be a good life. Like a hole in a donut."

"Strange metaphor, Sam. You must have food on the brain. Don't worry. We'll fix that. Dinner, I believe, is almost ready." Tom turned to his wife. "Is the lasagna done?"

She stuck a fork into the layered goodness. "I would just give it five more minutes to cool down. With all this emotional drama, we don't want burnt tongues in addition, do we?" She gave a quirky smile to Sam.

"Tom, I'm going to head to the bathroom and clean up a bit before we sit down to eat." He got up to leave, and as he left the room, Lisa and Tom looked at each other with worried faces. Sam was a good friend, and they hated to see him distraught. Perhaps it was good that he had immersed himself into college affairs so that his mind was distant from the personal. Valerie was nice, but she became flighty at times, if that was the right word. And Sam said it: She hadn't changed; she traveled a lot when he started seeing her. But her career had taken off the past three years, while he had remained the president of a good-but-not-exceptional university. It's better than what could be. One could only hope for the best and that the divide would not worsen.

After Sam cheered up a bit, he thoroughly enjoyed the dinner.

In his mind the lasagna was the most delicious lasagna that Lisa had ever cooked. She had seasoned the meat just right. Not too spicy and not too bland. The cheese clung to your palate in a good way. She had used a combination of cheeses: mozzarella, provolone, parmesan, asiago. Man oh man, that cheese really popped with flavor. Just using mozzarella will make okay lasagna. But will it be lasagna that makes you want to shout out "Mamma-mia, that's a some good pasta"? No. You want lasagna that comes together: the meat, the cheese, and, don't forget, the pasta (when it's not too thin nor too thick). At the end, your inner Italian will come out. And though you're satisfied and full, you'll feel like going out and having somebody whacked. Not that you're angry or anything. It's amazing what a good food experience will do to somebody's body and spirit. For Sam, this was Lisa's lasagna, though some good barbecue and slaw would also make him shout, "Soowee!"

Lisa cleared off and wiped down the table. As she brought the dishes to the sink, Sam and Tom walked to the living room. "You okay with the mess?" Tom asked. "I don't want you to think that we're leaving you to clean up after us like we're naughty little boys."

Lisa waved them off. "I know that you guys have a lot of college business to discuss." She looked at the clock on the wall. "It's almost seven-thirty. I don't believe that Sam wants to stay too long. So hurry to your little meeting. Tomorrow night you can do the dishes."

Tom walked over to his wife and kissed her on the cheek. A glimmer of a smile appeared from the corner of her mouth. Even if he got her sick, such affection was bliss. She went back to scrubbing the pan, and the two college administrators retired to the living room. As Tom settled onto the couch, Sam sat in the rocking chair across from him. As he began rocking gently, he sipped on some hot tea he had brought from the dinner table and said:

"Even though you primarily deal with student issues, I want to hear some feedback on some of the professors that started this year, as well as on some of the events the university has planned."

"No problem, Sam. You know that I'm there for you."

Sam set the cup down. "First, I know that Professor George Graves is still angry over his early retirement. In honesty, I really didn't want it to happen. He taught at the university for eighteen years." Tom nodded, and Sam continued. "Early in his career, he published brilliant articles. I can still go back to them today and find some new gem. And that book on Milton and his early Latin poetry. It's a bit quaint, but no one could deny that he did thorough research."

"I agree, and seventeenth century poetry isn't even my thing. I didn't completely finish the book even though you recommended it. But what I read was good."

"Yes, but that's my point." Sam shook his head as if in regret.

"What is?" Tom had his arms crossed in puzzlement.

"It was just too old." Sam gave a pointed look to his colleague.

"Huh?"

"Everything. Professor Graves himself, his research, his style."

"We have a lot of professors, full, assistant, and adjunct, who are senior members of the community, but we're not getting rid of them. I don't think so."

"Tom, it's a combination of things, as I said. George hadn't published anything new these past fifteen months. Not a sliver. And what he did publish the previous year—well, let's say we've read it before. Don't get me wrong. I like the man. However, with certain budget difficulties, sacrifices will have to occur."

"I agree that the university had to make a number of difficult decisions, but I don't think that the way it was handled last year was particularly right. George left your office screaming after throwing a stapler at Ms. Stewart. One of those heavy-duty ones too."

"And he's lucky that she's a kind, forgiving person as she didn't press charges." Sam raised his eyebrows as if affronted by the memory of George. "All I can say is that times change. And sometimes, even if you don't want to, you got to go along with them." Sam stared off into the distance as if having fallen into a visionary trance. The words of his colleague brought him back to the realm of the tangible a moment later.

"What about the Latino students?"

"Latino students? Huh? What does that have to with what we we're discussing?" Sam dropped the look of incredulity on Tom.

"Well, you know that I'm on the minority outreach committee, along with the assistant dean of admissions. In fact, I—I mean, we were able to increase the Latino population from five to seven percent last year."

"And so?" Sam wondered where Tom was going with this little factoid.

"I'm wondering what special arrangements there are concerning the grand opening of the Spanish House. You know how much it means to me."

"I thought that ribbon cutting already happened last week. According to my schedule, it took place last Thursday."

"Rain. Couldn't take place because of the rain. So they rescheduled it for this upcoming Thursday. The weather forecast said it was to be clear. Anyways, even if it's not, we'll then hold it inside the lobby."

"Mmm," said Sam. "I'll try to make it. Try to get some local media to the event as well. Some of those Hispanic groups hammered me last year about repairing the Spanish House. Well, they can't complain now. Still, I can't promise anything as to me being personally there as my schedule is booked to the hilt next week. I'm meeting with student groups out the wazoo. Also, I have that meeting with the board. If I cannot, I'll see if my secretary can go as another representative. She sure likes Mexican food—they will have Mexican food there, right?"

"I'm pretty sure that they'll have something from one or more of the Latin countries."

Sam turned again to Tom. "Is that it?"

"I guess so." Tom wished that Sam would take these things somewhat more seriously, but at least he said that he would do something.

"Good. Now we can get back to discussing some of the new professors for the term." He took a significant slurp of his tea, which had now turned lukewarm.

"Okay."

"It looks like we got a good selection this term. There's Robert Meyers. He's in physics. Astrophysics. We wooed him from William and Mary. Then, we received Priscilla Upton. Her work in neo-Freudian studies has made her the star of the psychology world. But if there's one person that doesn't have penis envy, it's her." Sam gave a short chuckle and then hushed, not knowing whether he had stumbled in humor. Tom just continued to sit there on the couch with a blank expression. Sam continued, "And most interestingly, we've received Brown from Brown. That's Herbert Brown. You must've heard of him?" With teacup still in hand, he raised his arms.

"Only notoriously."

Sam's eyes bulged out. "Notoriously? What do you mean? He's a rising academic star. Some say that he has already risen. We're lucky that we got him. Why do you think that we had to let go of George?"

"I'm talking about that incident that happened this past spring. You know the one that I'm talking about? You have to. It made the news."

Sam waved his free hand in dismissal. "Brown still kept him while he planned to transfer here. And that incident wasn't his fault. Young people, even bright Ivy League students, do stupid things. What if we got blamed for everything the students here did?"

"And his main focus of research?" Tom rhetorically inquired.

"What's wrong with his focus of research? We needed another professor in Africana studies. It's been slim pickings in that department since I arrived here."

"His research has focused on, what do you call it, natesology? I try to stay on top of these things, even though my focus is on student affairs. But is this even a legitimate field? The study of the buttocks. Come on!"

"It isn't the physical study of butts. At least, that's not all there is." Sam's mind tried to organize what he had heard from the departments in order to explain it to Tom as succinctly as possible. "Well, it's a new discipline. Very interdisciplinary. It combines biology, physics, history, geography, anthropology, media studies, English literature, and philosophy."

"And it focuses on butts?" Tom's eyes grew even wider in incredulity. He thought it sounded interesting, but he still couldn't believe this was a legitimate field, let alone a field where one of the most recently acclaimed professors would be an expert.

"Like I said, it's interdisciplinary. Take biology and physics. The student studies what makes human butts human butts in comparison to animal buttocks. The difference between the male and female is also studied. What draws males to female butts and vice versa. You obviously know that the female has that swinging motion in contrast to the male. Well why? The student finds out. Then, take history and geography. Views on buttocks size and shape vary according to period, ethnicity, and culture. The student studies how the majority culture has influenced the minority cultures in its midst. The reverse has occurred as well. Then there is genetics..."

"Does Herbert Brown have any specific expertise or is he a generalist?"

"According to my reports, he has taught on many subjects in the field. Although in the past couple of years, he has primarily published papers on Brazil. The influence of African, native, and European populations on shaping the physical female form and the attitudes surrounding it, within and outside Brazil. I heard he's really delved into the subject."

"He sounds like he's a really busy and engaged fellow. And that he knows his material."

"Let me tell you, Tom, he's even recorded an album. Not by himself. But last year he did a few guest tracks on a rap release. I can't think of the title right now. I'll try to look it up for you."

"I think that I can Google it." Tom leaned back and pondered what Sam had explained to him. It was innovative. The students would likely find it interesting. The Department of Women's Studies had even jumped on board, though it had initially made them hesitant. It's always good to keep an open mind. Still, skeptics would have multiple questions. "What about the board? I'm sure that at least half of them will have some concerns. Maybe not with the subjects themselves, but with any controversy associated with Brown. You said that you wanted positive results this academic year."

Sam pointed his finger at him. "That's part of the reason why I'm having that meeting with the board. Just trying to reassure them. But I'm sure that I can ease their concerns. I've even heard it from their mouths that I'm the most competent president of the past two decades. They trust my judgment." Sam finished with a Cheshire grin.

"Sam, I hope you're right." Tom leaned forward. He adjusted himself from side to side. He just couldn't get himself comfortable. He didn't know whether it was because he still had concerns or just that the couch material had started to irritate him.

"It's getting late. I best return home." Sam maneuvered himself out of the rocking chair to shake Tom's hand. "I hope you feel better."

Tom got up from the couch, and as Sam approached with his

outstretched hand, he raised his hand to stop him. "I don't want to get you sick. I probably already put you at risk having you here. Let's just say good night."

"Well, good night then." Sam withdrew his hand, nodded, and turned around to make his way out the door.

Lisa had stayed in the kitchen, but she had sat down at the table looking over a home and garden magazine. She looked up and said, "See you later. Have a safe trip home."

Sam nodded in acknowledgment. "You have a good one too. And try to make Tom well. I'm sure that he's going to be busy this year. I'm going to need his help."

"Don't worry. He'll be in tip-top shape with a few more days of rest."

Sam made his way out the door and gave a final wave to the embracing couple. As he walked to his car, he thought to himself that he wished that he and Valerie had relations as tender and sweet as those between Tom and Lisa. Perhaps he would try to call her tonight when he got home. It was almost lunchtime for her. Maybe she would be available, though Saturdays were a busy day for her art gallery work. As he started the engine and drove out of the driveway, he decided that he would try. He had to hear her voice.

* * *

Sam walked into his house and loosened his tie. He went to the fridge, grabbed a beer, and dropped onto the living room couch. He let out a long sigh and reached into his pocket to grab his cell phone. It wasn't there. He thought, *What happened to that stupid thing? It was just there. I know it was. I put it there before I sat down to speak with Tom.* At that moment the landline began to ring. He didn't feel like answering it. *Who would call a quarter after ten, anyways?* he thought. *People should have wound down.* After the third ring, he jumped up and answered the phone.

"Hello; Sam Castle speaking."

"Tom here. I hope I didn't disturb you getting ready for bed, did I?"

"No, I was just about to look for something I misplaced—"

"That's why I was calling. You left your phone on the floor. It probably slipped out of your pants when you got up."

"Thanks; I was about to worry myself silly looking for that thing. I'll just pick it up later this weekend. Okay?"

"That's fine. Well," he laughed, "I guess good night again."

"Good night." He set down the phone and let out a sigh of relief. He picked up his beer and went back to the couch. He grabbed the remote from the table in front of him and turned on the TV. *There's probably nothing on*, he thought. *Nothing generally is these days.* He flipped from channel to channel until he came across one of the local access stations. The image that he saw transfixed his eyes, and he set down the remote. A beautiful woman, sitting cross-legged in a chair to the left, came into focus on the television. She initially caught his attention. But then he noticed her guest, who, separated by a plain brown table and facing the audience, alternatively directed his attention to the host and the studio audience.

"Steff, I mean Shazzam Africa, have you noticed any growth in your organization the past year?"

"Brooke, I try not to focus on the quantity of members but on the quality. We have a lot going against us. The reactionary forces, as I said before. As mentioned, we're based in Cleveland.

We consider it our home. But we've recently tried to form chapters in Columbus and Cincinnati. I believe it's necessary. Although we have an African American president, the forces of reaction still work against us. Too many black youth seem lost. I've seen it in their eyes throughout the cities of Ohio. We give them community. We also give them hope and pride.

"But Mr. Africa, some individuals have claimed that your organization acts too militaristic. I myself am a little intimidated by your uniform. All black with that patch on the right side of the jacket and on the front of your beret. I'm not saying it myself, but some have said that it looks ridiculous. What do you have to say to your critics?"

Shazzam readjusted himself in his chair in obvious annoyance at the impertinence of the question as he thought about it. He got out of the chair and stood at full attention, hands clasped in front of him.

"The uniform represents strength. Black strength. And yes, it intimidates. That's by design. We won't let white dogs tear out at our honor and dignity. We say no to their violence and intimidation—"

"But Mr. Africa, has any recent violence or intimidation against the black community in the greater Cleveland area occurred? Any trend?"

"No, Brooke. And that's why we need the Black Arms. Especially here in Columbus. You see this symbol?" Shazzam pointed to the patches on his chest and on his beret. "The arm. The black arm symbolizes the power that we would use against those who would harm our community. See it surrounded by two rings? One red and one green. The symbols of our blood and our connection to Mother Africa."

"But we've received disturbing reports of members of your organization engaging in questionable behavior. I have some reports here about an incident at a local fair that took place this past July." She shuffled some papers to get to the newspaper clippings, but by the time she looked up, the angry face of Shazzam hovered above.

Shazzam, standing over her, pointed in accusation. "You call yourself a sister? How dare you! We're fighting for you. I don't have to take this bourgeois propaganda. You Aunt Jemima bitch!"

Before security could get to Shazzam and Brooke, Shazzam had already backed off and walked away, tearing out his microphone and throwing it in the direction of the audience. His bodyguards followed him as he walked off the studio floor, past the open dressing room door and out back, where his caravan of black cars awaited him.

Brooke readjusted her blouse and skirt. "That was exciting," she said to the camera. "We always promise exciting programming on this station." Still shocked, she paused until they restarted the teleprompter. "Coming up, we have local author Brad Cummings on the history of theater life in Columbus. He has a new book due out this winter. After a brief commercial break, we'll return to our scheduled program."

Sam turned off his TV and thought, *What a crazy person. You get some characters on these late night local access channels. And his manner and actions toward that attractive young host! What a shame. Thankfully, we don't have to deal with things like that at Central Ohio.* With his thoughts on the pretty interviewer, his mind shifted back to his wife. Was he going to call her or not?

He really wanted to, but that landline took a chunk of money for international calls. He decided that he had to hear her voice.

He dialed. *I hope that those curators haven't taken her out to a long lunch and business meeting*, he thought. *They took up so much of her time. She was always gone, even when he expected her to be available*. The phone continued to ring and ring until it finally went to voice mail: "Valerie is sorry that she missed your call. If you leave a message and it's important, she'll get back to you ASAP."

Sam always thought that voice recording prompt was rude and condescending, but what could he do? She was an artist with limited time. She couldn't waste it on trivial matters. He thought that maybe she had run to the restroom. It was almost time for lunch over there. He'd wait another ten minutes to try again. He looked at his watch, at the clock on the wall, and then back to his watch. This ritual continued until the ten minute point slowly arrived. He dialed again and got that same prompt. He hung up the phone and flopped back on the couch.

He stared at the half empty beer bottle in his hand. "Mr. Lager, I guess it's just you and me tonight." He took another swig and set it down on the table. Tears began to form in his eyes until a torrent of self-pity flowed. He wept until he had drenched his palms. He then fell asleep as he sat on that lonesome loveseat.

Chapter 2

Unfortunately, that Sunday wasn't as pleasant as Friday. It dripped, rained, and deluged the campus some more from morning until afternoon. Although on Sundays most students would be out, engaging in whatever activity could take their minds away from academic deadlines, that day most stayed in, unless they already had plans for the end of the weekend. Troy didn't have plans except to study until he could feel his eyes begin to bulge out, or at least until the rumbling in his stomach annoyed others.

"Troy?" Ian sat up in his bed. He yawned and rubbed his eyes.

Troy turned around. "What? You see that I'm studying. I have a test this Tuesday on this Roman history mess. The professor's a stickler for details, so I have to go over this information at least twice, until I get it down pat."

"I know, I know." Ian continued to yawn so that his mouth looked like a fleshy cavern. "You're always studying hard. Especially this year. Last year I don't think you hit the books as hard as you're doing right now."

Troy turned around his chair and stared at Ian. "You're right. I didn't. That's why I'm doing it right now. I turned some things around last spring, but my mom, and especially my pops, didn't like those first term grades. I didn't like them myself. They weren't bad, but they showed I wasn't taking things seriously." He turned around to get back to his work, but then he looked out the window at the steady downpour. "You're my bud, but at times, I don't think you can understand that. It's hard to explain."

Ian let out a snicker. "Why? Is it because I'm not always serious? Well, I'll admit it. I like having fun. Practical jokes and the like. But I understand the need to get serious. And yes, not just in lacrosse but in my classes too."

"Good. So you'll let me get back to this dry textbook. Although my body says that I need a break, my mind says that I must press on or face the wrath of Professor Jenkins."

"How long have you been studying?" Ian inquired.

"Coming up on three hours, I believe." He didn't have his phone near him. "What time is it?"

Ian grabbed his phone from underneath his pillow and turned it on. "Fifteen till eleven."

"So about three hours." Troy suddenly got out of his chair but didn't turn around to face Ian. Instead, he looked out the window.

"Troy? You thinking about something important? I know that you're thinking about something. I mean, you always are. But this time, I know that something big is on your mind."

"Nothing much. Just observing the rain. What it means."

Ian laughed. "It means that I can't practice today. Also, I don't feel like getting out of this bed unless it's to get something to eat. In fact, I might order pizza or Chinese."

Only paying Ian slight attention, Troy said, "I don't know why, but I always thought of the rain as a cleansing element. I know it sounds cliché. But when I'm talking about cleaning, I'm not just thinking about the physical. I try to think of all the bad that happened the previous week being washed away."

"But what if there is no rain? Does all the bad just pile up?"

Troy turned around to face Ian. "I don't know. I've never thought it all the way through. Maybe I should. Or maybe it's all just a bunch of crazy thoughts." Troy shrugged his shoulders.

"I never wanted to tell you this because I didn't want to upset you. I know it's strange—me hesitating so as not to offend. But I've thought that sometimes you think too much."

Troy just stood there not really knowing what to say. Having known Ian for over a year, he understood that they had different personalities, and he knew that Ian believed what he had just said, but he had never expected it to come out of his mouth like a bullet.

Ian continued, "I'm not saying that you're a nerd or anything like that. That's stupid. I'm saying that you're overly cautious. Don't get me wrong. Being cautious is a good thing. There've been times when I've wished that I had your personality. Having observed you, though, I see that you hesitate to say or do something—"

"And I think that's a good thing." Troy shifted his feet, leaning his arm on the chair. "It's kept me out of trouble."

"I'm not criticizing you, man. I'm saying that having observed you, I think that at times you don't do what you want to because you're afraid of what people will think. It's as simple as that. It's not that you're afraid of doing bad but that you're afraid of making an unwanted impression."

"I kind of agree with you there. I don't know why, but I've always acted like that. Even in small things."

Ian shrugged his shoulders too. He didn't know why either. It was just what he had seen.

"Since you're up, you want to get some breakfast? I'm

starving. I thought that I could wait it out another hour so I could get another twenty pages in, but you probably could hear my stomach growling in your sleep."

Ian waved his hand. "I'm a bit hungry, but it looks like you need to keep on. Listen, I'm going to head to the cafeteria for some takeout. I think they're still serving breakfast. I'm not sure. It's that in-between period. I'll bring you a bag of something, okay?"

"Sure. If it's breakfast, I'll take a bagel with cream cheese. Lunch, I'll have a chicken sandwich and fries. Hold on a sec; let me get my wallet."

Ian waited for a few minutes while Troy scrambled around the room to first find his book bag and then to scrounge for the wallet within. Finally he found a five and handed it to Ian. During the search Ian had slipped on a pair of jeans, a T-shirt, and shoes for his sprint through the deluge.

"I'll return in about twenty minutes. Don't pass out before I get back." Ian laughed and rushed out the door, making sure not to slam it as others down the hall were likely recovering from the parties of last night.

* * *

Ian arrived at the cafeteria soaked. He knew that he looked ridiculous and unkempt. But in all honesty, he didn't care. He was on a mission. So he strode to the station that had what Troy desired. After filling the two takeout bags and waiting a ridiculous amount of time to pay the cafeteria worker, circumstances finally freed him to return to the dorm to chow down on some good eats. He then saw somebody he hadn't expected to see that Sunday morning. Pure chance just arrived.

Milly Kwon stood in the midst of the cafeteria traffic.

Milly was a girl that normally wouldn't attract Ian. He didn't even know why he liked her. He went for the more voluptuous type. She wasn't a pine board, but she had a thinner shape that he overlooked. Almost a model shape, except with a shorter stature. She did have a wonderful smile. At least that's what he saw the times he observed her laughing with a friend in front of him in class. With that smile she could go places in Hollywood or on Broadway. She just seemed nice. But even with that impression, he never worked up the courage to say something to her besides "Do you have an extra pen?" or "Do you think the topic covered today will be a principal component of the midterm?" He thought, *It's a crazy, funny thing that I'm scared to say something.* But he never had these past three weeks. And now she stood a couple of cafeteria table lengths from him, and he hadn't even brushed his teeth before he had departed the dorm.

She caught him staring at her, but she continued in conversation with her friend. He recognized that friend from the same class. Now that friend showed the definition—no, the gallery of voluptuousness. Still, his eyes focused on Milly. He felt like turning around and sneaking out, though he knew that she had seen him looking, but she then held up a hand to halt her conversation with her zaftig friend and walked over to him.

"Hi, I'm Milly."

"I know. You're in my class." He tried to turn away, realizing that his breath was not as fresh as he wanted it to be.

"You know that it's rude to stare. I saw you looking."

A state of nervous agitation flashed over him. "I wasn't staring. I was just looking for a friend among the people seated down over there." He knew that lie wouldn't cut it, but he went with it.

"My friend over there has said that she's seen you staring at me in class."

"In class?" Ian thought that he had been covert when glimpsing. Apparently not.

"Don't worry. I'm not going to charge you with harassment." She gave a slight smile, flashing a crescent of those admired teeth. "It's just that you've stared at me before, and now I've seen you glimpse at me here. And even though we're in the same class, we're still strangers. Well, let's not be strangers."

"You're friendly."

"Well, I try to be. Even though I try not to be shy, I often am. That's one thing I feel I can't be."

Ian nodded. "Because of your career goals?"

"Huh?" She had a puzzled look. *How did he know?* she thought.

"My roommate—my friend told me that you wanted to act professionally. He saw you in a play. He said that you played your role well."

She bent her head down in embarrassment at the compliment. "It was just a bit role. My parents didn't even come."

Ian continued, "Still, I'm sure that you did well with it. During that time of the year, I don't really have time to attend events like that. I play lacrosse. Do you think that I look like a lacrosse player?"

"You look scruffy enough." She looked him up and down.

He laughed. "I didn't have a chance to wash up this morning. Actually, I woke up about a half hour ago. So sorry if my breath is a bit rough."

"No, it's all right. I heard that Clark Gable didn't always smell like lilies and cologne. He did okay. Now I'm not saying that you're Clark Gable, I hope you understand. But that's not a bad thing—"

"I get what you're saying. Anyways, you'd look this rough after you attended that party I did."

"Oh." Milly's eyebrows rose in faux wonderment.

"That's what I actually wanted to talk to you about. Not last night's party, but parties in general."

"Like my opinion of them and whether I'm a regular attendee?"

"Not really. I'm just wondering if you're going to Jay's little thing on the seventeenth. It's pretty much open to all."

"I thought about it, though I'm not really the partying kind of girl. Don't get me wrong. I like to throw down once in a while, but generally I like a quieter atmosphere."

"No, I understand. Still, you should come. Bring a friend too. Afterward we could see a movie or something, especially if you lose interest in the party."

"I'll think about it. By the way, have you met my friend? I've been rude leaving her standing there and not introducing her." Her friend had a tray of food in her hand. She looked off into the distance, watching as other students passed her by to find seats. She looked over to Milly, who beckoned her over.

"Ian, this is Rachael. You've seen her before. She often sits beside me in class. You've probably noticed her giggles at some of the professor's random digressions."

Ian thought, *I've noticed more than her giggles, but those were attractive too.* "Hey, pleased to meet you." Rachael and Ian felt awkward as they both had their hands full, so they slightly nodded to each other in acknowledgment.

Ian continued, "I just told Milly that you guys should come to Jay's party on the seventeenth. I heard that it's going to rock. Lots of music and beer. The works. It's off-campus too. I don't know if you know where he lives. It's nearby, though."

"I heard about it," Rachael said. "I wasn't sure whether I was going to attend or not. I have a paper due the following Monday."

"I bet you're smart enough to bust that paper out all on Sunday. I've heard your answers during class discussion."

Rachael blushed. "I'll think about it. Milly and I will let you know Thursday."

"Sounds good." Ian looked over at the clock on the wall. "I have to run. My roommate has been in the midst of a studying binge, and I think he's starving like I don't know what."

"We'll see you Tuesday." Milly flashed that great smile and turned around with Rachael to find a table. Ian by that time had fled outside, braving again the downpour as he headed back to the dorm.

"What do you think about Ian?" said Milly.

"What do you mean? Like, do you think he's a decent guy? Like you, I just know him from class. There, he's kind of quiet. But I've heard that he's the opposite outside of class from a friend from freshman year. He's into pranks and gags. Also, sometimes his mouth gets him into trouble. He's on the lacrosse team, isn't he?"

"That's what he just told me." Milly dipped one of her fries into a ranch-barbecue sauce concoction, which she had discovered when she was thirteen.

“I guess you could say that he’s kind of wild. But it’s in a good way.”

Milly nodded. And then she continued to dip and eat.

“Why are you asking all these questions? You like him or something. I mean he’s somewhat cute in a scruffy kind of way. Like a boyish Harrison Ford.”

“No—not really. I understand his attractiveness to other girls. I don’t know if he’s the player type or not, but I could see it if it’s true. I just didn’t know whether I should attend that party with him. I don’t know whether I should go at all. You know my parents.”

“You should let your hair down a little, Milly.” The irony of this comment was that Milly always wore her silky hair down in the same style she had worn since sophmore year of high school. Rachael’s long, curly hair, on the other hand, had been pulled tight into a bun that day.

Milly finished off the fries as she thought about her friend’s comment. She really hadn’t done anything special since matriculating at college. She had attended one party her freshman year, but she had left within an hour. The combination of the hookah smoke and the smell of fresh vomit didn’t really please her. Moreover, her theater work kept her busy. It had paid off in small dividends when she had gotten that role in the spring play. Still, her parents hadn’t attended. That upset her greatly. They didn’t treat her ambitions seriously. It’s why she always focused on her studies. If she could keep her grades up while continuing her acting, maybe they would accept her own goals and not their plans for her.

"In all honesty," Rachael said, "I don't think that he's your type. A little rough around the edges. But he sounds like a lot of fun. That's why I'm seriously thinking of attending. I can put the paper off for a day."

Milly knew that she wasn't particularly attracted to him. He didn't appear to be the serious type. That's for sure. But he had a friendly demeanor. Anyways, if she wanted to act professionally, she needed to put herself out there. Expand out of her comfort zone. Otherwise, she'd get bit roles for the rest of college. And with that lack of success, you could count Hollywood out of the picture. Attending another party wouldn't be so bad. Rachael would be there if anything happened. Her mom and dad didn't have to know either.

"We'll let him know Thursday," Rachael said, sipping on hot tea that was perfect for a drizzly day, "in case anything comes up later this week. Likely, we can just meet him there. He said that the house was close by."

Milly had just taken a bite of her chicken sandwich. She gave a thumbs-up. "I agree. Can't let life pass you by. I don't want to become another sophomore slump victim, driving in cruise control. I think I'll try to find a dress after class this upcoming week." She smiled one of those brilliant smiles and focused on the crispy goodness of the sandwich.

Rachael continued sipping her tea. She then dove into her food.

* * *

Back at the dorm, Troy had grown restless. He was hungrier than he had originally thought. His stomach bubbled, growled, and grumbled like a volcano. He had lost concentration on his schoolwork. How could you study when the sounds of the body washed over the brain? You couldn't. He again looked out the window to see if he could spot Ian. He had been gone longer than expected. He knew that a teammate or some other acquaintance likely was holding him up at the cafeteria. Definitely a usual circumstance. But couldn't he be punctual this time around? God! His stomach cried out for food.

Someone answered Troy's prayers as the door swung open and dripping wet Ian stood there like a returning champion.

"Thank God! I think hunger would have shriveled up my intestines if you had returned any later. What took you so long?"

"I'm only fifteen minutes later than I said I would be. You have to cut me some slack. It's raining like Noah's flood out there. I made sure to protect your food so that it wouldn't get wet and soggy. So you have to thank me for something." Ian looked at his own wet clothing. "And you're sitting there nice and dry. I'll probably have to change out of these things if I don't want to smell like a wet dog or worse. So here's your food."

Ian handed Troy his bag, into which Troy immediately began digging. He pulled out the bag of fries.

"Really, what took you so long? I thought that we agreed on an in-and-out mission." A fry fragment fell from his mouth, but he caught it before he could lose it and threw it back in his mouth.

"You won't believe it, Troy, but guess who I saw at the cafeteria?" Ian set his bag down at his computer desk, pulled out and turned around the chair, then sat down.

"Who?"

"Milly, that Korean chick in my class."

"Oh. Did you ask her out or not?" Troy, despite his

disinterested look, was curious about what had gone down at the cafeteria.

"Not exactly. I mentioned the party to her. She's currently on the fence about attending but said she would get back to me by Thursday."

Troy scratched his cheeks. He realized that he needed to shave soon. His face had become really itchy. It might've been that razor that he'd been using for six weeks. He needed to get some new blades. "You think that she'll come?"

"I don't know. She isn't the partying type. Not that I think she's a wallflower or a supernerd. From observing her in class and speaking with her now, she seems a tad introverted. But hey, that's all right. I just wonder how someone like that could pursue acting. She probably views it as a challenge."

"Well, I hope she comes, for your sake. I don't want my bud feeling glum. It's a new school year. You don't want to start things out crappy."

"I agree." Ian then realized he had forgotten to mention Milly's associate, that Christina Hendricks–like bombshell. "Oh, Milly has a friend. She's actually in the same class as Milly and me. Her name is Rachael. My oh my! You should see the mam-glands on her. Whoa! She's also nice. And more outgoing than Milly. I think that you'd like her. She'll probably attend the party if Milly comes. Think of it as a double date."

"Wait a moment. You were just telling me that there's nothing definite between you and Milly. Now you're talking double dates. Aren't you getting ahead of yourself?"

"Troy, a man can hope. That's what I've often said—a man can hope."

"How do you know that I'm even looking to date or anything like that?"

Ian shook his finger at Troy. "What do you mean, how do I know? We're buds, remember. Anyways, you're eyes are often transfixed on all the buxom beauties across campus."

"You're the one that's obsessed." Troy put down his sandwich and crossed his arms in playful defiance.

"Wait a minute. If I'm the one who's obsessed, then why am I interested in Milly? I mean, she's no ironing board, but don't expect her body to save you if you're floating in the ocean. For that situation, you'd need Rachael."

It was when Ian said things like this that Troy was still caught by surprise. He shouldn't have been. He had said very direct comments to people's faces before. He was brave like that. No, that would be the incorrect description. More like he was foolhardy at times. It was what was expected. Still, Troy wished that Ian would tone it down, even when it was just the two of them speaking.

In a more relaxed pose, Troy said, "I'll check her out if she comes."

"You should. I'm telling you, she's amazing. Well, her face is slightly above average. But everything else is stunning in my opinion. She has this thick, raven black hair, luscious ruby lips—I don't think that it's makeup—and again, those mounds." Ian stopped for a moment. "I'm probably sounding repetitive, am I not?"

"You actually are."

"Okay, I'll stop." Ian, after this descriptive portraiture, sat down at his desk to eat.

"I have one more question," Troy said.

"What's that?"

"What's her last name?"

"Buxbaum." Ian started breaking out in laughter.

"What's so funny about that?"

"Nothing. I was just thinking how close 'Buxbaum' sounds to 'buxom.'" Ian continued in muffled laughter while holding out his arms in a lifting motion.

"Oh, shut up," Troy said jokingly, throwing his empty paper bag across the room in Ian's direction.

* * *

"Yes, honey."

"Uh huh…"

"That sounds thrilling."

That afternoon, Sam Castle had found his luck. It was the most wonderful thing that had occurred that weekend for him. His wife had returned his call after he had left messages late Saturday morning, late Saturday night, and early Sunday morning. Although she had much to say on the phone, it came out slow and labored, as if all the day's activities had pushed her endurance to the limit.

"Listen, Val, I'm still not sure whether I should go to that ribbon cutting ceremony for the reopening of the Spanish House. I have a busy schedule that day. There's going to be that meeting with the board in the afternoon. I have a lot on my plate. Do you think that they'll be disappointed? I hope not."

"Who'll be disappointed, dear?" Her loud yawn shot into his ear.

"I don't know. Everybody. Tom wants me there, although

events like these are more of his affair. You know how he cares for the students. Especially the Latino students. Don't get me wrong. I care for them too. He'd just miss me if I couldn't make it, but I think that he would understand. The students, on the other hand, wouldn't. Last week I spoke with the two principal student planners for the event: Ms. Lola Flores, a resident at the Spanish House, and Ms. Rachael Buxbaum, who is secretary of the Spanish Club. Having heard the earnestness in their voices, I know that the event will be a big thing for them. It's why I was sad when I found out that the original event had been postponed due to inclement weather."

Valerie yawned again. "I'm tired, Sam. You know that I just got in. I've had a busy weekend and an even busier night. It can get hectic over here, even for an artist."

"I know, I know. It's why I want you quickly to tell me what to do. Like I've got many duties tomorrow, I know that you have a painting class to teach. Tell me. Is your class affecting your artwork?"

"What do you mean by that?"

"What I'm saying is that I'm wondering if your teaching is hampering your production time. Normally, when you're away, you send pictures of how your artwork is developing. I haven't received any updates since you left this time around. Your artwork makes you so happy. I don't want anything hindering it."

"Don't worry, Sam. I've been busy, but teaching hasn't completely swamped me. Just my priorities are a bit different right now. I realized that situation a week after I came over. Right now I want to work on presenting my completed work. The gallery has been more than satisfactory. Many people have stopped by this time. There's been more traffic than I expected. Critics and curious visitors. I even had some notable individuals all the way from Italy and Germany."

"You know I'm proud of you, Val. You've definitely worked hard for your success. I wish that I could be there with you in more than spirit."

"I know, honey. But from what it sounds like, the university needs you. Getting back to my opinion on the Spanish House situation, I suggest that you do what you think is right. If you feel that there are time constraints, you may just have to skip the ceremony. But anyways, I have to go. You probably don't want to hear my yawning anymore. It's after two, and I need to get some sleep. They want to meet early at the gallery, and I want to look bright and cheery when I get there."

"In contrast to your paintings."

"Dear, you're such a charmer. Anyways, have a good rest of the afternoon."

"Good night, Val." The phone beeped, and she was gone again.

I needed that, Sam thought. He was missing her voice. It had been a while since he had heard from her. He didn't know why. Although she was her own person, and he knew that when he first met her, she usually kept him up-to-date on her painting projects. Even if she didn't call, she would send a brief message along with a pic or two. But he hadn't heard from her at all during this Tokyo trip. Why? He hoped that she wasn't in a major depression. He remembered the last time she broke down when abroad. He had to take a leave of absence. He didn't mind helping her, but he had to catch up on a hefty workload when he returned.

She didn't seem too appreciative either. But that was likely the depression. He thought, *Maybe I'll try to call her again next weekend. See what's really going on.*

Sam sat down at his desk and pondered. Even though it was afternoon, he felt like going to sleep. He always felt tired when his wife felt similarly. Her yawns were contagious—even through the phone. Or maybe he was just an old man. He was sixty-one. A decade and a half older than Valerie. Most of the time he thought he was a man of vigor. He knew he was a man of vigor because Val said it herself. But she hadn't said it recently. She hadn't said much recently. At least to him. *I don't know why*, he thought. *I have to stop thinking about this, at least for now. I'm just going to go back over these papers. It'll take my mind off this nonsense.*

* * *

Lola lay down on her bed while she looked at her iPod screen. She picked a song that was bubbly and poppy and started humming along.

"Lola!" yelled a voice from the open doorway. Rachael stood for a moment with her hand on her hip. She yelled "Lola" once more as she walked over to her roommate's bed.

Lola finally turned around, though she still had earbuds in, and Rachael could hear slightly the music from the turned-up iPod.

"You're going to damage your hearing one day. I know that I sound like some old granny, but seriously, I could nearly hear that thing from the doorway. Why don't you turn it down?"

Lola pulled out the earbuds. "You know how I like my music." She jumped off the bed and moved her hips from side to side. She let slip a minor giggle, though she had a serious look that was neither stern nor mean. She just loved her music.

"I know. I also know that you'll regret it when you're older. But don't mind me; I'm just bossy old Rachael. Always hampering the fun." She smiled a little, knowing Lola wouldn't take her criticism seriously.

"My, my, Ms. Rachael. I always appreciate your warnings and caring considerations," Lola said with a mock Deep Southern voice, which was comical because her normal Miami accent reflected her Cuban and Nicaraguan roots.

"What would I do without you?"

"You would hang out more with Milly, not laugh as much, and I would be alone to help plan this open house."

"Sounds like a plan."

"Don't you dare skip out on this open house. You're secretary of the Spanish Club. You're needed more than anyone else."

"And you're actually Latina."

"I know. See the booty?" She shifted herself to give a better view.

"You're ridiculous. Completely ridiculous. But don't worry. I'm not going to skip out on you. I'll be standing by your side while we sing Spanish songs and have some great fajitas."

"I hope that I can skip out on that singing. I don't want to look too ridiculous."

"But why would you be ridiculous singing? You have a lovely voice. I should know. I always hear you when you're playing your iPod."

"Yeah, but your Spanish is better than mine. That's something that no one can doubt. Think of that. A sweet Jewish girl with a better hold on Spanish than a Latin girl from hot Miami. I should be ashamed of myself. If there were a rice-and-beans card, I'd have to turn it in or shred it."

Rachael laughed. She thought, *Lola can say some severely funny things off-the-cuff.* "I am the Spanish Club secretary, so I should know how to speak it *un poquito*."

"Don't rub it in." She tossed her iPod against the pillow and rose up from the bed.

"You're a valued member of the Hispanic Students Association."

"And one of the worst Spanish speakers. Funny that I have the accent but not the words."

"Girl, I'm not a member of the HSA."

"Cuz you're not Hispanic."

It was hard for Rachael to argue with that. It wasn't as if Rachael hadn't tried to join. She had. But again, she wasn't Hispanic. She'd just have to resign herself to being secretary of the Spanish Club and being a more fluent speaker than Lola was. Not that there was anything wrong with that.

"But don't worry about that. When was the last time you saw me attend their meetings?"

"I don't know."

"It's because I haven't. Not since last year."

"A falling out?"

"Sort of." Lola twirled her honey brown hair around her finger.

"Then why are you still a member?" Rachael was seriously puzzled. It showed on her face by her rippling her forehead for a brief moment.

"I don't know. I guess that I want to connect with my heritage, even if a few members of the HSA don't want to connect with me, even in a perfunctory way. It's funny, but I had another member bring my dues to the first meeting this year. It doesn't matter. It was my mama's money anyway. Still, I feel a little bad about wasting it. She was the one that encouraged me to join the HSA in the first place." Lola went quickly from being that bubbly pop princess to a downcast Chihuahua. She wouldn't have been offended by the metaphor. In fact, she would've come up with something like it if she weren't in such a funk.

"I think I know what will get your spirits up," Rachael said.

Rachael walked over to the CD player on her dresser. She found something that was even livelier than Lola's current selection. As the music began playing, she started dancing crazily.

Lola couldn't stop laughing. "Girl, you think that I'm crazy? Just look at you!"

Rachael changed from one set of dance moves to another. Well, if you could call it dancing. There was some rhythm here and there, but it was mostly wild motion highlighted by some flailing around.

"Come on," she said. "Join in!" Rachael continued twirling around like a whirling dervish on amphetamines. If anybody had looked on, the person would have wondered what madness was going on. The person would have had to admit that it was silly.

A hallmate did pass by the room and peer in. Her eyebrows rose. She shook her head and left, wondering if she should find living arrangements next year that weren't so noisy. Even if it was Sunday, people should have realized that others needed to study.

"No, you go ahead and dance yourself away," Rachael said.

Lola waved her hand in dismissal, though her glum disposition had all but left.

"Fine, I'll continue and be a spectacle by myself." A spectacle Rachael was. A number of the guys on campus knew it. She realized that most guys were probably just thinking about her curves, but she would just continue to dance away, even if they saw her.

* * *

In the Driving Park area, a preacher man was engaged in another spectacle and dance. The figure was swaying back and forth as the music played, the sound rising higher and higher until it burst into a euphony of excitement. Though nearly everybody in the congregation could belt out a good praise-to-Jesus, that preacher man's voice still rolled over them like a rumbling set of waves. It was as if some large cannon were blasting the congregation. Oh yes, a love cannon that would taketh away and giveth tears. Good God, he could get himself lost in some good gospel tunes. He would sway left and right, back to front, with his eyes closed half the time and his eyes surveying the crowd the other half. No wonder the congregation loved him. He was a physical man, not afraid to get down. He loved preaching the gospel. He felt that he had been born and bred for it. This made sense to him since his father and his grandfather and his great-grandfather and his great-great-grandfather had been preachers. He also felt that he had been called to it just as if God had given him a call on the telephone, saying, "Dill, I need you to soothe the souls of my broken people. Will you? I'll make it worth your while." So he felt that he had had no choice but to comply.

The song stopped, and Reverend Dill Johnson began to speak

from the platform.

"Thank Jesus for that song of praise to him! Don't you agree, my brothers and sisters? Now don't you agree?"

"Amen!" shouted the crowd. Up front, a strikingly dressed middle-aged woman, topped with a bedazzled, oversized red hat, led the amens. With her leading, the voices boomed throughout the church then settled down.

"Oh yes," Reverend Johnson continued. "Jesus has the whole world in his hands. There can be no doubt about it. He holds it just as a young farm boy, who, coming across a newly laid egg, gently picks up the precious young thing, cradles it in his arms, wondering in admiration at the gift of life, but then returns it to the hen to hatch it until it becomes a sweet baby chick and fellow child of God. Don't you agree, my friends?"

"Amen!"

"Aren't we all children of God?

"Amen!"

"My brothers and sisters, I want you to imagine God—I want you to imagine not as you normally do. No, I don't want images of bright light, lions, or Morgan Freeman; may God bless that sweet brother. I want you to picture him as Snuggle, that loveable bear we're familiar with. God wraps us in the warmth of his goodness. Can't you feel the sun beaming down on the back of your necks? Right now you can't. But look through the windowpanes on another day, and see how the sun shines through on you, my brothers and sisters. No one can doubt it. Now getting back to Snuggle, one may ask, isn't it blasphemy to picture God as a teddy bear? Isn't God all-powerful? *Why do you, Reverend Dill Johnson, weaken him with your words?* you may be thinking.

I tell you this, my brothers and sisters—I don't blaspheme. Oh no! And yes, God is still all-powerful. Never forget that. Your singing attests to that. However, in order to walk with God, we have to cling to his mighty hand. Think on this—would you rather cling to the soft arm of Snuggle or hold hands with the claws of a lion? Would you prefer the warm, clean embrace of a teddy bear or the firm handclasp of Morgan Freeman. Now I know that some of you sisters out there may hold out for Morgan Freeman." There was a roar of laughter from the seats. "But that's not the point. The point is that God can give us comfort in the days of troubles. He'll be that blanket that warms and dries us on wet days such as today. More than that—he'll be the softener that molds our hardened hearts."

"Amen!"

"My brothers and sisters, I want you to embrace the love of God in your hearts and lives. Express it aloud. Let you have the glory of Mephibosheth! Amen! Let me hear it!"

"Amen!" the crowd roared again.

Reverend Johnson motioned to the DJ and the choir director to start the music again. Reverend Johnson and the entire congregation burst out into an explosion of harmony. He started grooving as Yolanda Adams's "Not Giving Up" started to get really going. The sweat poured from his brow, as if he had stuffed himself into a sauna. He pulled out a handkerchief from his suit pocket and gave his face three wipes before returning it and continuing in the groove. He lifted up his hands as if he was holding up the sky from collapsing on his parishioners and yelled out, "Praise!"

After the end of the service, the shaking of his parishioners' hands, and the closing of the church doors, Reverend Johnson walked into his office and sat down on his chair, which was more like a seat from the high Bourbon era. Maurice, his choir director, was sitting cross-legged on a couch.

"Another good service, wouldn't you agree?"

"Amen!" he responded with a sly smile.

"The parishioners were really getting down to the Holy Ghost. I haven't seen movement like that in the aisles since last Easter service. There was a whole lot of shuffling and shaking going on. I thought the house was going to come down."

Maurice dangled his arm down. "Reverend Dill, I agree, but we have other matters to talk about."

"Oh, yes, yes," he said. He wiped his still-sweating brow, threw the handkerchief on a table, and turned around while loosening his tie, a fulgent piece that stood out even when matched with his equally colorful suit.

"I'm going to have to take a leave of absence in the next couple of months." While Reverend Johnson was loosening his tie, Maurice was tightening his to a stranglehold on his neck. He always wanted to look dapper, especially when a situation occurred where others would potentially yell at him.

"What!" retorted Johnson. He clutched at his bunched up handkerchief, turned it over, and began wiping in earnest with one hand while the other hand jerked his own tie from his neck. "What for? The people have been streaming in the past three months. Due to my recently more enthused preaching, I may say. I haven't seen numbers like ours since the summer of oh-six, when the community came together over that string of gang shootings in the neighborhood. After that, it seemed people really wanted God in their lives. Those barbecue dinners likely helped as well. But that's beside the point. And since I've hired you, we've been really rocking no matter which way you count it. Did you see the collection plates last Sunday?"

"Of course I saw them."

"Listen. Your direction of the choir has really taken this congregation to new heights. I can see the joy again in the people's faces. They light up, especially when we play those grooving hits. You've really caused both the choir and the congregation to lift their voices to Jesus. For that, I'm grateful."

"I don't want to leave either. But I have this new gig coming up. I heard that it's going to be fabulous. A little low-rent, but I think that I can fab the flab out of it when I'm done."

"What are you talking about?" Johnson stuck out his lower lip in irritation.

"Well, Reverend, I've been chosen to help out with a community project this coming February."

"What kind of project could be more important than helping the Oh Lord, Give Us Strength Baptist church?" He got up out of his chair and thrust his finger half a foot from Maurice's nose.

"Like I said, it's a community project. One for the underserved and underprivileged youth of our community." Maurice was irritated that he had to explain himself. He was the one that had put the choir back on the right track, and here Reverend Johnson was questioning him. The nerve of that pickle.

"You're still not giving me any details. You know how I don't like people leaving me out of the loop on matters that I consider important. Especially when it could affect the bottom line. You understand me?"

"It's going to be a black history program with the Columbus East High School students. I don't know what exactly is going to be on the agenda, but the school officials have left a large chunk of the program planning up to my discretion. I think that I might put my choreography skills to good use and create a dance sequence. I know that I want something that will both entertain and educate."

Reverend Johnson gave out a hearty laugh. "You're working with children? You're the one that nixed my plan of starting a youth choir. I even said that your assistant could be the director of that group."

"First of all, Reverend, these aren't children. They're young adults on the cusp of maturity. We're talking about youth who have to deal with the threat of gang violence, the reality of broken homes, and the possibility of unintended pregnancy. I feel that I haven't been giving back to the community as I should. This is my chance. So why don't you listen to their voices crying out to you?"

"All right, Maurice." Johnson lifted up his hand. "You've touched my heart. Don't you be getting all melodramatic on me! I don't want to see any silly tears." Johnson knew that Maurice could cry on command if he wanted. It was good performance material when he was in front of the choir.

"Thanks, Reverend. And don't you worry. The school says that they won't begin rehearsals until after Thanksgiving. I'll be available until then. DJ Slims should be able to take over when I'm on leave, though he'll be working with me when they have a set date for the event."

"Don't get me wrong, Maurice. I'm not mad at you. I was just a little surprised at the news. But good for you on getting this job. Keep me updated. I'll mark my calendar once you get a firm date."

"Trust me. The show will be fab-fab-fabulous. You'll love it."

Maurice left the room, and Reverend Johnson quickly shut the door. He pounced on the phone that he had been staring at and dialed like a madman.

"Sweet honey-child sugar lumps, it's your dilly-willy—I'll be right over. We're going to party tonight once you get me dried off."

Chapter 3

There were some concerns that the open house was going to be a washout again. It had rained early in the morning, and there were reports that fierce wind gusts would occur throughout the day. The trees across campus swayed about like drunken frat brothers and sorority sisters turning in after a Saturday party. Some university officials were afraid that there would be another incident just like the one that had caused the Spanish House to close last year, when a tree crashed through the roof and pinned a student inside a restroom stall. After that disaster the university had decided to go to war against the maples and oaks surrounding the building. There was only a single tree left hovering over the Spanish House, and like the residents inside, its roots were strong. So it was unlikely that the giant oak would crash their gathering.

Rachael was up much earlier than Lola was. Although both took an average amount of time to get ready, some days Lola got dressed and put on her makeup more slowly than usual. Likely that day it was because of the overcast weather. The skies were gray as ash, but the weather forecasters had said that it would clear up by late morning. Lola was still waiting for that to happen.

"I guess that it's too late to cancel now." Lola was sitting in her chair, checking her phone for any missed messages.

"Lola, the guests are going to be arriving in an hour. Anyways, we've been setting things up so that the gathering can take place in the lobby. Did you see the bunting? Jose picked it out himself. It looks classy, to me, for bunting. I'm surprised at his taste."

Lola nodded in agreement. "I don't want to cancel either. It's just that a dampened atmosphere is no good for a celebration. Have you ever seen a group of Latinos gathered together under gray skies? Let me tell you: It's no fun. I remember one time there was a birthday celebration for one of my uncles. It was just a light drizzle outside. Guess what happened? Somebody stabbed somebody. Luckily, it wasn't a fatal wound. Still my motto's been since, see the gray, no play."

"You're being dramatic, as usual. I hardly believe that incident occurred because of the dreary weather. Things just got a bit heated in the yard or what not." Rachael touched Lola's shoulder. "But we're getting off the main point. The fact is that the day has arrived, and we're going to have many important guests."

"I know, I know. Dean LeBlanc is supposed to show up. The vice president of the Columbus Area Hispanic Business Owners said that he was a definite. We may even have President Castle come, although at that last meeting with us, he sounded indecisive. He said that he'd been extremely busy but he'd still try to make it. I don't know how that situation will turn out, but we still have a number of important people coming."

"Don't forget about the band."

"You're right. They'll probably be here even sooner."

The Spanish House had tried to book the *norteño-corrido* band, The Empanadas. They were the hottest group in Mexican music in the Columbus area. They even had a couple of self-released albums, and there were rumors that they had just signed a contract with a major record label. None of this mattered as the lead singer had come down with a stomach bug that had caused The Empanadas to cancel all their gigs. The rest of the band members weren't sad that they would have to miss playing at a ribbon cutting event. With The Empanadas about to hit the big leagues, it was just too beneath their dignity.

Fortunately, the Spanish House found a quick replacement band. Unfortunately, they didn't do their research on the band, and they were stuck with Machaca Machete, a notorious *narcocorrido* band. Some of the young women in the Spanish House had gone online and found the band's webpage after they had found out The Empanadas had to cancel. They didn't really look at the band's lyrics in depth. All that they saw was that a cute fourteen-year-old boy fronted the band. He reminded some of them of their little brothers at home. How could such a sweet-looking boy sing about prostitutes, drug trafficking, and the torturing and the wasting of his enemies? There was a disconnect. Or maybe there wasn't. It didn't matter because the band would soon be there to play ballads.

Nobody consulted Rachael or Lola, so the two wondered if the situation would throw another wrench into their plans to have the best open house ever at COU.

"I hope that the band won't offend too many," Rachael said. "Yesterday I looked up some of the lyrics, and boy, they're some crazy stuff. To be honest, I didn't think stuff like that existed in *corrido* music. I guess that I've been ignorant because what I read reminded me of gangsta rap. Except with instruments."

Lola nodded. "Yeah, it's some crazy music. Many of the performers' lives are even crazier. I heard in the news that the police had recently busted one of the bands due to the connection with the Zetas. Like there was violence and stuff. I don't want that in my life."

"I hear you, girl," Rachael said, walking away to look in the mirror to make sure her hair was straight before she headed downstairs.

"I need to finish getting ready," Lola said, getting up from her chair at the makeup cabinet. "I'll meet you downstairs in about fifteen minutes. Okay?"

"See you in a little, then." Rachael walked out of the room and down to the lobby.

* * *

That morning Tom had an argument with his wife. They didn't argue much, but when they did, it could get nasty. Nasty like a cold sore on chapped, crusty lips. Definitely something that you wouldn't want to be around you. The couple had thrown things, stomped around like petulant children, and slammed doors. It was an hour of chaos. Then it stopped. But there was still a sense of uneasiness in the air, so Tom left early for work. Tom didn't have to go into the office that morning. Because the Spanish House expected him at the ceremony, and he wanted to go, the administration said that he could come in later, say around two. He was fine with that.

As he drove to the campus area, he thought about his wife. He loved Lisa. She was a good woman. But at times she was too white bread. Too vanilla. He guessed that it made sense. Maybe he was too vanilla as well. It fit with his name. But even though she had been acting nice lately, it seemed a bit phony to him. The Stepford wives came to his mind. *It's a funny thing that you can get angry with someone because hidden away in your head you think that she's too nice,* he thought. Well, at times, she was too nice. She always let her mother walk all over her. He wanted to yell at her, "Get some backbone!" But he didn't. She just didn't have any spice. And he wanted spicy. Still, he could never leave her. He loved her. So he was stuck in a conundrum and thought about this conundrum until a loud horn sounded behind him.

Tom lifted up his hand in apology. "Sorry," he said, even though he knew that the angry driver couldn't hear him and likely didn't care about his "sorry" or why he had been lost in thought at a green light.

As Tom pressed hard on the gas, he continued to think. *I don't know what's been getting into me lately. My mind has just been wandering from thing to thing. Maybe it's just me getting over my cold. I don't know. But I have to focus. As Sam said, the university needs me this year. I can't have my head going all wishy-washy. The students need me, and my wife still needs me. Even if she is white bread vanilla. But first things first. I'm going to make a good impression with Manuel Garcia. I'm sure that he's as interested in the welfare of our Latino students as I am. Hopefully, Sam can make it too. But I need to stop worrying so much about that. I just have to fix my mind on the celebration.*

Tom turned on the radio, switching to a station that had on a talk radio personality. After five minutes he turned it off in disgust and switched to La Mega 103.1 to get him in the mood. He was humming along as most of the Spanish went over his head. A giant grin returned to his face as he cruised to his destination.

* * *

In the Spanish House, Jose and two other residents were busy making final touches to the decorations and the setup of the furniture. They hadn't realized that it would be such hard work.

The purchasing of the bunting and the associated party favors had been much easier, although there had been a dilemma on what color ribbon to buy for the cutting ceremony. Some students wanted it to be red, green, and white. A few of the residents complained that this was too stereotypical. Others complained that not only was it stereotypical but that it also didn't take into account other Latino ancestries. What about Colombia, Honduras, Venezuela, among others? Lola Flores herself was half-Cuban, half-Nicaraguan. A student had spoken up, saying that Lola didn't matter. She hadn't been to the HAS meetings at all this year. Besides, Cubans don't count. At least that's what his mom said, as well as a textbook, *Chicano Intertexuality and the Delineations of Sociopolitical Class*. Another student spoke up, reminding him that Lola was the principal planner. Another student reminded her that Rachael had also taken charge of the arrangements of the open house. Another student then said that she didn't know why that Zionist oppressor of persons of color was even allowed in this house. A final student reminded her that Rachael spoke better Spanish than most of the residents. After this uproar all were silent for an uncomfortable minute. The group thus decided to get a rainbow ribbon, although another resident wondered if it would confuse people into thinking that it was the open house for the GLBTQA House, which was positioned near the Spanish House (not that he was homophobic, he quickly added). The rest of the group waved off his concerns, and they settled on the colorful ribbon.

Lola was at the foot of the stairs, looking around at the decorations, and heard the chatter of the residents as they made their way to the kitchen to retrieve the food and beverages. She followed them to ask a question.

"How are things going?" she said. "Looks like almost everything is set up. Looks great. I like all the decorations. They look really professional."

A number of the girls ignored her. One of them whispered into the ear of another and giggled. The whisperer turned and looked at Lola with a look of disdain. She flipped her hair, continued with her covert conversation, and walked with the gaggle of girls to the opposite end of the kitchen.

Jose, however, turned around with a tray in his hand.

"Thanks, Lol. I tried my best. Some of other guys helped. Still, moving that furniture around killed my back. I think that I'm going to sit after I set these enchiladas down. I'm really tired."

Lola smiled. "Don't fall asleep before our guests arrive. We don't want to give Mr. Garcia the impression that we're a bunch of layabouts. He might cry at the future of Latino youths, saying, 'Where's all the hard work ethic that your papas and mamas showed that helped you get to where you're at right now? Where is it?'" She lifted her hands in a gesture of mock outrage.

"Don't worry, Lol. I'll be standing at attention when he and the other important guests arrive. Why do you think they call us Mexicans and not Mexicants?"

"You forget. I'm not Mexican."

"I know, I know. It's just a joke on me." Jose shifted uncomfortably as a sharp pain ran down his back, and the tray suddenly felt twice as heavy. "Let me put this down over there before I drop it and make more work for myself or the cleaning staff." He shuffled away.

Lola noticed that Rachael was at the countertop pouring lemonade into some throwaway plastic cups. As Rachael picked up the cups and turned away to bring them into the lobby, Lola nearly ran into her.

"So glad that you've come down to help with these finishing touches." Rachael took a sip from one of the cups.

Lola laughed. "I just came down to find something to eat—and to sample some of this tasty lemonade." She grabbed the other cup from Rachael's hands and took a giant slurp. "God, I'm thirsty."

"Hey, that was for Marie for over there."

"Forget about that *puta*," she said before she took another sip and wiped her mouth with her fingers. "Did you see how she treated me? I felt like knocking her out. Ignoring me like that. I would've knocked her down hard if there hadn't been anybody else around. I know that she heard me!"

"Calm down, Lola."

Lola had finished her drink and continued, "But did you see the nerve of her? I've tried to be decent with her. But she's always starting stuff. Getting into people's business. I don't have to stand for her mess. I should go over there and knock those cheap extensions off that fivehead of hers. The dirty—!" A flourish of crimson flashed across her face. She looked like she sounded: a firecracker shot off in celebration of a revolution.

"Calm down, girl. We don't want a scene here. Remember, we've got important people showing up." Rachael patted her on the back. "Why don't you sit down? I'll get you another lemonade after I finish pouring the rest of the drinks."

Lola huffed and sat down on one of the couches in the lobby. She crossed her legs and stared off into the distance like a cat not wanting to be held.

Tom LeBlanc was the first guest to arrive at the Spanish House. He had pulled into the COU Hall parking lot, and the walk was only about one fourth of a mile from the hall to the language house. Tom was pleased that in the sky the battle between the blue and the gray had finished and the victor had been the blue. The weather conditions were clearing up, which provided for a pleasant walk. He whistled a short tune as he made his way to the front door. All outside doors on campus dorms used an ID key card lock system. This was to prevent the pervy and scurvy of Columbus from trespassing and molesting the students. Occasionally, a sketchy individual slipped in, but yells and shouts would quickly drive them out. Unfortunately, Tom, because he had rushed out the door that morning, had forgotten his ID card at home. He began looking through the sliver of a window on the door and started rapping his knuckles against it. A face stared back at him through the window. He knocked again. Finally, the door opened.

"Hello, sir," the student said. "May I ask who you are?" The student continued to look him up and down.

"Who I am?" Tom replied. "I'm the dean of students and multicultural affairs."

"Are you on the guest list?" The student still had the door partially open. His face was half out of the building while he firmly planted the rest of his body inside.

"Of course, so can you please let me in? I don't know if this weather will become nasty again. It's been volatile outside. Okay?"

The student relented, and Tom walked in, making his way to the cups of lemonade lined up on the table. Although all the cups had an equal amount of drink, he chose the cup that he thought was the fullest. While sipping his lemonade, he walked around the lobby, trying to make conversation with the students.

Fifteen minutes later there were multiple loud bangs on the front door. Rachael, who had been working in the kitchen, walked to the door. Seeing six figures dressed in black, she opened the door and welcomed them in.

"Hola, senors." The five men and one boy walked past Rachael. They were carrying in numerous musical instrument cases when one of the men spoke up.

"Senorita, can we have some help? Our amps are still in the van parked in front of your house."

"*No problemo*, senor. I'll have some of the young men get your stuff and set it down over in the corner." Rachael pointed to the corner of the lobby that they had designated as the performance spot for the band.

"*Bueno*, senorita." He smiled a toothy grin. "And *muchas gracias*."

Rachael gathered half a dozen young men and told them the band's request. The half dozen gathered the band's remaining equipment and brought it inside. The equipment wasn't heavy, but it was somewhat unwieldy. Fortunately for the upcoming performance, they dropped nothing.

Rachael noticed the youngest band member, whose name was

Carlos, in the corner. He had finished setting up his space. Now his eyes stared off into the distance as if he were in a trance. She didn't know if he had fallen asleep while standing up or if his mind had become focused on the upcoming performance.

She walked over, touched his shoulder, and said, "Senor."

"*Si*," he said, his head turning slowly toward hers.

"It looked like your mind was on something. Is it anything important? I hope that the accommodations are pleasing to your band. All at the house are looking forward to your playing."

"Everything is fine, senorita. I was thinking on Mexico."

"Mexico?"

"I haven't been there since I was a little boy. Since I was seven."

"That's very sad."

"You know, senorita, about my father?"

"No. Know what?"

"He was murdered in Mexico."

"That's terrible!" Rachael wondered what horrible backstory this boy had. He appeared so rigid and stoic.

"That's why I left and came to America. Well, that's why my mother took me and left. We spent a few years in Texas, but we've spent the last four in Columbus. I like it a lot here."

Rachael nodded in agreement that it was a wonderful area.

"I do wish to return to Mexico and seek vengeance against my father's killer. One day that *maleton* will have a knife in his belly! I swear *por dios*!"

Taken aback by young Carlos's vehemence, Rachael, with wide eyes, stared at the animated boy. *This young man*, she thought, *means serious business*. She stepped back a bit.

"I hope that you will be able to visit your homeland soon, I think," Rachael said hesitatingly.

As she was walking away, young Carlos said, "By the way, senorita, me and the band were admiring your *curvas*. I hope that you don't mind me saying this, but you have lovely *agarraderas*. Oh, and your friend that was sitting over there—she has a nice *calabazo* too." He raised his arms up as if he couldn't help but notice an attractive woman, whom he also had to compliment to her face.

Rachael walked back outside to greet the late guests that were sure to arrive soon. Outside the house stood the band manager. She spoke up.

"I was just speaking with young Carlos. He seems to be a lively young man. A real firecracker."

"Senorita Buxbaum, you wouldn't know. He's the best thing to happen to Machacha Machete." He shook his head while looking down. "Senorita, before, we were adrift. There was no direction, and there was no money." The band manger gave a perfect example of a "show me the money" gesture. "It didn't help that our previous lead singer was killed in a robbery. He was involved in some bad stuff. I didn't know it at the time. It was tragic. Poor young man. Thinking back now, I realize that he had no real talent to take the band to the top. But he was lively too. One could say—how do you say it—that he was the life of the party?"

Rachael nodded to show that that was the right expression.

"But he had no real leadership abilities," he continued. "Now Carlos, young though he is, he has what it takes to make Machacha Machete one of the top, if not the top, *corrido* bands.

Are you a fan of *corrido* music, senorita?"

"I've heard some bits and pieces here and there," she said. "I can't say that it's on my regular iPod rotation playlist." She chuckled a little before the band manager began speaking again.

"*Corrido*, senorita, is the music of the people, by the people, for the people. Yes, sometimes they mention naughty things in the lyrics. But it's necessary as it deals with the struggles of the people. Life isn't pretty for the people, you understand, don't you? Even though you're not Latina, you've read history, haven't you? Many deaths and killings. Lots of poverty. It's through these lyrics that listeners turn their poor lives into fantastical retellings. All mankind is in need of fantasy, don't you agree?"

Rachael nodded her head, not knowing whether the band manager was telling the truth or was a masterful storyteller himself.

Both of them noticed that a man was walking toward the house from a path. Even from a distance, they could tell that he had a distinctive style. He was wearing a pinstripe black suit with a cornflower-and-royal-blue striped tie. His shoes looked immaculately shined. And his face. Look at his face. The most glorious horseshoe moustache covered the bottom half. This had to be Manuel Garcia. He stood about five-ten, had broad shoulders, and walked with an air of knowing business, running business, and being the business.

"Good afternoon, senor and senorita." Manuel motioned to them. He shook both of their hands. "May I come inside?"

"Oh yes, Mr. Garcia." She let him in, and he made his way to trays of finger foods.

"I see more people arriving," Rachael said to the band

manager. "One looks like a middle-aged woman. And there are some other students. I believe that it's about time for us to gather outside." She motioned to those off into the distance, as if to say, "Come on, you sloths, you're holding things up!" She then walked in with the band manager as she saw the crowd continuing in their boisterous conversations. She motioned to them that the ribbon cutting ceremony would begin in about five minutes and that they should all head out to the front of the house.

Outside the house the ribbon stretched across two small trees about fifty feet from the front door. The ribbon itself was large, with its width being about a foot. A crew had put up the ribbon two hours before. There had been some struggle to wrap the ends of the ribbon around the tree trunks. After a half hour of struggling, the ribbon crew decided just to nail the ends into the trees. A student walking by while they were hammering freaked out, believing that they were harming the remaining trees. They had removed most of the trees from the area because of last year's accident. Jose told the student to screw himself, and the student ran away down the path, looking back and frowning at the ribbon crucifixion scene. Jose had been right. The ribbon had led to some confusion. A number of students had asked if this was the GLBTQA open house. Jose had to continue telling the passersby that no, this wasn't the GLBTQA open house, first of all. Their house was just down the path to the left. Second, the GLBTQA had no open house this week. Their event was next week. Others who would have attended thought the Spanish House was the GLBTQA House because of the colorful ribbon. They thought to themselves that they must've received the wrong date, and thus they passed by and headed back to their dorms or onward to other events.

The huge crowd was making its way through the door to the ribbon when Ms. Jane Stewart tried to step into the house.

"Sorry, miss," a student said. "But we're heading over to cut the ribbon."

"But I just need a drink. My throat is parched. Can't I get some water or something?" Her hand was gripping her throat as if it had been just cut by bandits.

"No can do, miss. All must make their way to the ribbon." He pointed in that direction. The crowd shuffling out the door did as the student's voice commanded, and they swept Ms. Stewart back away from the front door. She stumbled a bit, but soon she was standing straight, marching to the trees.

Rachael and Lola were positioned in front of the ribbon as the crowd approached.

"Friends and guests," Rachael said, "we appreciate your presence at this momentous event."

The crowd clapped for ten seconds and then stopped, realizing that Rachael had much more to say.

"We remember last year's tragic incident, which damaged our home and killed our dear friend, David Gutierrez." Rachael pointed to the plaque that commemorated the late student. "Last year's memorial was such a beautiful celebration for such a tragic end to a young life. This year we dedicate this repaired house to him and those devoted to Spanish language and culture."

There was further applause.

"We welcome as guests Mr. Tom LeBlanc, dean of students and multicultural affairs, and Mr. Manuel Garcia, vice president of the Columbus Area Hispanic Business Owners. Unfortunately, it appears President Castle could not be here physically with us today. But I believe that he's here in spirit."

"What about me?" said Jane Stewart. She was still trying to catch her breath from the hustle and bustle of the crowd's rushing to the ribbon.

"Excuse me, miss?" Rachael said, wondering who this woman interrupting the ceremony was.

"I'm Jane Stewart. I'm President Castle's secretary, and I'm here as his representative. He let me know on short notice that he wouldn't make it. I'm sorry, but he sends best wishes to the Spanish House."

Nodding, Rachael continued, "So I guess that we welcome Ms. Stewart. Please send our regards to President Castle when you see him."

Further applause ensued. Some students were beginning to wonder how red their palms would be by the time they actually cut the ribbon.

"Fellow students and guests, I hope that you enjoy your time at the Spanish House. We have delicious food prepared by caring hands and entertainment provided by the lovely band Machacha Machete." She began to think to herself that "lovely" was probably not the choice word to say, but it was too late now. "After we've cut the ribbon, please enjoy the chorizo, burritos, taquitos, *bolillo*, and *cabrito*. We've provided quite a feast thanks to members of the university staff, as well as some of the students before you."

There was another round of applause as a student brought Rachael a pair of scissors.

Taking the scissors, Rachael whispered into the student's ear,

"What are these?"

The student had been in a rush. She had forgotten that there would be a need for scissors at the ceremony. In her haste, she had grabbed the first pair in front of her. Unfortunately, she had picked up some blunt-tip kid scissors that could barely cut notebook paper. She hadn't realized her mistake until she had stepped outside with the crowd rush.

"Sorry, it's all that I could find." The young woman shrugged her shoulders.

"I guess that it'll have to do," Rachael said, speaking to herself, although the crowd overheard her. "Lola, will you do the honors, please?" Rachael handed off the scissors.

"How can I work with these baby things?" Lola said, looking askance at the object.

"Please just cut the ribbon, Lola. I believe that everybody's a little hungry right now."

Lola took the scissors and started cutting. It started fraying the ribbon, but the scissors kept sticking. Lola looked up at the crowd, and she noticed Marie snickering to her friend. Obviously they were making fun of her. The rest of the crowd just wanted the ribbon cut so that they could go back inside. Lola looked at Rachael for help. They decided together to tear the ribbon at the spot where it had frayed. It wasn't pretty, but eventually they got the ribbon into two pieces. The crowd was relieved that the ordeal was now over, and they all hustled back inside.

Machacha Machete had finished setting up and positioned themselves to play. Carlos welcomed the guests and started announcing the playlist.

"We're going to begin with one of our classics, 'Ortiz and

Morales.'" The band started getting into the groove after an initial rough start. The voice of Carlos started soaring like an eagle released from a cage. The accordionist really gave the song a danceable beat, while the *bajo sexto* shot out a strong rhythm. Even some of the non–Spanish House students started tapping their feet and clapping their hands. Rachael listened and became shocked when she heard Carlos sing about how Morales gutted his cartel rival, Ortiz, like a pig and placed his entrails on his woman's laundry line. She walked away, not really wanting to hear anymore.

She walked over to the center of the room and overheard Tom speaking with Manuel.

"Mr. Garcia, may I call you Manuel?" Tom said. "You've done well for yourself."

Manuel nodded in agreement.

"As you know, the Hispanic community has exploded in the last decade," Tom said. "I'm impressed, watching how you've maneuvered things in Columbus. Driving around Columbus, I've seen many Latino shops. It seems that things have gone up for your community. Wouldn't you agree?"

"Yes, I've negotiated a lot of loans for new businesses. Unfortunately, a rash of crimes has taken place recently. Mainly break-ins and vandalism, but what do you expect? We live in the biggest city in Ohio. There are bound to be problems. But I believe in looking at situations from the positive angle. We have a vibrant community. Primarily Mexicans, but we also have Puerto Ricans, among other immigrants, moving in lately. I believe that a renaissance along the West Side will occur in a couple of years. Listen, I'm not just doing this for self-interest. I want the community to have a better life."

"I agree with you, Manuel. That's why I'm devoted to the students here." Tom looked over to one of the students and back to Manuel. "Especially those of Latin heritage. Many of their parents didn't have opportunities like their children. I want to make sure that they make a success of themselves during their time at Central Ohio. That way they can make a contribution to their community."

"It sounds like you're really devoted, Mr. LeBlanc. We need allies and advocates like you in our community."

"Thanks. I'm just trying to make the world a better place. And I know that it's the small things that count. Now if you'll excuse me, I have to go speak with Jane. I saw her somewhere. Knowing her," he smiled, "she's probably already off for second helpings." Tom left Manuel's side for his grand search.

Lola's attitude had changed once she had put some food in her belly. Her hunger had likely been one of the causes of her irritable manner during the morning. Still, Marie was a *puta* in her mind, and even good eats and lively music couldn't change that opinion.

"Enjoying the day?" Rachael said and noticed Lola resting in an armchair, chowing down on a plate of rice and beans and chorizo.

Her mouth full of rice, she said, "I'm feeling a bit better." She swallowed it down. "This is some good stuff. Who made it?"

"One of the cafeteria staff made the chorizo." Rachael pointed in the direction of Machacha Machete, where a couple of middle-aged Latina women were dancing energetically to a song in which a cartel member had slit the necks of dozens of his rivals. They really let out a shout at that section, and Carlos gave an affectionate wink back to the whooping grannies.

"Well, I love it. I'll tell her thanks later."

"So you think that the open house is going well?"

"Looks like it's fine to me, even if my eyes and mouth are preoccupied right now." Lola ate another spoonful of the rice.

"You know that in about an hour, I've got to get ready for class?"

"Don't worry, Rachael. I have everything under control. The open house probably won't last much longer. Everybody's really going through the food quickly, even though the staff and students prepared a lot."

"Okay, I'm just reminding you."

Rachael left Lola to speak with some of the other guests, and time quickly passed. The hour had rolled around, and soon it was time to head off to meet Milly before they walked to class together. She grabbed her bag, said goodbye to Mr. Garcia, and headed outside.

Lola had noticed that Mr. LeBlanc had headed upstairs about ten minutes before and hadn't returned since then. He probably had to use the bathroom, she thought, but wondered why he hadn't used the currently vacant facilities downstairs. She put down her drink on the table and headed upstairs. She spotted Tom with a nervous look on his face. His hand was resting on the knob of one of the rooms when he looked up at her.

"Mr. LeBlanc, what are you doing up here? All the fun is taking place downstairs." Lola cocked her head to the side.

"Well, I needed to stretch my legs—and my belly. Some of those dishes took a toll on my stomach. Good, but heavy." He rubbed his stomach, but Lola wasn't buying his explanation.

"But I saw your hand on one of the student's door knobs, like you just left or something. I don't mean to be rude, but what were you doing, if you don't mind me asking?"

"In actuality, Ms. Flores, a student sent me to retrieve an item. She wasn't feeling well. She's rested herself on the couch for the past twenty minutes. She told me that she didn't know if she could make it up those steps." He whispered, "I think that it's cramps or some other lady troubles." Continuing in a normal voice, he said, "So I decided to get the thing for her after I made a pit stop at the restroom."

Lola still had some doubts about Mr. LeBlanc's actions. But what could she do? Call the police and hold him until they arrived? Administer a lie detector test? All that was absurd.

"Come on, Dean LeBlanc, let's go downstairs for dessert. I also think that Machacha Machete is about to play their final song."

They walked downstairs, and just like clockwork the students and staff started to serve the various sweets. Machacha Machete also finished up with their last song, "Cocaina y Bacalao." A number of the students simultaneously lost their appetites.

* * *

Professor Herbert Brown woke up screaming. It was midnight, and normally at this time he was fast asleep. He had been dreaming his regular dreams. These dreams usually centered on his daytime work. Simply put, they focused on butts. Generally, nice, curvy, heart-shaped *bumbums* and *bundas*. Often, he dreamed about his lovely wife. Occasionally, he dreamed about other women. Generally, after these dreams he felt initially good.

Then he'd turn over and look at his beautiful Sophia and feel horrible. This night his dreams began as usual. Bottoms bouncing like a basketball during the NBA Finals. His dream then turned into a nightmare. The buttocks began deflating, until the woman looked more like a New York runway model than a contestant for the annual Miss Bumbum Competition. That's when he woke up screaming, clutching his wife.

"What's wrong, *meu querido*?" She yawned, turned over, and embraced him. "It's late, and you have work tomorrow."

Still trembling, Herbert said, "I had a horrific nightmare. It was horrible." He gripped his wife even closer.

"What was it about?" She opened up her eyes and gave him a quick peck on the lips.

Herbert hesitated. He didn't want to mention that he had been dreaming about another woman. The fact that the woman in the dream wasn't real didn't matter. In fact, he had completely imagined her. He didn't even recall the dream woman's face, or even if she had a face. He just knew that Sophia could be so irrational when jealous. He didn't want to upset her. He had to get some sleep tonight. Herbert remained quiet.

Sophia, prodded by her husband's silence, continued, "Was it about me? If it was, what happened to your *querida* in your oh-so-frightening nightmare?" She gave him kisses all over his lips, cheek, and forehead.

Herbert lied. "Yes, it was about you, sweetheart."

"What happened? Did I die? Did something tragic happen to your sweetheart?"

"No, it's a bit ridiculous to recall. You'd probably laugh at me. Why don't I just go back to sleep?"

"No, Herb, I want to know." Sophia had moved on from displays of affection to poking her husband in the shoulder.

"All right, all right." Herbert sat up against the backboard and turned on his lamplight. "I dreamed that you were dancing around on the beach. I don't know what beach. It was somewhat blurry. I think it might've been Apoador. It doesn't really matter, though, and it's beside the point." He continued, "You were dancing and that lovely bottom of yours was bouncing like crazy." Sophia giggled and put her hand over her mouth. "Well, all of a sudden, it started deflating. Really started going down until you looked like one of those waifish New York runway models. I could've cried. Then I woke up in a cold sweat."

"How tragic!" she said playfully. She took the corner of one of the cover blankets and wiped away the sweat.

"I told you that it sounded ridiculous." He slinked back down onto the bed and pulled the covers tighter around him. He felt an uncomfortable combination of heat and cold wash over him.

"Hush," she said, looking deep into his eyes. "You're probably just worried over work. Didn't you say that you had large enrollments in all of your classes this semester? I know that some of your students can be exasperating."

"It's not that, sweetheart." Herbert paused in thought, his mind going back to the proceedings of earlier in the day. "Today, there was an important meeting with the board of trustees. There have been some questions among some of the parents and the alumni about my research. They believe it's a novelty and not serious academics. I heard that some were after my head. I feel that I'm going to be chased away, as I was from Brown. How am I ever going to get tenure at this rate?"

She inquired, "Did they come to a decision? I mean, the board?"

"The thing is, sweetie, I wasn't even expected to appear before the board. It was a meeting between them and Sam Castle. He was supposed to argue a defense on my behalf. With his recommendation, I could likely start on the tenure track at the university. But the thing is that I don't trust him."

"Why, *meu querido*?"

"He's a liberal." His visage switched from a picture of worry to one of sternness.

"But isn't that a good thing? Won't that mean that he'll give you some latitude to pursue your research? When I first met him, he seemed like a nice man. His wife seemed a bit flaky, but they seemed like a nice couple."

Sophia had truly enjoyed the hour she had spent with Sam when she and her husband had visited the Castles' home. He was personable, had asked her many questions about her hometown in Brazil, and appeared to be very interested in her husband's research. On the other hand, Valerie had spent the majority of the hour talking about herself. She seemed a little self-centered. She had brought out a few of her paintings, which were somewhat interesting, if not pretty, at least according to Sophia. Then while she and her husband were conversing with Sam, she flitted around the house like a butterfly that had just gained its wings. But Sam, from Sophia's observation of his interaction with Valerie, seemed to love her. Hopefully the marriage would stay happy as it was Sam's second marriage and he wasn't getting any younger.

"That's the problem," Herbert said. "The president at my last university was a liberal. The thing is, when things come down to the wire, they betray you. They throw you to the dogs. I prefer dealing with reactionaries. At least you know where they stand. It's better to know your enemies than to have some person playing games, being friendly, and then betraying you, leaving you at the mercy of your enemies. It may sound crazy, but it's true. Remember what happened last year with that student? They put all the blame on me. I was the scapegoat, and they threw me to the wolves." Herbert had worked himself into a state of righteous indignation. The perspiration on his face had turned from a cold sweat of fear to a hot sweat of anger. Anger at the reactionaries who sought to destroy him, anger at the liberals who always failed to stand up for him, and anger at those academics who failed to the see the revolutionary power in his pioneering the field of natesology. In time they would see. In time they would understand.

"Don't worry, *meu querido*, my little radical. I know that you'll be successful here." She gave him a big, wet kiss on his cheek. "I love you. I have faith in you. One day the haters will eat crow. You just need to persevere in your work."

He turned the frown into a smile. "You know, Sophia, you always know how to turn my moods around." He returned the kiss.

"I just want my sweetheart to be happy." She continued to look at her husband as she readjusted the sheets to keep them both comfortable.

"I know." Tiredness returned quickly and washed over him like a tsunami. Being worked up had taken the energy out of him. "I guess that we both should get some sleep. Like you said, we both have an early day tomorrow."

"All right, *meu querido*, have sweet dreams." Sophia turned over, positioned her pillow, pulled up the comforter, and settled into a sweet rest.

With his wife turned to her side, Herbert gave her flesh a giant squeeze. "Good night, my bodacious Brazilian bombshell." And soon he fell asleep, snoring, mi-mi-mi-miing, and all that soporific jazz. It was good night, Professor Herbert Brown. And the rest of the night was good for him.

* * *

Earlier that day Sam had become as scared as Professor Brown would become that night. One might say that he was even more terrified as he was the person scheduled to meet with the board of trustees. Very few faculty members and administrative professionals remained fearless when they were scheduled to come before the hovering eyes of the board. Some have quaked in their presence, while others have shook. A person would think that they had stepped into a nineteenth-century religious service if they observed the questioning. They restricted the proceedings, however, and thus the testimonial remained strictly between the questioner and the respondent. The board wouldn't have it any other way. It showed that the board still had some influence, despite the lack of knowledge about who the board was by the majority of the public, including alumni and parents. On the other hand, the university professors and administrators, when they didn't have to appear before the board, spent a significant amount of their time disparaging the board, which they claimed was out-of-date and old-fashioned. Why should a bunch of old white men have a significant say on how COU was run when every year the student body and the Columbus area became more diverse? It didn't matter to them that a black member, an alumnus, had served for the last five years, or that a woman, whom some say was the preeminent member, despite the fact that all board members were to be viewed as equals, was serving. Many said that her personal crusades took up most of the agenda at board meetings. It also didn't seem to occur to the faculty and the administration that the majority of the faculty and the administration were old white men. This was the situation as it stood when Sam Castle walked down the hall of the third floor of the University Center to meeting room B.

Meeting room B was trouble. Everybody on campus knew that. Administrators, faculty, and students skipped past the room like it contained the bubonic plague. On that hall, three meeting rooms existed: A, B, and C. Meeting room A was inconsequential. First, people considered it too small to count as a true meeting room. It hadn't held more than one conference since the university had first established the place. The university tried a gathering there once. The sight became as silly as could be. They packed the attendees in the room like sardines in a tin can. And the room smelled like it—the mustard-based sardines, in fact. Many complaints issued forth from the university community. The organizers of the event had even threatened to take their conference down the road to another university the following year. After that incident they mostly abandoned meeting room A. Not completely abandoned as the administration decided to bestow it to the janitorial staff as a new work closet as a late Christmas gift. A few grumblings issued forth from the staff.

Meeting room C, on the other hand, was for the all-important task of fun. Fun for the faculty, fun for the students, and fun even for those not associated with the university. It had the same dimensions as meeting room B. It thus could hold a great number of people. When the university has its Winter Festival Extravaganza, nearly every faculty member can fit with wiggle room to spare. The student Spring Bonanza also uses the room for the date auction, another popular event. One time, the university allowed the Sexual Health Education Alliance, a Columbus area community partnership allied with a campus organization, to use the room. An unsuspecting professor walked into the room and witnessed an extensive orgy occurring. He said, "Pardon me" and quickly walked back downstairs, blushing and muttering to himself. When the word got back to the news media, and thus circulated around the Columbus area, and when the students' parents heard, a terrific uproar started. In reply, the president issued a statement saying that the university had had ties with the SHEA for many years but apparently a misunderstanding had occurred between the two concerning the day's planned activities. He apologized but then mentioned that maybe "all could learn about respecting the lifestyle choices of others." Some parents had said that that wasn't an apology. It didn't really matter as the outcry died a couple of months after the event. This was the brief history of meeting room C.

Sam, however, trembled before meeting room B. He didn't know why the room scared him so easily. He was the president of Central Ohio University. A respected man among his peers and in the Columbus area. The previous two years, he had been pioneering reforms that other colleges, not only in the Midwest but across the country as well, were taking notice of. There were a few malcontents, but there would always be a few grumpy grandpas trying to take a man of vision down. It was the way of the world. The board, however, could break a man, even an extraordinary man like him. There was rumor that one year the board had called in a professor for questionable conduct. Among other professors they disputed what the conduct involved. However, the fact known was that after the meeting with the board, the man had left the room screaming and had run down the hall. A few professors had said that they saw him unpacking his desk. Others said that they never saw him again. The funny thing was that he was tenured so it was unlikely that they would up and fire him. Most of the staff agreed that he had just lost his mind.

Sam paused for another minute before he opened the door. In the meantime he pulled out and collated the papers within his portfolio. He then put them back in and situated the portfolio underneath his armpit. He took a deep breath, put his sweaty palm on the door handle, gave it a good twist, and entered the room.

The lighting inside the room was dim. It gave off a dull-brown-hue-feeling across the space. The room was emptier than usual. Normally the room served also as the place for honor council proceedings. When these cases occurred, curious students filled the seating to the brim. That day, around the quiet courtroom of meeting room B, there hovered a sense of loneliness. This made Sam even more nervous as he approached the front. In front of him, however, was not emptiness. There sat the ten board members waiting, waiting to dispense judgment on Sam Castle and Herbert Brown. Sam adjusted his tie and looked to see if there were any stains on it. He realized that it was too late to return to his office to exchange the possibly stained tie, so he stopped fiddling with it.

"Mr. Castle!" a voice rang out from among the seated decalogue. It was board member seven.

"Yes?" Sam responded. He lifted his head as he had focused on the floor as he had shuffled in.

"Time!" another voice boomed out, coming from board member nine.

"What about time?" Sam inquired. He truly didn't know what that board member was talking about.

"Look at the clock on the wall!" board member nine said.

Sam turned his head to the left and looked up at the clock. The clock ticking seemed to be getting louder in Sam's ear as each second went by. He turned his attention back to the board. "I looked at the clock." He was really getting nervous now.

The same booming voice replied, "What does the clock say?"

"Um, it looks like it says that it's two-twelve." Sam hoped that was the correct response.

"Two-twelve, Mr. Castle. Two-twelve. What time is your appointment with us today?"

"Um, Mr. Board Member, it was supposed to be two o'clock. I was running a little late. I wanted to make sure I had all my papers straight—"

"Silence, Mr. Castle. Do you believe that we have time to waste? Our time is precious, as we believe yours is. That's why we believe in punctuality, Mr. Castle." The voice changed tone and lowered its volume. "Now please have a seat before us."

Sam sat down at the desk and chair waiting before him. He was sweating a little less than he had been when he had walked in, but his brow was still glistening. He removed the portfolio from under his armpit and placed it before him, situating it a little to the left. He looked up cautiously as he took a number of papers out and placed them in their proper order before him. He wondered if the board was irritated at the sound of shuffling and didn't know whether to hurry up and continue to create a loud noise or to slow down and irritate them with the continuing delay of the proceedings. The board had put him in a difficult situation. Between the devil and the deep blue sea. He didn't know how he'd get out of it, but he knew that he wanted to get out of this meeting as soon as possible.

"You've come before us to discuss the fate of Mr. Herbert Brown," board member one said.

"Ah yes, board members. I've come to recommend that Mr. Herbert Brown be allowed to be put on tenure track by his fellows."

There was a lull in their responses. Then the board members looked from side to side at each other and whispered into each other's ears. Sam didn't know which was more terrifying: the silence or the scratchy buzz of whispers that followed. Thirty seconds later they responded.

"Mr. Castle, we have some concerns about Mr. Herbert Brown," board member four said. "Some questions need answering before we are satisfied and can rule either way. Will you indulge us?"

"Of course—of course. What do you need to know?" Sam lifted his arms up in a questioning manner.

"Mr. Castle, please have your hands at your sides or folded in front of you during the proceedings," board member two said.

"I'm sorry, board member. I'm just a little nervous and excited. Excuse me." Sam adjusted his arms to the appropriate position. "Now, again, what do you need to know?"

"First, Mr. Castle, there's the question of Professor Brown's so-called field of expertise," board member four said.

"Ah yes, board member. Professor Brown is considered to be the leading researcher in the field of natesology—"

"Natesology," board member four said. "What kind of academic discipline is that?" He waited for Sam's response. There was a delay, so he continued, "Mr. Castle, don't forget that we have your information before us. Therefore, please give us your straightforward, honest answer. It will make these proceedings not only go smoothly but also quickly. Your answer, please."

"Sirs and madame," Sam nodded in board member one's direction, "natesology, simply put, is the academic study of the buttocks." He paused to look at the reactions on the board members' faces. There were none.

"Go on," board member six spoke up.

"Actually, it can't be simply put. It's a complex field of study involving biology, physics, history, geography, and anthropology, among other subjects." Sam went on to explain to the board, as he had explained to Tom, how all the abovementioned subjects interacted to form the interdisciplinary field known as natesology. He told them how long the field had existed in the academic world. He also tried to explain why others considered Professor Brown a pioneer in the field. He even stepped up to the bench and provided them with some copies of research papers that Professor Brown had written. Still fearful of the board members, he quickly stepped back behind his desk.

Sam stood with his hands folded in front of him for a little less than five minutes as the board members shared the papers with each other and whispered to each other about the research. Sam's forehead was still drenched. He looked down at his tie and saw that it was a little wet as well. He thought, *God, it's hot in here. I wonder if they've turned on the air conditioning. All this perspiration is making me look so untidy. It's probably giving a bad impression. I wonder if they're sweating. No, they can't be. They're the board. They're human, but they appear so superhuman. Especially number one sitting up there. That's one tough-looking woman. I bet that she's a real witch to her husband, if she even has a husband. Probably not. Or she probably did and devoured him down to bone and gristle.* He gave a slight smile, imagining in his mind board member one transforming into some monster and crunching down on some unfortunate old man. The voice of one of the board members staring down quickly brought him back to reality.

"Mr. Castle," board member eight said, "is there something funny that you would like to bring to our attention?"

Startled, Sam replied, "No, board member. I was just thinking of something my wife told me over the phone. It had to do with something that happened to her in Tokyo."

"That is of no concern to us, Mr. Castle," board member one said, her eyes like surgical lasers shooting through Sam's head. "Your focus is to be on us and these proceedings. It will do you well."

"Yes, ma'am—I mean, board member," Sam said. He really wanted to remove his hands from in front of him, but he was afraid of the consequences. Perhaps the she-monster and her fellow he-monsters would spring from their chairs and snap his neck. Then what would his poor wife do?

Board member one set down a paper that she had been reading. She folded her hands and laid them on the paper. She then spoke with even greater authority. "Having gone over the information concerning Professor Herbert Brown's research prior to these proceedings, as well as briefly at this juncture, we have decided that his academic research may have a place at Central Ohio University. We still have some small concerns, but I believe that Professor Brown's academic efforts at Central Ohio will help solidify his position not only with this committee but also with the university community and with the Columbus area."

Board member six raised his hand. "I—I mean, we have just one more concern before this meeting is adjourned."

"Yes, what is it, board member?" Sam had hoped that it was the end of questionings. He was nervous about what they were going to ask him next.

"There's the matter of that incident that happened at Brown University."

"Incident? What incident?" *Oh no*, Sam thought. They're going where he knew that they would but had hoped that they'd forget to go. But the board doesn't forget.

"We're almost through, Mr. Castle, so no games, please." Board member six had straightened himself in his chair as he continued to peer down on Sam.

Sam gave his brow another thorough wipe. "I think that I know what you're referencing, sir. You're speaking about the tragic death that occurred at Brown."

"It wasn't just that it was a tragic death, Mr. Castle. The incident occurred in the classroom of Professor Herbert Brown. It, of course, happened when this university was already in negotiations to hire him. We didn't stop the proceedings. But we still have a minor concern that something similar will happen here. We don't want that, do we?"

"Of course not, board member. I've spoken to Herbert during my own free time. I had him over for some lunch a few weeks ago. He explained to me that Brown University had settled everything. The student had been in a major depression. Herbert had noticed it, and he had tried to help. Then one day while Professor Brown was teaching, the student decided to open one of the windows in the back, and he leaped out. Obviously, the students in the classroom were extremely distraught, but Herbert recommended to them the mental health resources available. The thing is that the student had been going to the school psychiatrist the previous three weeks. I think that's the only irony."

The board members nodded as Sam finished relating the Brown University tragedy of spring 2011. They spoke among themselves as Sam patiently waited for dismissal. He had stopped sweating like a hog in line for the slaughterhouse. He was still fidgeting a little, and he looked up at the board members to see if they had noticed. They hadn't this time.

"We've heard all that we wanted to hear at this time, Mr. Castle," board member one said. We'll be getting back to you near the end of spring term to weigh our final decision, in accord with the other faculty members, of course. We may require further meetings with you on other matters later in the year. If so, you shall hear from us first by telephone. You haven't changed your home telephone number, have you?"

"No, I haven't."

"Good, Mr. Castle." Tapping her fingers, she continued, "I believe that this meeting has been satisfactory to both you and the board?"

"Definitely." Sam was so happy that he would soon be out of the presence of the board that he almost couldn't help but remove his hands from in front of him. "I just have one more question, board members."

"Yes, what is it?" board member six said.

"When will Professor Brown be notified about this decision?"

"Professor Brown will receive a telephone call no later than eight o'clock tomorrow night," he answered. "Now is that all?"

"Yes." Sam jumped the gun and began picking up his portfolio.

"You are now dismissed," board member six said. "Have a pleasant afternoon. And remember, though we expect great things from you, President Castle, keep humility in mind."

"I'll remember that, sirs and ma'am," Sam said. He immediately began putting his papers back into the portfolio. He said his valedictions to the board, turned around, and quick-stepped out of meeting room B like a soldier in retreat during a rout.

Sam could breathe easier now that he was out of the clutches of the board of trustees. He could say that he had triumphed. At least for now. He had given a brilliant defense of Professor Brown. Brown would now have time to prove himself. He knew that he would. The man was brilliant. He could be a potential star in the academic world. Sam pictured Brown's face on numerous academic journals across the nation. He smiled as he continued to make his way to the staircase. If Brown made the cover of a journal, imagine what they would say about Central Ohio. They would say that "President Castle knows how to take charge of a university. He's our model on how a president deals with the complexities of a rising academic community. He's our man!" *Yes, we're on our way up*, he thought. He then strolled downstairs.

Chapter 4

The following night Professor Brown was resting in bed, having arrived home from work a couple of hours before. He was suffering from the most incredible migraine he had experienced in the last six months. He had turned the lights off and tucked his head deep beneath the set of pillows on his side of the bed. He was first groaning and moaning, and then he was tossing and turning. He couldn't get any relief, despite having taken a couple of pills an hour earlier.

A figure stepped into the bedroom. It was his wife, Sophia. Knowing his agony, she didn't turn on the light but instead tiptoed to her side of the bed and sat down on the edge.

Gently placing her hand on his shoulder, she said, "Are you still feeling bad, *meu querido*?"

Groaning, he replied, "Oh yes, honey cakes. The pain is unbearable. I haven't felt like this in months."

"Tell me where your head hurts?" She rubbed his shoulder and kissed it.

"I feel like my eyes are going to explode. It feels like they're expanding and contracting. Those stupid pills haven't done anything. I feel like I'm going to die. I don't know what to do," he moaned out.

"I'm so sorry, *meu querido*. Would you like some hot tea? I can go brew some right now if you'd like."

"No, no," he yelled out, which was a mistake because the

agitation heightened the pain. He covered his head even tighter, groaning into the stack of pillows. "I just want to be left alone."

"Okay, my little radical. If you need anything, holler." Sophia thought to herself that might not be such a great idea as the loudness of his own voice might prolong the agony. She left the room and was heading toward the kitchen when the phone began to ring. She quickly jumped to it before the second ring.

"Hello? This is the Brown residence."

"May I speak to Professor Herbert Brown, please? This is of utmost importance."

"Okay. May I ask who this is and what this concerns? You see, my husband is not feeling well right now. He came from work very stressed and with a bad headache. A very horrible headache. He's been in bed for the last—"

"I'm sorry for his discomfort, but I must speak to him immediately. It concerns his career prospects at Central Ohio."

"Oh dear," she replied. "I'll get him on the phone right now." Walking with the phone back to the bedroom, she saw her husband already grabbing for the phone beside the bed. Apparently, Herbert had overheard the brief conversation.

Herbert picked the phone up and said, "Hello, this is Professor Herbert Brown. I heard that you wanted to speak with me." Sophia then cut her phone off.

"Professor Brown, this is John from the board of trustees."

"Yes?" Professor Brown knew that there had been some concerns among the board members about his research. Some overzealous parents or reactionary alumni had contacted them when they heard that he was transferring from Brown to Central Ohio. Although his colleagues accepted him, he was afraid that pressure would cause them to vote against tenure. He would then again be adrift in the chaotic sea of academia. No home, no love. Except from his lovely wife.

"The board has reached a decision for now. You've probably heard that we met with President Castle. For your sake, the meeting went very well. Mr. Castle appeared to be nervous, but one expects that at times. He really went to bat for you. It almost sounded like he believed that the success of this university depended upon your success."

"To a certain extent, I believe that President Castle is an accomplished man. Sometimes he's behind the times, but I believe that his support of the field of natesology shows that he's willing to bring this university beyond the dregs of the past into the future."

"Those are mighty words, Professor Brown."

"Well, John, I hope to find my place here. It's a lovely area, even if there is much room to grow, at least in my opinion—" Professor Brown halted. He didn't know if he was sounding too arrogant. He knew that his work was important and vital. But the board might not share that opinion. In Professor Brown's mind, the board was only a corporate leader of the Columbus area. What did they know about striving for, seeking, and finding truth? Usually, their minds only focused on staying in the black. It wasn't their fault. That's the only life that they knew.

"As you likely could guess, we had some concerns. First, there was the nature of your research. Second, the incident that occurred last spring term. And third, some of the alumni had issued reservations about further contributions to the university."

"If you need me to explain, I can—"

"There is no need for any concerns on your part, Professor Brown. As I said before, the meeting went well. We believe that you may make a fine member of the academic community here. We of the board will thus reserve judgment until the finality of the spring term. We may call a meeting then as to your final status at Central Ohio. Of course, your fellow faculty members will vote whether to award you tenure track or not."

Herbert took the phone away from his mouth and breathed a sigh of relief. He was on his way up. He had passed the first hurdle. Now all he had to do was make an impression upon his fellow academic brothers and sisters.

The board member continued, "I officially welcome you on board at Central Ohio. We hope that you will make waves here."

"Thank you, John—I mean, board member. I believe that I'm already reaching my students in my classes. I hope to reach the masses as well through my research."

"Well then, have a good night, Professor."

"Thank you again." Herbert hung up the phone and stretched his arms upward. He hated being so gracious to those corporate putzes. But he knew that they held his future within their little piggy hooves. *It wasn't fair, but who said life was fair?* he thought.

"Good news, I hope, honey?" Sophia said, walking back into the bedroom.

At least my migraine is dying down, he thought. "Yes, I believe so. The administration is getting off my back for now. I won't have to worry about that mess anymore. They will review my file in the spring, but I seriously believe that they're going to give me tenure."

"That's so good, *meu querido*!" Sophia ran over to Herbert to give him an embrace, her backside swaying from side to side.

Herbert thought, *O, what a lucky man am I!* Then it was sweet nights and sweet dreams for both of them.

* * *

That Saturday night had arrived like a strike of lightning. Ian had strained his body during morning practice. Coach Leonard really liked those Saturday practices to be real backbreakers. Ian thought, *How would we do good this upcoming season if by the time it arrived, we were broken men? I feel like my back has been detached from my head. I wonder if Coach is going to let up a bit. It almost feels sadistic. I wonder if we as a team could talk with him about it. Nah, then he'd really make us suffer.* This ran through Ian's mind as Coach pushed him and his teammates through push-ups, side shuffles, prisoner squats, lateral hops, burpees, and planks. By the time the three-hour torture session had ended, the strenuous exercise had coated the young men's bodies in sweat. They could've been their own Crocodile Mile if they had body flopped and slid across the practice field. Ian had been glad to hit the showers that afternoon, and soon after returning to his dorm, he took a nice nap until it was time for Jay's party.

Troy was waiting in the lobby. He had his keys in one hand, while the other held a soda. Between taking swigs of the drink, his fingers were twirling the rings on his keys. *As usual*, Troy thought, *Ian's running late. We're supposed to meet Milly and Rachael there. Even though Jay's place is only five minutes away, they could be already there. Maybe they've left, having seen that we weren't there.* All these thoughts ran through Troy's head when he then saw Ian ambling downstairs.

"Hey man, what took you so long?" Troy said. "I thought you took a shower earlier. You're making us late."

"I wasn't in the shower, dude. My back is still killing me from that suicide workout. He really gave it to us today. I probably won't recover for weeks, and in the meantime Coach Leonard will likely have us do another." Ian rubbed his side, and his face had an intense grimace. "You know how Leonard can be, and you know how lacrosse workouts are."

"First, my coaches in school were never as homicidal as Leonard. And second, there's a reason why I don't play anymore."

"Because you would never be able to keep up with me, right?" The grimace had turned to a sly smile, and Ian gave his friend a punch-tap on the shoulder.

"Hey, what are you doing that for? I thought that you said you were aching so bad that you would collapse. That hurts."

"Oh, shut up, Troy!" Ian bantered him. He continued, "Now, are we going to get ourselves to Jay's or what?"

"What do you think I've been waiting down here for? The end of the world?"

"Coach's practices are more like the end of the world. Come on, let's go."

The two of them walked to Troy's car. With his aching body, Ian struggled to get in, but soon they were off to Jay's gathering.

It was a little after eight, and the party had been in full swing since seven. They started things early at Central Ohio. Especially at Saturday night shindigs. And especially when Jay, the soon-to-be-graduated king of parties, hosted. Around the house a trio of fraternity brothers chased some sorority sisters with water guns. Although it was temperate outside, it was still too cool to go out and plug somebody with a Super Soaker. This didn't stop the frat brothers from plugging away at the young women until their shirts gave a hint of what their favorite bra brand was. A number of the senior students were out on the porch drinking. Most of the underage students were hiding inside from any potential invasion by law enforcement. Generally, a police raid on his parties was nothing to worry about. There was an understanding between the Columbus police and Jay. If there was no disturbing his neighbors, there was no disturbing the good times. Luckily for Jay, situated on both sides of his house were other students' residences. And they weren't Indian or Chinese visa students either. So they knew that when a man (or a woman) had to let off some steam, they had to let off some steam in the most fun and crowded atmosphere, at Jay's place. To be honest, although everybody said Jay's place when speaking about Jay's house, it, of course, wasn't just Jay's house. He shared it with four other young men, who were seniors as well. There was some expectation concerning which group of students would get first dibs on the house next year. The cost of the place meant that the students heavily dependent on financial aid weren't even in consideration. Still, there was pending competition between the various partying sets who could afford the two-story, five-bedroom, three-bathroom home.

Milly and Rachael were sitting on a double rocking chair, taking in all the shenanigans around them. The entertaining sights didn't embarrass them, but they were getting nervous that Ian and his friend would be even later than they already were. Milly craned out her neck and looked around, while Rachael tapped her fingers on the arm of the chair. Rachael then saw a vehicle pulling into the driveway. She noticed that Ian was in the passenger seat but also saw that there was a rather nice-looking young black man in the driver's seat. The car drove past them and parked around the back. A couple minutes later, Troy and Ian walked to the front porch.

"Hey, Rachael. Hey, Milly." Ian waved at the two girls.

"How're you doing, Ian?" Rachael said. "We were getting worried that you had bailed on us. That's kind of why we didn't go in."

Milly got up from the chair and stood beside Rachael. She smiled at Ian, and he smiled back.

"Oh, we were running a bit late," Ian said, not mentioning that he was the reason. "But anyways, this is Troy." Ian motioned to him. "I heard that he and Milly have already met, so I guess you guys don't have to be introduced." He chortled. "I told you that I was bringing a friend. I consider him my best friend at Central Ohio. I might've mentioned him to you in class. He used to play lacrosse too. Not here at the university, but back at his high school. One of the things we have in common."

"Nice to meet you," Troy said, holding out his hand.

She shook his hand. "Pleased to meet you as well." She turned her attention to the three and said, "Since we're all here, I guess we can go in and check things out." They went in and found some places to sit around the living room, while Jay carried a conversation in the midst of them.

Who was Jay? Jay wasn't an athlete. He wasn't extraordinarily wealthy, but his parents had enough cash around to allow him to rent the residence. He usually sported a surfer look: the bleach blond and gelled hair, sandals even in autumn, board shorts, and a clean smile. He, however, never had surfed before. Never had been to the California coast. And when he had made a trip to Virginia Beach during the break between his sophomore and junior years of college, Jay had spent the time strolling on the shore looking to schmooze the bikini beach babes. This doesn't mean that Jay was a poser. He just liked the look, and apparently most people liked the look on him since he was a popular man on campus. Or it could be that he opened his house for parties.

As the four walked into the living room, Jay offered them some beers. Only Ian accepted, and he began sipping on the cheap stuff before he found a spot on the couch. There was a couple making out beside him. But a few minutes later, they left to go outside.

"So, how do you like the atmosphere?" Troy asked Rachael, who was sitting across from him in a chair.

She got up and sat beside Troy, who was now on the couch as well, and answered, "It's something. It's not like I haven't been to parties before, but still they were a little more sedate than this."

Troy could see someone in the kitchen holding two cups of beer. That person then slipped on the floor, spilling the two cups on his own shirt. Another student ran to get some paper towels, while another helped the stunned student up.

"Yeah, some crazy things can happen here, but Jay's a cool dude," Troy said. "No one gets seriously hurt. At least, I haven't seen or heard anything. Anyways, I heard that you're in Ian's class."

"Yeah." The noise level was rising, so her voice had to keep up.

"He told me that you're a real go-getter in there. You know, you raise your hand a bunch. Know a lot of stuff."

Rachael didn't know whether this was a complaint or a compliment, so she blushed. "I'm not really a brownnoser or anything like that. My mom just always told me to speak my opinion. I guess that's why my hand's always been up high since elementary school."

"No, I didn't think you were anything like that. I actually find it admirable. Many students, I'd say most girls, would be content to sit back and not question things, or they're too afraid that they'll say something stupid. You don't appear to be that kind of girl."

"No, I'm not."

"That's good." Troy turned his head from Rachael and noticed that they had cleaned up the mess in the kitchen. The student was at a kitchen table, still nursing his hurt head.

"Hey, Troy, you say that you and Ian are best friends?"

"Yeah. I have another friend that I've known since middle school. He's going to Ohio State down the street. But since college we haven't really met up but two times. I guess that's the way college is. Your past friends move on. And then you move on. It's somewhat sad when you think on it. But that's why I'm glad that I met up with Ian during the freshmen orientation. He wasn't even on the same hall as me, but we just clicked."

"That's good to have friends like that. Milly and I are like that. Except we met during the spring semester while engaged in some community service work—hosting a barbecue event."

"Sounds like fun."

"It was more work than fun, but we did get some great food afterward." She paused. "I also have another really good friend. She's actually my roommate. She didn't walk over here with us, but she's around here somewhere. She's a junior."

"Speaking of that, Rachael, I heard that you lived in the Spanish House. How's that?"

"It's actually kind of nice. It fits with what I want to do. Most of the people living there are pleasant. You do have some questionables, but most people are nice. Actually, this past Thursday we had an open house because, as you may have remembered, there was that tragic accident last year. It went better than I expected. There were a few mishaps, but what can you expect? We're all imperfect. If I'd known you before today, I would've invited you too."

"Thanks, but I think that I would've been busy with class. But back to the Spanish House itself; you said that it fits with what you want to do. What do you want to do?"

"I guess like most people, I've had a lot of dreams. Some of them very silly."

Troy nodded in agreement. He remembered that when he was six he wanted to be an astronaut. In high school he found out that he had neither the aptitude nor the desire to pursue higher mathematics, so he nixed those dreams.

"But now I want to be a pediatrician for underprivileged children." Rachael knew that whenever she told a person this goal, it sounded really cliché. Even though deep down, she knew that it was a noble goal, she still felt silly mentioning it to certain people.

"So why are you majoring in Spanish then?"

"Oh, I really want to work down in one of the Central American countries. I visited Guatemala back in high school, and despite the poverty that I saw, I really enjoyed the warm smiles of the people. I knew then that I wanted to give back to such people. But anyways, I've been taking science classes too to prepare me for med school. I don't know which one I want to attend yet, but hopefully, depending on my grades, I'll get into a good one."

"It seems like that you've got pretty much everything worked out. I hope that all will come into place."

"Now what about you, Troy? Do you have any plans for the future?"

"To be honest, not really. I know that that sounds bad. I'm here on my parents' money, and I'm adrift. Well, I'm not adrift. I know that I'm majoring in history—I think—but I don't really know what I want to do with it."

"You could go to graduate school."

"It looks like that's about all I could do with a history degree at this point. I just like studying history. You could say that I'm sort of a history nerd. Maybe, though, one's likes shouldn't overshadow one's needs. I don't know. I'm still in a dilemma."

"Don't worry, Troy, you still have until spring to declare a major."

"That's still leaving a lot of pressure, but thanks anyway."

In the meantime Ian was trying to woo Milly with his own brand of humor. Even though Ian had been speaking with Milly for just twenty minutes, he knew that he really enjoyed her company. She was somewhat demure, but he could tell that she wasn't a pushover. How could she be? She had explained how she loved the theater. She had been in love with it since she was in the seventh grade. At times she had to keep this love hidden because her parents didn't really approve. It wasn't that they didn't allow her to perform here and there. When she was in middle and high school, they regularly came to her performances, and they clapped at the end every time. However, her freshman year at the university changed all that. Over fall break she told them that she knew that she must become an actor. It was in her blood. She felt it. Her parents told her that she was crazy. Her father yelled, "How can acting be in your blood? You're Korean. You need to be a professional. Acting's not professional." She tried to explain to him that there were many Asian actors. Even many actors who were Korean. She even showed him many of the titles on Netflix. Still, he wasn't having it at all. He called her a disgrace to the family and said that all she would ever get in Hollywood or on Broadway was Madame Butterflyesque roles. He said that he didn't want to be angry with her but that he was just looking out for her welfare. Milly's mother agreed with the father, but she wasn't so vocal and instead tried subtle ways to change her daughter's mind: For instance, she started buying her daughter subscriptions to doctor magazines; however, because the mother's English wasn't that good, in addition to *International Health News* and *Doctormag*, she also purchased her daughter a subscription to *Doctor Who Magazine*. Instead of nurturing in Milly a desire to practice medicine, her mother increased Milly's interest in science fiction roles.

Milly explained all this to Ian, who admired her willingness to stand up for what she believed. Although Milly still took biology classes to appease her parents, she said that when she graduated she was still heading out to LA or to New York. And she was going to prove to her parents that there were good roles for Asian women even if she would have to make them herself.

Ian then fell into his habit of telling jokes, which often occurred immediately after he felt relaxed around someone.

"Hey, Milly, are you into jokes?"

"What kind of jokes?" Milly was nervous. She still didn't know Ian very well and wondered if he was the type to put the moves on girls by breaking them down with dirty humor.

"Well, let me tell you this one: What do you call a bunch of Koreans in a pool?"

"What?" Although Milly knew that the answer was likely something stupid, she was truly curious.

"Rice Krispies."

"Ha, ha." She thought it was hilarious in an un-PC way. She thought that her parents probably wouldn't have found it amusing, but they weren't here. They would've said, "Why are you hanging out with that stupid boy? Do you want to get stupid too?" So what? She could enjoy herself. School and her parents could wait until Monday.

"I've got plenty more. I usually only tell them around a select group of people. You don't want to get a bunch of people's panties in a bunch. You don't appear to be the panties-in-a-bunch type, so that's good."

"Wouldn't you want to know?" She smiled.

"Ha, you're funny, Milly. People might not recognize it at first, but you've got a jokester hidden in you. It's a shame that your parents don't want it let out."

"Don't get me wrong, Ian. My parents are good people. They just want what's best for me. The only problem is that I have a different idea from them. I still respect them and all. I just hope that they see that my dreams and goals are just as legitimate as those that they believe I should pursue." She paused to think on what she had told Ian. "I guess that there is a crossroads that all have to reach at a certain point in their life. My point is right now. Or at least I hope so." Milly crossed her arms, although the impression given wasn't that of toughness but rather that of certitude.

Ian nodded in acknowledgment.

The four friends talked among themselves for the next half hour. Others said brief greetings and introductions too as they passed by the four in the living room. Jay then popped up.

"Hey, Troy and Ian," he said, standing over them.

"Hey," Troy said. He scratched the slight hair growth on his cheek.

"I'm sorry that earlier I didn't really say hello," Jay said. "Just been pushing beers into people's hands. But you guys have been doing okay?"

"Yeah." Ian spoke up. "We've just been dealing with classes and stuff. It's kept us busy. In my case, Leonard has been really pushing it lately, but besides that, I've just been settling into my sophomore year. I don't want the slumps to take hold."

"I hear you, man. But you're enjoying this small shindig?"

"I wouldn't call it small. I would guess that you've got about sixty to seventy people here right now. More will probably show up."

"Yeah, but may I ask who these lovely ladies are beside you guys? I offered them some drinks but didn't ask their names." Jay smiled his surfer-style grin at the two girls.

"This is Rachael, and this is Milly," Ian said. The young women shook Jay's hand; his smile still flashed across that tanned visage.

After these introductions a commotion happened. A young man stumbled, and, laughing heartily, he tripped over the table leg and spilled his drink on Rachael's dress. The young man fell to the ground, still laughing, oblivious to the mischief that he had caused. Rachael began dabbing at her dress with a bit of a napkin left on one of the couch's arms.

Jay grabbed the intoxicated student from off the ground and said, "What are you doing, man? Why don't you watch yourself?" He set the student on a chair in the corner to sober up a bit.

While Rachael was getting up to clean herself off, Jay lifted up his arm.

"I'm sorry about that," he said. "Your first go at one of my gatherings, and it looks like your dress is now ruined because of that jerk-wad over there."

"Don't worry. I'll just head to the restroom and dry myself off." She waved her hand as if to say that there was no problem and that this happened all the time, even though this was the most exciting party that she and Milly had ever attended.

As Rachael walked away, Troy got up from the couch and said to Jay, "I think that we're going to go."

"Hey man, I'm sorry about the spilled drink—" said Jay.

"No, it isn't that. We planned on heading to the movie theater. I don't know what we're going to see yet, but there's probably something good."

"That's cool, man." Jay put his hand on Troy's shoulder as if to assure himself that no hard feelings existed between them.

There were no hard feelings. It was just time to go.

Ian and Milly jumped up from their seats and joined Troy.

Jay said to them, "Don't forget to come to our Halloween party. It's occurring on Halloween, of course. I think that's a Monday, but don't worry, I think that our professors know that we'll be sleeping off the good times."

"Cool, I think we'll be down for that," Ian said. "If I don't see you until then, have fun in the meantime."

"You know that I will, man."

Upstairs, Rachael had just left the bathroom. Most of the spots on her dress she cleaned and dried out. She didn't care. She'd just have to take it to the dry cleaner sometime next week. Walking down the hallway, she came across Lola.

"Hey girl, have you been up here the whole time?" Rachael asked. Rachael noticed that she looked a little tipsy. Tipsy, not drunk.

"I'm fine, Rachael. I've just been up here playing some video games. I haven't been playing that great, though." She hiccupped and laughed.

Rachael thought to herself, *I wonder why*. "If you're finished, we were planning on going to see a movie."

"What movie?"

"I don't know yet, but I think we're going to leave soon."

"Sounds great, Rach. Let me just go back and get my purse. All right?"

Lola walked back to the room and returned to Rachael with a tipsy grace. Rachael walked downstairs with her arm in arm.

"Rachael, we're about to head off," Troy said. He looked over to the girl on Rachael's shoulder. "Is that your friend Lola?"

"Yeah," Rachael replied.

"She looks like a spitfire."

Rachael didn't reply but escorted Lola outside the house. The three others followed.

The five of them decided to pile into Troy's car. They could drop the girls off back at their car afterward. Before they left the driveway, Ian decided to look up what was playing at the Lennox Town Center.

"Crap!" Ian exclaimed. "There isn't much to see. I guess it's the slow season. Lot of cheap horror crap showing."

Rachael spoke up. "What about *I Don't Know How She Does It*? I heard that was good. I've read the novel."

"That'll be a no," Ian said, looking over at Rachael. "Although Troy and I are outnumbered three to two, we want no chick flicks."

"Hey," Troy spoke up, "what about the movie *Drive*? I heard that it was action-packed. A real retro-thriller."

"Sound's all right to me," Rachael said. "What about you, Milly? You are our resident actress."

"I heard some good things about it, so I'm down," Milly said, indifferent to the choices and not wanting to cause a stir.

"I guess that's settled," Troy said. "Let's go. I think that the next showing starts in about fifteen minutes."

And so the five were off to the movie theater.

Afterward the five drove back to Jay's house to drop the girls off. Ian had really enjoyed the film and enthused about it on the way back.

"At first, I didn't know where the movie was going. It started somewhat slow. I was thinking to myself, 'Oh boy, another boring art house film,' but then a third of the way through, I was like, 'Oh man, and this is what I'm talking about.' And all the action sequences, oh my. And that chase scene with Christina Hendricks. I was on the edge of my seat. I like action, but I've been bored lately with all that's come out."

"I thought it was interesting, but it was a bit violent for my tastes," Rachael said. "What about you, Milly? How did you find the movie?"

"It was okay. You're right. I think that some of the violence was overdone. But it was very stylish. As Troy said before, it was very retro. That's what I found interesting."

"That's what I'm talking about," Ian said. "The retro feel. That's what I loved about the movie. You know that I'm a fan of eighties movies. I almost wish that I had been born then so I could've enjoyed them in their first run. I especially love those Greg Stone flicks. Those are great. This movie gave me the same feeling I have when I watch something like *To Live and Die in L.A.* or an episode of *Miami Vice*. I don't know what the movie told you, but it said to me that unlikely heroes are often the most courageous. I like that. Most people don't know what situation life will throw them into. Here's a regular but talented working guy, and he's put in a situation that he never expected, but once he knows what he needs to do, he just does it. Most people today are just a bunch of talkers, but they never get anything done, and they want people to praise them for it. I know that I'm boisterous at times, but I prefer to be that stoic guy who does what he needs to do and then goes home. I have to say that the overhead shots of LA really got to me too. I wonder what Columbus looks like right now from the sky."

"Probably not as amazing," Troy added. "But although I'll not rave as much as you about the movie, I'm glad that we went to see it. But I do agree with the girls that some of the scenes went a bit too far. I get what they were trying to do, but it'll probably be off-putting to most people."

Everybody thought that Lola had fallen asleep in the car, but she spoke up. "I liked the music."

"Yeah, that was an interesting choice. I'll have to check out more of the style when I have a chance."

"It's called 'new retrowave,' I believe," Ian said.

"Well, I think that it's kind of cool." There was silence as the car group pondered the night. They looked outside at the buildings, the lights, and the individuals who were walking to their destinations, wherever that may be, as they drove through the downtown.

To break the silence, Ian spoke up. "I have a bunch of jokes for all of you. Are you ready?"

"Oh no, Ian," Troy said, looking over at him. "What nonsense do you have for us? You better cover your ears, ladies."

"No worries, Troy," Milly said. "At the party, Ian displayed his type of humor."

"Okay," Ian said, "so why doesn't Mexico have a competitive Olympic team?" There was a slight pause before he answered his own joke. "Because all the people who can jump, swim, and run are already in the States."

"Hey!" Lola said, roused now. "My family's not even from Mexico. I'm Cuban and Nicaraguan."

"Okay then," Ian said, pulling another joke out of his repertoire, "what's the Cuban national anthem?"

"What?"

"It's 'Row, Row, Row Your Boat,'" Ian answered, laughing.

"I'll give you that one," Lola said.

"Now for you, Milly," he continued. "What do you call a Korean woman with one leg?"

"I don't know," she replied.

"Irene. Ha ha, don't you get it? *L* and *r*."

"I get it," Milly said. She let out a faint smile.

"I just have a couple more before we turn in. Okay, what's the new movie that is frightening Jewish women? Well, it's called 'Debbie Does the Dishes.'"

"Hey," Rachael said, "I resent that."

"And for you, my good friend Troy, why don't blacks like Tylenol? Because you have to pick cotton to get to them."

Troy smiled because he had already heard that one before and it was pretty lame.

The car had pulled into the driveway. There were still people lounging around the place, and it was obvious that the party was still going on, although it was somewhat diminished.

"Before you girls get out, I've got one more—for myself. Being that I've got some German ancestry: What do you call a pissed off German?" The three young women all said, "What?" Ian replied, "Sauerkraut."

Everybody burst out laughing, as the girls were gathering their purses and the cups that they had carried from the movies.

"Well, guys," Rachael said, "I guess we'll see each other later on, sometime next week."

"Good night," Ian said. "And it was nice meeting you, Lola." Lola was still a tad drowsy, and she hung onto Milly and Rachael as they walked away to their car.

"Hey, man," Troy said, turning to Ian. "Did you have a good time tonight?"

"Yeah."

"Do you think that Milly likes you or not?"

"I don't know. She didn't run away after I told her some of my one-liners."

"I was kind of worried about that, but all the girls seem chill; wouldn't you agree?"

"Yeah."

"Well, let's head home and get some shuteye. I haven't done much myself, but I'm whipped."

"Like a slave?"

Troy shook his head in amusement. "Yeah, like a slave."

"Well, if you think that you're tired, remember that I had the grueling workout earlier."

"Let's just get home so I don't have to hear anymore about Coach Leonard." Troy backed out of the driveway and headed back to the dorm.

* * *

That weekend had proved to be a period of needed rest for Sam Castle. With the board meeting off of his shoulders, he could sit back in his recliner, have some wine, and read some of the magazines that had piled up on his coffee table. It was Sunday night, around eight-thirty, when he finished reading the latest *Harper's* magazine. *Man*, he thought, *that Singer fellow has a lot to say. I don't agree with all of it, but I see where he's going with his reasoning. That's why I had to bring Brown on board. I need someone who's going to shake things up a bit.* Sam mused on this for a few minutes, before he realized that he had said that he was going to call his wife before the week ended. He looked at the clock on the wall and reasoned that it was about nine-thirty over in Tokyo. He'd try her landline first, and if she didn't pick up, he'd call her cell phone. He then wondered if she was still asleep. It didn't matter. He had to speak to her about his triumphs.

After two rings, he got a response. It wasn't what he expected.

"*Ohayou gozaimasu*; this is Katashi," a male voice said on the other line. "How may I help you?"

"Hello? Who is this?" Sam said, bewildered by the unexpected voice.

"Yes, this is Katashi. How may I help you?" he repeated.

"I want to speak to my wife, Valerie Castle. Where is she?" Sam's face was turning beet red now as he licked his lips.

"Just a moment, sir." Sam could hear shuffling and rumbling as he realized that Katashi was handing off the phone.

"Hello," Valerie said.

"This is your husband, Val."

"Yes?"

"Whose that man that I was talking to just a minute ago?"

"Oh, that's Katashi."

"Katashi? Who the hell is that?" Sam got up from his recliner and began pacing the living room.

"He's my student here. I met him at the gallery."

"Well, what's he doing in your bedroom?"

There was a pause before Valerie continued. "Oh—and he's my lover."

"What!" Sam couldn't believe it. He knew that Valerie liked to do her own thing, but he couldn't believe that she would cheat on him. He realized that there had been some distance between them, but that occurs in all marriages at one point. He'd been married for eight years, for God's sake. You can't expect a relationship to stay all lovey-dovey the entire time. *But with a Japanese man?* he thought. *What does he have that I don't?*

There was further space of silence as neither person really knew what to say. Both felt awkward, but believed that they would feel even more awkward when they recommenced speaking. Finally, Valerie broke silence.

"Sam? Are you still on the line? Hello?"

Ten seconds later he said, "Yeah, I'm here."

"Are you upset, dear?"

"What do you think? Of course I'm upset. You expect commitment out of people, and this is what you get. Just tell me this: Why did you do it? No, tell me why you're doing it. Basically, I just found you in bed with him."

"It's hard to explain, Sam. Maybe it's the artistic temperament, as silly as that sounds. I don't know. I just fell for Katashi. As I said before, he's an art student. His technique—in art—I found very good. I began mentoring him to help him improve a little, and things just happened."

"Is he a younger man?"

"Yes—he's in his late twenties. But it doesn't matter to me. You're older than me."

"I know, Val, but you're my wife. I know that I haven't always treated you nicely. I've tried to give you some space, though. I've always allowed that. But this? I don't know what to think. I'm so sick to my stomach that I don't even want to think about it anymore. I'll let you figure out what you want to do with your life because obviously you don't know yet. I don't know when I'll call you again, but it may be a while. Because I'm not such an ogre, I will say best wishes on your gallery. Goodbye."

Sam had hung up the phone, and he was still shaking all over. Shaking with anger. Shaking with embarrassment. Even shaking with fear for what the future would entail for him and Valerie. After getting off the phone with Valerie, he realized that he hadn't told her about his meeting with the board of trustees. She had caught him completely off guard. Well—she didn't deserve to know. Let her paint pictures with her little Jap boy if that's what suits her. Sam grabbed the stack of magazines on the counter and threw them up against a wall. *Oh man*, he thought. *I'm going to have to clean this mess up now. If Valerie were here, we'd do it together. But she's not here. And she may never be coming back.* He left the magazine pile on the floor and sank back down into his recliner. He grabbed the wine bottle and poured a large portion, which he swiftly drank down. He then wept until he fell asleep from the combination of the wine and emotional exhaustion.

Chapter 5

For the next four weeks, Troy and Ian threw themselves into their schoolwork to the point that they couldn't meet with their friends with regularity. Troy had two papers due the second week of October. He wrote an easy five-page assignment, which he knocked out early. He procrastinated on the second paper. It dealt with Japanese feudal history of the eighteenth century. Interesting stuff to him, but it wasn't his forte. He'd rather watch a Kurosawa film instead. But of course that wouldn't fill his history major distribution requirements. He finally busted the research paper out the twelfth and thirteenth and turned it in that Friday. Relieved, he decided to celebrate with a couple of shots of Old Granddad. Just a couple of shots. Ian wasn't that fortunate. Not only did he have a paper due that same week (in the class he attended with Milly and Rachael) but he also had a midterm exam that Friday in another class, which caused everyone to call out for divine assistance to pass—and that was just to pass. Ian did pass, barely. Unfortunately, what mental toll his academic work took, the physical toll of lacrosse matched. Regular season wouldn't start until the end of January, but that didn't mean that the conference didn't schedule preseason games that fall. A one-day Fall Classic mini-game tournament had occurred that Saturday. Central Ohio did well. Maybe not as well as expected, but they did well. Coach Leonard wasn't too pissed but said that if they didn't improve by the time spring rolled around, consequences would fall hard on them. Afterward Ian collapsed on his bed and didn't wake until the next day in the late morning. He thought that resting that day would give him some needed energy, but he still felt exhausted. With all their major work completed, Ian and Troy thus decided to skip class Monday and devote much needed time to catching up on their video games and TV.

As Ian rested in his bed, he flipped through the channels. There wasn't much on TV, but he did come across *Indiana Jones and the Temple of Doom*. He loved the movie. He loved all the *Indiana Jones* movies, but for some reason he loved this one the best. It was strange because most people said that they loved *Raiders of the Lost Ark* best, or maybe they had a friendly feeling for *The Last Crusade*. It was probably because this was the first one that he had found his dad watching. The movie held a special magic for him. Mainly because he loved eighties films, but most people didn't get that, in his humble opinion.

"Hey, Troy!" Ian said, trying to get his friend's attention while he read a book.

"What?" Troy looked up from the novel, which he set aside on his desk.

"You like *Jones*?"

"Yeah, the series is pretty cool. I haven't watched them many times, but I see how many people view them as modern classics."

"Did you know that a lot of critics hated *The Temple of Doom* when it came out?"

"No. I knew that the latest one didn't get good reviews. But *Temple of Doom*? It isn't as great as *Raiders*, at least according to IMDB and what some of my friends back in high school say, but I found it enjoyable."

"Yeah, most critics seem to hate it. Funny thing is that I ran into that hate my freshman year." Ian turned down the volume before he explained.

"Did a hallmate diss it or what?"

"No. In my freshman seminar, my professor said something. Now that I think about it, I realize that the class sucked donkey balls. Media Interpretations of Southern Asia. We watched many good films in there. Well, some of them sucked in my opinion, but who cares what little Ian thinks. Anyways, one day he said that he was assigning *The Temple of Doom*. And I was like, 'Oh, good.' We had a class discussion following the assigned film watching, and then the professor spewed a lot of nonsense about *The Temple of Doom*. I felt like spewing chunks at his bloviating. He said how Spielberg was misrepresenting the Indians. Portraying them as otherworldly, or some other nonsense. I told him that his view reeked of crap. The serial films that he grew up with influenced Spielberg. Yeah, some of those seemed a bit racist, or at least obtuse concerning different cultures. Spielberg, however, wanted to make then modernized versions of films that he had grown up with, and that included the innocent naiveté in those films. It's pulp, not reality. That's what made the eighties movies so great, and it's why most critics hate them the most. Yeah, they give praise to *Raiders* and others, but if they could, they'd tear it down like they tore down *The Temple of Doom*. And it's obvious those critics don't even actually watch the movies they review. Going back to that professor, he said that Spielberg showed insensitivity by portraying those Pankot Palace residents as meat-eaters, when in reality they practiced vegetarianism, being Hindu and all. There it shows: The critics don't watch the movies that they supposedly watch. The people at Pankot Palace were under the influence of Kali and Mola Ram. So obviously they wouldn't be good little Hindus. After that incident I said that I'm never taking another film criticism class again. It ruins the enjoyment of the movies. Don't get me wrong; I like messages at times. But please don't let it ruin the movie."

After this rant by his friend, Troy just nodded. He didn't really know what to say. Sometimes, Ian didn't make much sense. On occasion, he did. Although Ian's rant had come out random and out of nowhere, he could see where Ian was coming from.

"I hear you, man," Troy added. "Thinking is good. People should think a lot more about a number of things. But sometimes, I think, people overthink things. This leads them to some pretty stupid conclusions."

"We think a lot alike. I guess that why we're friends," Ian said, laughingly. He turned the volume back up on the TV. Indy had just finished escaping from the spike pit, and Ian settled in to watch the rest of the film while he healed up from his lacrosse exertions.

* * *

Up in Cleveland an angry man sat in a dingy warehouse. He almost always felt angry. But for the past week, he had been livid. His plans had not progressed despite his thoughts that he had pushed very hard to make them succeed. That disastrous television appearance on that cheap local access channel had occurred. He had acted angry there too. But that woman had pushed him into a corner with all those questions. What could he do but snap back like a rottweiler who felt threatened? The stagnancy of the Black Arms movement brooded in Shazzam Africa's mind. How could the organization grow, he thought, if he had to deal with criticism like that—and from his own people too? That won't do.

While brooding, Shazzam sat on a throne. It wasn't a particularly expensive throne. The red and green stones that covered the arms were imitation ruby and emerald. The back of the chair did feature actual obsidian, but it only covered a sliver, and very haphazardly at that. Beside his chair stood two of his personal guards. If they hadn't had personal names, an observer would've just called them Bulk and Hulk. Being proud of their strength, they didn't care at all what people called them as long as people respected them. When they walked the inner-city streets of Cleveland, people respected them. But those people respected more than their strength; they respected whom they walked with. Even if they didn't respect Shazzam in Columbus yet, many respected and feared him in Cleveland, despite his youth.

Shazzam Africa's first name wasn't Shazzam. However, his given first name had embarrassed him since when he was a preteen. When he found his racial awareness, he knew that his Christian name needed to go. His mother had named him "Steff," an unusual name for a boy in his community. His mother had been a fan of *Pretty in Pink* when she became pregnant. She went to the theater thrice to see it and later owned the film on VHS and then on DVD. In her neighborhood, though, no Duckies or Blaines existed, let alone Steffs. She had to choose from just Marcuses and Andres. She chose an Andre. Afterward, Shazzam's mother decided to give her baby the opportunities that she hadn't received. He needed a name that would give him success. Thus, she named him Steff after her secret *Pretty in Pink* crush. After college Shazzam then also changed his surname to Africa. He knew that he had to get back to his roots.

Shazzam got up from his throne and walked around inside the complex. He admired his comrades as they worked hard. Most of them engaged in weapons training, but others diligently scrubbed the floor. They had engaged in a gathering of like minds the night before, and on the ground there were still some food stains. Flanked by Bulk and Hulk, he told them to keep up the good work as he marched past them.

Shazzam wasn't the original leader of the Black Arms, of course. They had formed back in the midseventies after they had broken off from the Black Panthers. The then leader had said that they needed a more militant position, and so he took a few members and formed a new organization. Later that leader died of AIDS, in the early nineties. The second leader of the Black Arms led the organization from then until 2008, when he decided that he wanted to retire and pursue something else. He thus handed over the leadership to Shazzam, still in college at the time, and went away to Boulder, Colorado. Since those three years ago, Shazzam had increased the membership of the Black Arms by 50 percent in the Cleveland area, but elsewhere in Ohio they hadn't had much success. The Black Arms did have a slight association with the Black Students Organization at COU through a student from the Cleveland area. But besides that, nothing. Shazzam wanted that changed.

After making the rounds at his warehouse, Shazzam sat back down on his throne. Despite his satisfaction with his members, he still pouted at his situation. He thought there had to be some action somewhere. He had restless members. He felt it in the atmosphere. He knew that they had to march on some injustice, but he read the various Cleveland newspapers and watched the local news, and nothing had caught his attention. Some of his members might have to go back to shaking down some of the local businesses, but he knew that they didn't have much capital. If there wasn't another mission soon, some of his more rowdy members might even go back to sticking up people in the neighborhoods. And then he'd have to deal with a lot more than a nosy television host. Still sad, he reassured his guards that something would come up soon. They would just have to wait.

* * *

"Look at this, Rachael," Lola said. Lola stood over her dirty clothes hamper with a look of disgust on her face.

"What?" said Rachael, who was reclining against the wall on her bed and was reading a women's magazine. Most of the articles exemplified trash, but once she started reading, she couldn't stop until she had flipped through the pages from cover to cover.

"I think that somebody's broken in and entered our room. I just know it." Lola continued to dig around in the twisted pile of clothes.

"How do you know?" Rachael flipped to another article.

"It's kind of embarrassing to talk about. It's kind of gross too."

"And?" Rachael looked up from her magazine, staring at Lola and waiting for her to continue.

"Let me ask you this, Rachael: Have you noticed that your undergarments—your panties—that they've gone missing?"

"What? Why, no. At least that I don't think so. I haven't noticed anything strange." Rachael got up from her bed and stretched.

"Well—I think that there's something strange going on. I've noticed it for the past three weeks. It started with that black thong. Then I couldn't find one of my boy shorts. And now one of my favorite pairs is missing. I think that we have a pervert running around our dorm." Lola stopped digging through the laundry, stood up straight, and folded her arms in certitude.

"A pervert? Really, Lola? First, you've probably just misplaced your stuff. Did you try looking around the entire room? Or you might have left them in the dryer. So you should check there as well. Second, how could someone get in here as we usually lock the door, even when both of us leave just for a few minutes? I think that your mind is playing tricks on you. Maybe if you just calm down and think straight, you'll find them." Rachael tried to reassure her friend.

"I am calmed down! I just want all my items back." Lola stomped her foot. "And to answer all your questions, I did look in all those places. Even back in the laundry room. And guess what? I didn't find my underwear. I know that I hadn't even put them in the wash. So yes, some pervert has gone and stolen them."

"Well, I told you, Lola, that I've accounted for all mine these past three weeks."

"You might not have checked fully. Somebody could've snatched yours when they snatched mine."

"Okay, so if you believe that there's some panty bandit around, do you think that it's any of the guys in the house?"

"What about Jose?"

"Jose? That nice guy? I don't think that he's that kind of person to go around rummaging through people's stuff. And no offense, but second, I don't think that he's really into you. I think that he has a crush on me. I don't really like him that way, and I've tried to explain it to him, but oh well—he still follows me around the dorm like a lost puppy dog." Rachael shrugged her shoulders as if to say, *What can I do?*

"Well, then who?" Lola said, generally perplexed at the situation.

"I don't know what to tell you, Lola. I guess—keep your eyes out for any guys approaching our room. And I guess we can make sure to remember to lock our doors all the time, even if we're just running downstairs to get a snack."

"I guess that's all we can do right now," Lola said, resignedly.

"Don't worry. If any strange, freaky guys show up, I'll tackle them, and we can then beat them up together."

Lola smiled. "Speaking of guys, have you spoken with Troy lately?"

"No, unfortunately not. He did call me about a week ago, but we haven't even seen each other during lunch. I think that he's been busy with a number of papers. Hopefully we'll meet up before Halloween."

"You must really like him. You're always mentioning him to Milly when she stops by."

"I like him. I don't know if I like him in a romantic way or anything like that. I mean, he's attractive to me somewhat. But I've known him for about five weeks. And for most of that time, our classes have kept us so busy. No real time for conversation. We just keep missing each other."

"You mentioned Milly—how's she doing? She never really stays when she comes by. And she's rather mum with me lately."

"Oh, don't worry about Milly." Rachael waved her hand. "You know she's not really the drinking type, and when she saw your state that night we went to the movies, she felt somewhat uncomfortable. She doesn't have anything against you or anything like that. But that's beside the point. Ian initially interested Milly, but she told me one day, when we went out for lunch, that she thought that Ian was funny but too immature for her. She has enough on her plate with school and theater. Dating wouldn't work out anyways. If her acting upset her parents, how much more so would they rant and rave when they found out that she had a boyfriend and one who liked to tell Korean one-liners? Not that the jokes weren't funny."

"Oh," Lola said. "Well, I'm cutting back on the partying myself. It's affecting my studies too much. That midterm last week in statistics class really kicked my *culo* to this week. I'll probably not even make it to Jay's party if I don't get things in order soon."

"Well, I'm sorry to hear that. Your costume last year looked pretty awesome."

"You had a good one too."

"I know." Lola's mind had gone from her missing underwear to her La Meurte costume from last year. *It would be too bad if she couldn't attend*, she thought. *I'll blow them away with my costume this year.*

* * *

The next week the students at COU relaxed as much as they could. They had finished midterms and had turned in most of their research papers. Most of the students' minds then focused on the upcoming holiday. Even though most of them had outgrown the need to beg for goodies, they still appreciated the aspect of make-believe, and so most had already picked out their costumes for the following Monday. Troy sat down at the table in the cafeteria with Milly and Rachael and discussed his plans that Wednesday.

"I don't know why you girls won't tell me what you're wearing for the party this Monday. Does it have to be some big secret?"

"Yes, it does," Milly said with her hands on her hips. "We want to surprise you and Ian."

"Let me see if I can narrow it down," Troy said, his arm positioned like Rodin's *The Thinker*. "Is it another one of those slutty costumes?"

"Troy!" Rachael said.

"Well, it's true. Every year girls portray themselves as sexy this and sexy that. Not that I really mind it, but it gets predictable. I just looked online, and the costume store even has a section saying 'Sexy Costumes.' It is what it is."

"That's right," Rachael continued, "they're called sexy outfits, not slutty, and anyways most girls just want to show off what they got on special occasions."

Troy smiled. "I believe that would be on every occasion. But anyways, I'm going as a centurion. You know, as a Roman soldier."

"It fits your name," Milly said.

Realizing the joke, he smiled. "That's true."

"What about Ian? Does he already have his outfit together?

I'm surprised that he isn't here too."

"Oh, he wasn't feeling too well. It might be some short stomach bug, or it could be just the lacrosse practices kicking his butt." Troy knew the real reason why he had declined to come to lunch with the three of them.

Milly hesitated. She fidgeted around, played with her peas on her tray, and then said, "It's because I said no to going out with him, right?" She looked up at Troy.

He nodded.

"I told him that we could stay friends, but my parents just wouldn't accept me dating him. Thinking about it, they wouldn't accept me dating anybody at this point. They'd say that it would take away from me becoming a doctor. They probably don't want me to date until I've set up a prestigious practice somewhere. That would mean that I would never marry."

"He told me that it was because you're Korean. That's why it's a no-no."

Milly let out a sigh before continuing. "My parents do want me to eventually marry a Korean guy when I start dating, so there could be some problems. But do you think that if I'm willing to go against my parents' wishes and pursue acting that I would have their concerns halt who I wanted to marry? Yes, I'd respect their wishes, but I'm not going to be forced into some narrow constraints on what a Korean girl should do. No, I decided that although I enjoy Ian's company, he is a bit immature for me. I believe that he's been a good friend to get to know. But I'm not declining him because he's not Korean. I wished that he'd understood that, and I hope that he can continue to feel comfortable around me."

"Don't worry. I know Ian well. He'll eventually get over it. He just feels somewhat stupid, though. I'm sure that he'll join us at the party. I'm not sure exactly what costume he'll be wearing, though. He said that he wanted to keep it a secret, like you guys. He did give me a hint that it was *Miami Vice*–themed. You know how he mentioned that he likes eighties pop culture?"

They nodded.

"I'm sure that whatever it is, it will be the talk of the party. Last year he was dressed up as redneck pageant princess. I nearly busted my guts laughing when I first saw him."

"It will probably be great," Milly added.

The three ate their lunch, conversing about classes and the potentiality of Milly getting a role in an upcoming fall production. The three then went their separate ways, and Troy headed back to his dorm before going to his feudal Japan class.

* * *

Early that evening Ian and Troy were intensely involved in some video game matches. Normally Ian dominated matches, but that day Troy had been whupping up on him. During one of the matches, someone knocked loudly on their door. They ignored it, but the knocking continued. Troy got up out of his chair in a huff and opened the door.

"Hello, Mr. Troy Thomas," a young woman said; she had a backpack and carried a clipboard and pen.

"Oh no, you again," Troy said, shaking his head again.

"You must know what I'm here about, Mr. Thomas."

"Hey, Troy," Ian said, with the game controller still hot in his hands. "Are we going to get back to the game? I want a rematch now." He lifted the controller up above his head to show that he was impatiently waiting.

"Just a minute, man."

"Now Troy, I was wondering why you haven't joined the BSO. You came to one of our meetings earlier in the year, but I haven't seen you around since then. What's going on?"

"Nothing's going on, Dominique. I just haven't joined. Haven't felt the need to."

"Why not?" Dominique looked over at Ian, who had set the controller down on his lap. "You feel that you're too good to be with your people or something? I see that you don't have a problem hanging out with him."

"No, I actually do associate with a number of 'my people,' as you put it. But I don't feel like that I have to join your organization to do so." He stared at her as if to say, *What?*

"Well, Troy, we need as a community to be a strong front. To counter the voices of reaction and bourgeois complacency on this campus. Every member counts in this struggle."

"Let me ask you this, Dominique: How many blacks do you see strung up on campus? Any dogs getting let loose on the students?"

"Just because they are not stringing us up bodily doesn't mean they aren't stringing up our brothers and sisters mentally. It seems like they've already strung you up in mental chains. The BSO can free you from those chains if you let us. We have many programs, including a lecture—"

Troy lifted up his hand to say, *Let me stop you right now.* "Listen, I've heard your whole spiel before. I'm not joining the BSO. You can continue to be a member if that's what you like, but it's just not for me. Now I have to get back to more important things."

"Like living and playing in the world of fantasy while our black brothers and sisters are dying in the real world? You should be ashamed of yourself."

"Well, Dominique, I'm afraid that I'm going to have to live and die with that shame. I wish you well with your organization's recruitment efforts, but I'm going to have to say good night to you. Goodbye." With that, he shut the door, leaving Dominique standing there with her mouth agape.

Seeing that the distraction was gone, Ian picked up his controller and unpaused the game.

"Hey, man," Troy said. "What are you doing? Wait up a second." He jumped back into his seat and began playing again.

"Troy, what was all that nonsense about?" Ian looked over at Troy.

"Oh, nothing. Just a rabble-rouser who's always coming around, it seems. Don't worry. I don't think that she'll be coming around much anymore. God, I hate when people interrupt me like that. That mess gets on my nerves."

"I hear you, man. I hear you."

"Let's just get back to me whupping up on you."

"I don't think so, dude. You're going down like Mr. T in *Rocky III*."

"Ha, shut up, man."

* * *

That Friday President Castle prepared for any mayhem that might appear that weekend. He had all campus police on call—even though this pissed them off. The president issued an email stating that the university would take all criminal mischief seriously.

That included egg throwing, TPing the neighbors' trees, and random fighting in the streets. He didn't want to spoil their enjoyment of the festivities, but he wouldn't hesitate to use the local police in addition to campus police to quell any behavior that could lead to an unsafe environment at COU and the surrounding areas. Most students agreed, but a few malcontents believed that President Castle just liked pissing on their parade, and they sent the email message straight to the trash.

After getting the majority of his paperwork done, Sam called Tom to his office. He had a couple things that he wished to speak with him about, both personal and private. As Sam put his papers away in his desk, Tom stepped into his office.

"Oh hey, I'm just finishing things up. I'm behind as usual, but that's the life of a president."

"You said that you wanted to see me, Sam. You said that it was important, but that you couldn't mention it over the phone. What's wrong?"

Sam got up from his seat and walked over to Tom. He let out a huge sigh. "I've got something bad to tell you, Tom." He shook his bowed head.

"Don't tell me that you're planning on leaving the college next year."

"No, it isn't as bad as that. Actually, yes it is. But it's on a more personal level." Sam paused as he collected his emotions. "I've found out that Val has been cheating on me over there." He shook his head again.

"What? In Tokyo?" Tom's mouth was agape.

"Of course in Tokyo. Where else do you think she is?" Sam had become snappy.

"I'm shocked, Sam. Really shocked." Tom patted Sam's shoulder to comfort him, but he could still see the agitation in his friend's eyes. "When did you find out? Just recently?"

"It was after my meeting with the board of trustees. I was on such a high note afterward and then I found out this news."

"That's some weeks ago now. Why didn't you tell me sooner? You know that you can talk to me. We're good friends."

"To tell you honestly, Tom, I was embarrassed. Embarrassed about the whole situation. I thought that she loved me—and then to cuckold me while I'm working hard here. And with a Japanese man? I know that it sounds prejudiced, but I never knew that she found them attractive. I asked her, 'What does he have that I don't?' And do you know what? I never got a straight answer. I got some crap answer about how she fell in love with his art technique or something like that. It's typical of Val to come up with some flaky answer like that. Still, I don't understand."

"Sam, is she coming home? I know that the gallery run was supposed to end sometime in December. Did she say anything?"

"To be honest, after what she told me, I wasn't really even listening to her. I said that the choice was hers. If she wanted to stay with her Japanese boy toy lover, then there wasn't much that I could do. I didn't even mention divorce or separation. I hung up the phone and let it be. I haven't spoken with her since. The whole situation is still up in the air. We've had fights before when she's been away, but I still usually get photo updates of her work. However, since this incident, I haven't received anything. I actually wonder if she's doing any painting over there. When I think on it, she's probably been spending all her time with Katashi. That's the guy she's been seeing."

"Um," Tom said, "I don't know what to tell you. Let me ask you this: Do you still love her? I mean—are you willing to take her back after all she has done?"

Sam shrugged his shoulders. "I don't know yet, Tom. I'm still thinking about it. I think about it almost every day. But like I said before, the ball is in Val's court, and there's not much else that I can do."

"I feel bad for you. It breaks me to see you down in the dumps. Just let me know if you need anything. Lisa and I will be there for you."

"Thanks." There was a lull as Sam looked up and then back at Tom. "I need to talk to you about something else that has come up."

"Is this serious too?"

"Yes, it kind of is. It involves the students. Particularly, the female students." A troubled look washed over the face of Sam.

"What's been going on, Sam?"

"I've received reports and complaints from female students that there has been a trespasser in their rooms…" Sam cleared his throat.

"And?"

"And that trespasser—or trespassers—has been making off with the students' undergarments."

"So we have a panty thief on the loose at Central Ohio?" Tom gave off a chuckle.

"This is serious business, Tom. We want all the students to have a safe and harassment-free environment here. Now many of my students are afraid that some pervert is loose on campus. They don't know whether it's another student, a faculty member, or even a random stranger from the Columbus area."

"So what are you going to do? You can't put cameras in the students' rooms. Obviously, there would be complaints from them about that. Ha!"

"You're right. We have limited options at this point. But we have narrowed down the perpetrator's modus operandi. Here, take a look at the names of all the victims." Sam grabbed a sheet from off his desk.

Tom scanned his eyes over the list, and he then looked up at Sam.

"Do you notice a pattern?" Sam said.

"I believe so."

"These names are all ethnic names, specifically names of Hispanic origin: Fernandez, Flores, Mendoza, Ramos, Vargas, et cetera."

"So?"

"I believe that we have a hate crime situation on our hands." Sam put his hands on his hips.

"A hate crime?"

"Yes." Sam looked at Tom with determination.

"Maybe more like a love crime. You can't be serious. This is probably just some student prankster with too much time on his hands."

"I am serious. It's my job as head of this university to take things seriously. In fact, I'm surprised that you're not taking this situation more seriously than I am. You're involved in multicultural affairs. And I know that you have a strong attachment to the Hispanic community. I would think that you would be more outraged about what's going on than I am."

"Sam, I understand that it's a problem. I was joking around a bit. Sorry, but I'm taking it seriously."

"Good. That's the Tom that I like to hear. Like I said before, there's not much we can do at this point. We'll see if the perp continues with his activity in the next few weeks. If he does, we'll seek stronger measures. Hopefully, though, the man, if he's a member of this community, will halt his actions after the university sends out a warning to the students about the past activity. I believe that should nip it in the bud."

"Sounds like a plan." Tom looked again at the sheet with the list of names. "I believe that I'll have to get going. My wife is making dinner tonight, and I still have some work to finish up as well. Plus, she wants me to buy some ice cream. She forgot all about it when she was at the store. I don't want to keep you from finishing what you have to also."

"No worries. Some of this business can wait. I just wanted to get some of my problems off my chest. Thanks for taking the time to listen."

"No problem. What else are friends for?" They shook hands, said goodbye, and Tom left for his office.

Sam slumped back down into his chair and looked at the list of names again. He shook his head and took a sip of his coffee.

* * *

Halloween night set the campus abuzz with activity. COU promoted many university-sponsored activities. There was a horror movie night, various games, and even a lecture on the importance of Samhain to Celtic and American cultural life. Very few attended the lecture, although more students went to the movie night than in previous years. Most students, however, celebrated their own way: private parties and alcohol. The standard university way for years.

Troy and Ian were getting ready to go to Jay's place. Before they hit Jay's house, they were going to go pick up Milly and Rachael, whom they hoped would be ready by the time that they arrived. Ian, still in the restroom, put the final touches on his costume. Troy was sitting on his bed impatiently. He pulled down on his tunic and thought to himself that he probably should've chosen a costume that included pants. It had sprinkled earlier in the day, and although it wasn't frigid outside, the temperature had dropped enough that anybody with exposed legs would feel a significant chill. He was glad that the costume came with a *paludamentum*, so at least his shoulders and chest wouldn't be cold. Troy looked up when the door opened and in stepped Ian.

"What are you wearing, man?" Troy said, taken aback.

Ian strolled in the room. "Who do you think I am?"

"I have no clue at all." Troy leaned in, still wide-eyed.

"I'm The Noogman," Ian said in a pose, as if to say, *Ta-da.*

"The Noog-who?"

"The Noogman. You know, from *Miami Vice*. His name was Nugart Lamont on the show, but he went by Noogie or The Noogman. I prefer 'The Noogman' because it sounds much cooler."

"But your face. Just look at it."

"I just came from the restroom mirror, Troy. So I know that everything's fine."

"Um, I don't think that everything will be fine." Troy looked over his friend. Those red vent glasses, the neon turquoise T-shirt, and the tan Merc Harrington jacket, however, weren't the only thing standing out. He noticed that Ian's face was covered in paint. It was blackface. No, blackface was the wrong term. It looked less Al Jolson and more Laurence Olivier. But it was definitely not Ian's natural hue.

"What's the matter, Troy?"

"Are you really going to go to Jay's like that? You know—with that brown makeup on?"

"Hey, I had to get the right feel for my costume. If I just went as some white guy, they'd think that I was just some random douche from the eighties. They wouldn't know that I was the Noogman."

"I still don't think they would know who you were. I didn't when you walked through that door."

"Just chill out, man. I have everything under control. I really don't think anybody would be offended. Let's just stop worrying and head out."

"If you say so." Troy lifted up his arms as if to say, *Whatever*.

Troy was grabbing his keys and his wallet when he realized that he had no pockets. "I guess these will have to go in the glove compartment when we go inside the house."

"Come on! We have to pick up Rachael and Milly." Ian rushed out of the room ahead of him.

* * *

The ride to the Spanish House didn't take too long. The only thing holding them up was a few intoxicated students who had stumbled into the road and were blocking traffic. Troy was parking on the side of the road when the two girls walked up to the car. Troy unlocked the car, and the girls jumped into the backseat.

"I knew that you would choose a sexy costume," Troy said with grin across his face. Milly was dressed in a sexy Shotgun Sally costume and Rachael was dressed as a Parisian showgirl. Both women looked pleasing.

"Hey, we're modern women," Rachael said. "We can choose what we like."

"What about Lola?" Ian said as he turned around to face the young women.

"Um," said Rachael, "she has a lot of studying to catch up on. I think that she has a test on Wednesday."

Ian turned around.

"I'm sorry. I don't want to put down your costume, but who are you supposed to be?"

Ian smiled. "I'm the Noogman. You know, from the best show of the eighties, *Miami Vice*."

"I thought the best show was *The Cosby Show*," Milly said.

"No," Ian said. "That's a good show, but I wouldn't call it the number one of the decade."

"You do know that you're wearing blackface?" Rachael said.

"First, it's not blackface. It's obvious that I'm wearing a more brownish tint. Second, if I didn't have this getup on, then how would people recognize me as my character?"

"Who is this Noogman that are you talking about?" Rachael said.

"Like I told you before, he's a character on *Miami Vice*. He's this convict character that helps out Rico and Tubbs."

"That's even worse," Milly said.

"How's it worse? He helps out the good guys." Ian shrugged his shoulders.

"Um, you said that he was a convict, and you're wearing blackface."

"It's brown," Ian said and crossed his arms. "Listen, I don't think that anybody will really get offended. I'm just portraying a character. Listen, if anybody says anything, I'll just scrub it off. Okay?"

The girls were still a little wary about the reactions that they might receive when they walked into the house, but they set most of their concerns aside when they thought of the good times ahead.

They arrived at the party a little after nine. The car pulled around back, and they got out and walked to the front of the house. They noticed that the bushes and trees in the front yard had been covered with toilet paper. A passed-out young woman slept underneath one of the bushes. She had checked out early this night. Troy rang the doorbell and was greeted with a euphonious "Come in!" The four stepped in and soon were speaking with the other attendees after they had grabbed their drinks and found seats.

Jay, dressed as a buccaneer topped with Charles II locks, came downstairs followed by an entourage. He was speaking to another young man as he walked into the living room.

"Hey, Troy," Jay said. "Glad that you could make it. I see that you're a Roman soldier."

"A centurion, specifically."

"That's cool." Jay pointed out Ian. "Who is Ian supposed to be? I can barely tell who he is in that eighties getup."

"He's supposed to be The Noogman."

"The who?" Jay cupped his ear as if he couldn't hear Troy

over the party sounds.

"The Noogman. Apparently he's a character from that show *Miami Vice*." Troy shrugged his shoulders. "I didn't know who he was either at first. And I was kind of skeptical about the costume anyway."

"Why?" Jay took a swig from his cup.

"He's got this brown face makeup. It doesn't really bother me too much. I know Ian. But I was worried that somebody else would take offense. But I haven't seen any problems yet, so I guess that it's just my overactive imagination."

"Don't worry, Troy. It's Halloween. Everybody's doing something a little crazy. Look at the couple over there."

Troy looked.

"I guess that I'm sounding a bit stupid. Maybe I'm just hungry, and it's affecting my nerves. I didn't really have a chance to have dinner. We were thinking of getting something before we came over, but Ian wanted to get here to show off his self-made costume." He rubbed his belly.

"Here, man." Jay pulled four twenties out of his wallet. "I'm not that hungry, but why don't you order some pizza for you and the rest of the guests. I'll leave the topping choices up to you. Just no anchovies. That mess will really stink up this house badly."

"No worries. I hate that stuff too. I'll get my phone and make the call right now." Troy got up from the sofa and headed outside to his car.

Back in the living room, Ian was speaking with another male student, Milly, and Rachael. He asked them if they needed another drink. Milly said that one beer was good enough for her. Rachael asked for another, and he got up from his chair to retrieve it. When he got back to his seat, he continued telling them about his crazy professor, Herbert Brown.

"I'm glad that he's not here to see me in this costume. I think that he would have a heart attack. That man is obsessed with race issues. I guess that I should've known what I was getting into when I signed up for his class, but I really didn't."

"I heard that he's a leader in his field," the male student spoke up. They were near the sound system, and it was a little hard to converse over the bass.

"I guess so," Ian said. "Speaking of his field, he might not like my costume, but he would love the music selection here. So far I've heard 'Ass on Deck,' 'Thick Ass Hoes,' 'Ass Clap,' 'Booty Meaty,' 'Big Booty Judy,' 'Shake Yo Booty,' 'Shake Ya Booty,' and 'Shake That Azz.' Those are some real diverse selections there."

"Yeah, I heard that he was a bit obsessed with the subject," the male student said.

"And get this, along with some choir director he's planning on doing a black history show at one of the local high schools. I'd love to see what he tries to pull off. Ha!"

"I try to give most of my professors the benefit of doubt," Rachael said.

"Me too," Ian said. "But this guy is crazy. Bonkers. If I make it out of the class with a C, I'll be happy. Personally, I don't even know why they hired him."

"Well, I guess that you'll just have to stick it out for the rest of the semester," Milly said.

"I'm trying." Ian took a sip of his beer and reclined.

Ten minutes later in walked a set of football players. They

were high-fiving and backslapping all they met as they made their way through the house. D'ante Smalls led the crew. His last name contrasted with his physical attributes as a middle linebacker. He was tall and filled to the max with bulkiness. He was generally popular around campus, especially with a number of the ladies, but Ian really couldn't stand him. Rivalry existed between the lacrosse players and the football players, but that wasn't why Ian avoided his company. Ian got along with the other football players. D'ante, however, was to be avoided, in his opinion. Why? D'ante had revealed himself to be the biggest braggart on campus. Ian realized that flashy showmanship manifested itself in the sports world. He played lacrosse, of course. But D'ante took it to another level. And that level equaled obnoxiousness to the nth degree. D'ante recognized himself as an alpha on campus and made sure that everybody knew his status and that others knew theirs, and he used that to get what he wanted.

When the football players walked in and made their rounds, they shouted, "Number one! Number one!" That Saturday the football team had played one of their most anticipated games, against East Indiana College, and they had massacred them, 44–13. Now Ian appreciated whenever the Titans did well against rival colleges. But he knew that with every win the football team got, D'ante's gloating became even more obnoxious. And that annoyed him beyond his limits.

Ian was still reclining back when D'ante and his crew walked over to him.

"Yo! How's it going?" D'ante said. He smirked at Ian.

"I'm fine—I guess."

"You've been enjoying yourself at the party?"

"Yeah, actually I have. But I was kind of in the middle of a conversation."

"Speaking of that, who are these lovely ladies? I don't believe that I've seen them around campus. Let me introduce myself. The name is D'ante. I'm a linebacker."

"They already know that," Ian said pointedly.

"Listen, Ian, I wasn't talking to you." D'ante shook his finger at Ian. "I was talking to them."

"Okay then. Chill out."

"Who are you telling to chill out? I should bust you in the mouth, especially since you look ridiculous in that outfit."

"Well, you and your crew look mighty original yourselves." The football players had come dressed like Cincinnati Bengals football players.

"Shut your mouf, or I'll shut it for you!"

D'ante had drawn back his fist when Milly spoke up. "Why doesn't everybody just calm down? We're here to have a good time."

"I'd have a good time if your friend wasn't harassing me, but maybe you could change that." D'ante reached for Milly. "Why don't you get up and have a dance with me. I like this song."

Ian jumped up from his seat and got between Milly and D'ante. "Why don't you just leave us alone for now? If not, we're probably both going to do something we'll regret later on. Okay?"

D'ante didn't say anything to Ian. He just stared at him for a few seconds, and then he looked back at his crew. "Come on! Let's not waste any more time with these chumps. Let's get some more bottles." The football crew went into the kitchen to rummage through the fridge.

"God, I hate that guy!" Ian said.

"He seemed like a jerk," Rachael said.

"Yeah, I'm kind of glad that you stepped in," Milly said. "He became too aggressive for my taste. I wouldn't have wanted to dance with him after the way he acted anyways."

"Don't worry," the male student said. "D'ante does a lot of posturing. But I think that he's a coward. Without his crew he wouldn't have made a move against Ian. The best thing is to not pay him any mind."

Milly nodded in agreement.

The four returned to their previous conversation. The music continued to blast, and their voices continued to try to keep up. The football crew walked on by again, and D'ante glared at Ian, who paid him no attention.

Troy, meanwhile, had come from another room. He headed downstairs as he heard the doorbell. He knew that it must be the pizza guy. He clutched the money in his hand as he opened the door.

"Hello," the delivery driver said. "How's it going tonight?"

"I'm all right."

"Looks like it. You students are keeping me busy all night with orders. It looks like this party is really going on."

"Yeah, we're pretty much enjoying ourselves."

The delivery driver nodded. "Well, the total is going to be fifty-three dollars and fifty-seven cents."

Troy grabbed the pizzas and set them down on the floor. He put a twenty back into his pocket and gave the three others to the delivery driver.

Troy was about to close the door when he heard the delivery driver.

"Mmm! Look at them tittays on her!"

Troy turned around and then back to the delivery driver. He knew that he had noticed Rachael.

"I bet that girl's got them pancake nips that make you want to pour some syrup on them or something. You know what I'm talking about?" The delivery driver had a pervy grin scrawled all across his face.

"No, I don't. Listen, that comment was uncalled for, and I'm probably going to call your manager after that remark."

"Hey man! Don't do that. I just couldn't help noticing. Let's just keep this little matter between us. Okay?"

Troy didn't say anything except "have a good night," and he shut the door, shaking his head. *Some people*, he thought.

Troy picked up the pizzas and walked over to his friends.

"You seem like you guys are relaxing good," Troy said. He glanced over at the three, who all had cups in front of them. "Care for something to eat with that brew? I know that I'm starving."

"What do you got?" Ian asked.

"Some pepperoni, some bacon, and one cheese. Here, have a slice."

Ian, Milly, and Rachael grabbed slices out of the boxes. With the smell of pizza wafting in the air, a crowd soon gathered around the four. Ten minutes later the only thing left in the boxes was the grease.

"I heard some yelling when I was coming downstairs," Troy said. "What was going on?"

"Oh, it was nothing," Ian said. "Just D'ante trying to start some trouble. He backed down though. I'm surprised that he hasn't slunk back for some pizza." Ian dunked his slice in his beer.

"The guy is a pain," Troy said. "But hey, you're always going to have punks like that. You just have to find ways to deal with them."

"Yeah, I get you. Roll with the punches and all that."

Troy turned his attention to Rachael and Milly. "You having fun or not? You seem to be just like bumps on a log. You probably haven't moved from those seats."

"We're good," Rachael said. "I like people watching, even if it's just the drunken antics of some frat boy. You can take in a lot if you just sit back and observe. I sometimes think that it's better than jumping in on the action. Plus, after these two beers, I don't think that I could get up and dance. I'm a lightweight. The music has been somewhat repetitive, though. If Lola were here, it would be more her style."

"Booty all around," Milly said.

Rachael laughed. "Definitely." Then they all chuckled as Troy settled down onto the couch.

The rest of the night was eventful but not particularly exciting. A freshman girl did stumble down the stairs, but she didn't break anything except her pride. A crowd gathered around her to make sure that she didn't have a concussion, but she just asked for another beer, and the crowd laughed at her nonchalance. Following that, they played "Monster Mash." It was quite a change from the hip-hop. A number of students formed a conga line, and they did the cha-cha around the first floor. Some were still in the hip-hop mindset, and these grinded against each other as they went. It was a bit disgraceful, but the perpetrators continued, too drunk to know what they were doing or to remember their actions. The attendees later threw away their costumes after they returned home as beer and food had stained them, but it didn't matter as next year they would buy new costumes to surprise or titillate others. By one-thirty in the morning, all the food, except for some whole wheat crackers, and drinks, except for a bottle of Two Buck Chuck, had dropped into the bellies of the students of Central Ohio. The students had shuffled out like zombies. Some of them had looked like it. And another celebration had ended.

Chapter 6

Over the next two weeks, the students got back into the hustle of academics and extracurricular activities. With Halloween in the past, the students were already looking forward to the Thanksgiving vacation period, which was a week away. They knew that once their parents filled them with stuffing back at home, it would just be another two weeks before they would return home and their parents would stuff them again with stuffing. It seemed like the cycle was never-ending, but it was just the fall-winter season for a college student. The colors of the leaves had already changed, and with that so did much of the fashion of the campus women. At times, it was hard to keep up, but that's why they read *InStyle*, *Cosmo*, and *Lucky*.

Rachael had received a new issue of one of the magazines, and she was steadily devouring it like it was premium fudge. Lola was also reading a women's magazine, though it had completely opposite fashion advice. Rachael took half of it seriously; the other half she left as nonsense. To the average man on campus, it was as confusing as most politics. So most just took it as a form of magic to which they weren't privy. While Lola was looking at the clothes, she began to speak to Rachael.

"Do you know that there hasn't been an underwear snatching incident since Halloween?"

"Wow, Lola, I'm jumping for joy," Rachael said in a deadpan voice as she continued to read.

"No, I'm serious. I haven't been missing a pair for a couple of weeks. The icing on the cake was that Marie had two pairs stolen that Saturday. Boy, she was pissed. But after that, nothing. I think that the email the president sent out really scared the perp."

"Or maybe he just moved on and found a new fetish." Rachael looked up from the magazine, used a tissue as a bookmark, and placed it beside her.

"You wouldn't be so blasé if it were your things being snatched from right under you."

"Maybe I'm just not so desirable to the perv. That's why he wants none of my lacy things."

"If only I could be so lucky." Lola switched topics. "Rachael, are you going anywhere special for winter break? I know that you like going on those service trips. I thought that you were going somewhere special this year."

"Actually, I'll be home this year. My parents said that my grandparents are coming over for Hanukkah. They'll probably arrive that Sunday. I'm looking forward to seeing them as I haven't seen them since last December."

"That's good."

"What about you?"

"The only place I'm going is home. I can barely afford that. But it will be nice to catch up on some sunshine when I'm down there. It's always so rainy and cold up here. I must've been crazy to choose this college, being the hot-blooded Latina that I am."

"Well, if you hadn't come to COU, I wouldn't have met such a feisty Cuban friend."

"And Nicaraguan, don't forget."

"Yeah."

"Let me ask you this, Rachael: You and Troy getting along?"

"What do you mean?"

"I might've asked you this before, but are you two dating?" She winked at Rachael.

"No!"

"Why not?" The topic had piqued Lola's interest.

"We're just friends. We enjoy having lunch, but he's always so busy, and I'm always so busy. Even if he was into me like that, I just don't think that it would work out."

"Is it because he's black?"

Rachael looked at her friend with a sense of shock. "I didn't know that you thought like that."

"I personally don't. I've been on dates with people of many different backgrounds, but I don't know other people's preferences. I don't even know how your family feels."

"I've never thought about it either way. Of course, if I hooked up with somebody from the streets of East Side Columbus, they might voice their concerns. But Troy isn't like that. But that's beside the point. Troy hasn't made any moves. He's somewhat timid. I like that a little, but then at other times, I don't."

"I think that you're confused. It's probably good that you're not dating anyway. You'd probably leave the guy's head spinning. He wouldn't know whether you were coming or going."

"I still think highly of Troy. He's a nice guy. I just think that like his friend Ian, he's lost. It doesn't seem like that from the outside, but I can feel it."

"Are you sure that's not the psychology class from last year talking?"

"No, I know that I have good intuition."

"Since it seems that you don't even know yourself, I don't think that you can judge Troy."

"I'm not judging Troy, and you're right to a certain extent that I probably don't know myself. I know my career goals, but I don't think that anybody really can know himself or herself completely. How could you in this world of distraction and confusion? I think that the best one can do most of the time is hope that one knows himself or herself a little and then find others that will help you put that puzzle together."

"Like putting an outfit together."

"Sort of." Rachael picked up her magazine again and looked over an article on makeup tips.

* * *

Sam had received an email the previous day. At first he had thought that it was just spam and then he had taken a closer look. It was from Dominique Fisher of the BSO, who was demanding an urgent meeting with the president. She declared that the black community represented by the BSO was tired of the slights and insults that they suffered at this reactionary university. She listed a chronology of these "insults," and then she got to the final item. A student had appeared at a party in blackface. An appalled fellow student had observed the attire of the student and had become quickly offended by the microaggression. The offended student, disgusted by the sight, had removed himself from the living room and eventually felt that he had to leave the party. According to the offended student, the behavior had offended others, but they had been afraid to say anything. The whole thing had put a damper on the party. Dominique concluded the email saying that if the university didn't take immediate action, she would write a letter to WBNS-10 TV news and the university would pay a heavy price.

So Sam set up a meeting that Wednesday, and he was almost as nervous as he had been when the board of trustees had called him before them.

There was a knock on the door, and in walked Dominique Fisher and another student, who was a behemoth of a young man.

"Hello, Ms. Fisher." He stretched out his hand to shake, but she failed to reciprocate.

She got right down to the point. "Mr. Castle. You've read my letter that I've written on behalf of the BSO. I'm here on serious business. The treatment of the students of African descent on this campus—apparently, it's gone from bad to worse. And we're here to demand action."

"From your letter, I read about that nasty little business at the party."

"Yes, we're shocked by it too. In fact, D'ante here can tell you about it from personal experience. He's the one that had to deal with the assault—at a time when he was celebrating his and the football team's victory over East Indiana. A victory of which I'm sure that this university is proud. For a respected member of this university like D'ante Smalls to be treated so horribly is obscene. What are you going to about it, Mr. Castle?"

D'ante stood there like a statute. Not like that he was stoic, but more like that he was just taking up space.

"Mr. Smalls, is this truly what happened?" Sam looked into his eyes, and he could tell that either D'ante didn't like the staring or that he was nervous to stand in the president's office.

"Yeah, it's true. Do you think that I'd lie about this? When I walked into that house and I saw Ian Mueller, I felt like I had entered a Klan barbecue or something. And then he antagonized me. Trying to fight me and stuff. But I held back. I made sure that I showed restraint, even though I've never been more hurt in my life. Sometimes, that scene comes back to me when I'm at practice. I can't even concentrate. Coach doesn't like that. I don't like that. So what are you going to do about it? What consequences will Ian face after this racism toward me and the black community?"

"I want to speak with Mr. Mueller first, so that we can sort matters out. We don't want to run ahead of ourselves, do we?"

"We want justice, Mr. Castle!" Dominique said. She stabbed her finger at him. "We expect a proper resolution by this weekend, or we will retrieve our allies, and we have plenty in the community who would come to our defense if they felt that we weren't being taken seriously. How does that sound?" She put her hand on her hip and glared at the president.

The situation worried Sam now. He didn't want a media uproar blowing up in his face. He knew that the football team was popular on campus and that many would rally to the defense of a football player. He knew that he needed to handle the controversial situation tactfully. He didn't want to slam a sledgehammer on Mr. Mueller, but he knew that if word got out that the university was a place of intolerance, next year's enrollments might plummet. That would be the end of the ascent of COU and him. How could he wade through this minefield without blowing himself up? Sam sat back down at his desk. He tapped his pen on the desk while he thought carefully for the next couple of minutes.

Both Dominique and D'ante had their arms crossed. They stared at Sam while they waited for him to say something. Finally, Dominique broke the silence.

"We want an answer as to what you're going to do. Do you want the rest of the BSO to march down to your office? We can do that, and we will if there's no justice. We believe in no justice, no peace. What do you believe in?"

"Ms. Fisher, there's no need for rash words. Here's what I'll do. Mr. LeBlanc and I will have a meeting with Mr. Mueller this Friday. We'll discuss with him in depth what took place on Halloween. If it's serious enough, we'll decide the appropriate consequence."

"I ain't threatening," D'ante said, "but I better have a resolution to this, or we'll go to the news and see what they have to say about it. I like this school, Mr. Castle. I'd hate for something bad to happen to Central Ohio, but if I don't get justice, then I won't hesitate to go to other sources. We'll have more than the BSO marching to your office, and there'll be nothing that you can do about it."

Sam rose from his chair and placed his palms on the desk. "I don't like your tone, sir. I said that I'd do everything possible to resolve this unfortunate matter. I told you that I would get to it swiftly. But your words sound threatening, and we don't tolerate such behavior here. You understand me?"

"Listen," Dominique said, "D'ante isn't trying to be antagonistic. He just wants a safe environment for students of color. It's why he joined the BSO. He didn't expect that he'd be at the end of such a horrible racial assault, but he was. He just wants the university to recognize this and for them to levy the appropriate punishment."

"I understand," Sam said. He walked around the room with his hands behind his back, and he then turned to the two students. "You don't have to worry. Justice will be done."

"Thank you," Dominique said. "We look forward to hearing from you by next week." The two students walked out and shut the door behind them.

"Curse them!" he said to himself. "What mess have I waded into?" He walked back over to his desk and opened the drawer. He pulled out a flask of gin. He looked around the room and then took a swig. "God, I needed that." He put the flask back and flopped down into his chair.

He was glad that Jane hadn't seen the previous scene with D'ante. It was embarrassing enough for him. He wondered when she would return. She had gone out for lunch, and then, she had said, she had to make some copies of an agenda. He hadn't asked her to, but she had taken the initiative. Jane's actions were normally like that. He thought to himself that he didn't appreciate her enough. She almost did everything asked of her. She had been at the university before he took the helm, but she stayed even though she had been devoted to the previous president. *I should give her a bonus this Christmas*, he thought. *She'd love that.*

As he reclined, Jane walked in with a stack of papers.

"Sam, I've got the items in order. Where do you want me to set them down? They're about to drop from my hands."

"Put them over there." He pointed to a tray in the center of the room.

She put the papers in the tray and walked back to her desk and sat.

"Jane, don't tell any of the other staff, but you can expect a little bonus this upcoming holiday season. I've thought on it, and I realize that I don't appreciate your efforts enough. If it weren't for you, I'd lose myself in a maze of envelopes and letters."

"Thank you," Jane said, starting to blush.

"No, really. I have a lot on my plate, and sometimes I get so overwhelmed. A certain incident has come up now, and my mind has become focused on that. I realize that without the minor details covered, the major work would never get done."

"What about Valerie? I haven't heard you mention her for a number of weeks. Is she still in Tokyo? She normally soothes you when the work of the university bears down hard."

Sam shook his head as a mournful disposition overshadowed his face. "I don't know about Valerie. I haven't spoke with her in weeks." He looked up at Jane. "She's been seeing someone over there. I didn't know what was going on. I was a fool." A tear formed in the corner of his eye.

"I'm so sorry, Sam." She rose from her chair and walked over to him. She then put her hand on his shoulder.

"I think that I was blinded by my ambitions. Maybe I wasn't paying enough attention to her. It doesn't matter now as she's getting all the attention she wants. I don't even know if she's coming back since things are still up in the air."

"I know that you love her, Sam, but I think that she treats you horribly at times. I think that she loves you in a sick kind of way, but she doesn't respect you. I've seen it when she's around. It must be hard to live like that."

"I still believe that her actions are partly my fault. Maybe I didn't take her seriously enough. Her lover takes her seriously.

He has to. She's his art instructor." Sam brought a tissue to the corner of his eye and wiped.

"Listen, Sam." Jane brought her face lower and then her lips touched the corner of his lips.

"What are you doing?" Sam leaped out of his chair, frightening Jane, who then stepped back.

"I'm attracted to you, Sam. I can't help it. I've tried to fight it. I've tried to. You may not see it, but you've always treated me well. Yes, there are times that you've been gruff, but you were under pressure. Now that I hear about Valerie and her cheating on you, I understand how you've felt. I just can't let her take advantage of you like that. I want you to feel better. I can make that happen. Just let me."

"I can't do that, Jane. You're a good secretary to me. My work would falter without you, but I just can't do that." He continued to back away from her, his hands saying no.

"Why not?"

"I still love my wife. Yes, she's been distant at times, but overall she's been good to me. I don't feel like throwing away a decade's worth of effort over some Japanese boy toy. I love her too much. I made mistakes in my first marriage. I've made mistakes in this marriage too. Val likely knows in her heart that she's made mistakes. I'm, however, still going to fight for her if I have to. I won't repeat my past. I'll learn."

"But what if she doesn't return to the States? What are you going to do? You're just going to pine for her until she loves you again?" Jane, normally calm, stewed over Sam's rejection of her advances.

"She still loves me. I know it. She's just confused at this point.

You'll see when she eventually returns. This is just a phase. A painful phase to me, but I can rise from my ashes. That's why I have to say no to you, Jane. You're a lovely woman. A kind woman. But I can't betray Val, even if she's forsaken me for now. To you it may sound crazy, but I know what's right. I'm sorry."

"As I said before, I love you, Sam. But I'm sorry to see you so delusional. I don't mean that in a bad way. It means that you have a good heart. I don't want you to get hurt, but I can't make your choices for you." She shook her head from side to side. "I'm afraid that since I expressed my true feelings to you, I don't believe that I'll feel comfortable serving as your secretary. I'm sorry. I'll serve out the rest of the term, but after final exams this semester, I'm going to have to move on. In the meantime I'll try to be friendly with you, but I'm afraid that the final weeks we have together will be awkward."

"I don't want there to be awkwardness between us, but as a grown woman, you need to do what you need to do." Sam looked over to the door and back to Jane. "If you're worried that the bonus I promised you will be withdrawn, I'm letting you know that my gift still stands. Think of it as severance pay."

"Please, Sam, I don't want to talk about money right now. I don't want your money. I want you. As such, I can't accept your gift anymore. I just want to move on. In honesty I don't believe that it'll be appropriate for us to work around each other if you're still devoted to Valerie. I'm sorry, but this is going to have be my last day. I'll type up that report that you requested by the end of the day, but I'm saying goodbye forever."

Jane went to her desk and grabbed her bag. She looked around for her keys inside, and when she found them, she walked out the office without waving goodbye.

Sam thought to himself, *Women are always leaving me. What's my problem? Oh well, I guess that I have to call Tom to see if we could arrange for some sort of meeting with this Ian character.* He dropped back down onto his seat, and he began dialing.

* * *

"Troy, look at this letter that I received from the college."

Troy walked over to Ian's computer desk and looked at the monitor. He scanned the letter and then he looked at his friend.

"What does this mean?" Ian said.

"It looks like you're screwed, my friend."

"But I didn't do anything wrong. Silly. But wrong?"

"I told you that I had reservations about that costume, but you didn't listen to me. And now look at the trouble you're in. You have a meeting with both the president and the dean of students. It can't be good."

"But the rest of it is a load of lies. Accusations from students saying that I intimidated them and that I've helped create a climate of prejudice and hate. I don't hate anyone. Maybe I extremely dislike D'ante and those that go along with him, but I don't hate anybody. I want to know who these accusers are."

"You'll find out when you go to that meeting on Friday." Troy looked over the letter again, shaking his head. He then went to his bed.

"You feel for me, man, don't you?" Ian turned around in his chair and looked for Troy's response.

"Yeah, I think that it's complete garbage too, but what can you do? You have to go to that meeting and explain yourself."

"What do I explain? What do I say? 'Hey, look, I'm not a racist. See, I've got a black roommate, whom I consider my best friend.' That'll sound more stupid in that office than it does right now. So what do I do?"

"Just tell him that you went to the party. You thought that you had a cool costume that you wanted to show off. You ran it by me. I said it looked fine, but I didn't know who you were supposed to be. We didn't see any problems at Jay's place. No one came up and told us that they were offended. We didn't get any mean looks from the guests. Everything was cool. Just tell them that this letter was a surprise to you but if anyone was offended, you'll be willing to apologize."

"That sounds good, man. I'm still worried about Friday, but you've helped me out a lot. Thanks."

"I don't want you running into any trouble, at least not any trouble that you can avoid."

"The thing is that if anything serious does happen, my scholarship is on the line. Coach said that he didn't want any controversy this year, as well as desiring top playing from us. If I'm kicked off the team, I'd lose my scholarship. I might not be able to pay for school afterward."

"Listen, you're not going to lose your scholarship. I was at the party. Nothing happened. I didn't see anything. And even if I hadn't seen someone offended, I would've heard it if it happened. So don't worry. You just need to head over to the president's office with a proper attitude and the truth. Afterward, all you'll be thinking about is that Thanksgiving turkey and gravy, stuffing, cranberry, mashed potatoes, mac n' cheese—the works."

"Stop it! You're making my stomach growl, and I haven't had dinner yet."

"Come on, you filthy racist!" Troy joked. "Let's head down to the cafeteria. I think they're serving burgers tonight. And if we wait any longer, they won't be fresh."

Ian's gloom turned to joy at the anticipation of greasy, hot food.

* * *

That Friday afternoon the approaching four o'clock meeting filled Ian with nervous anticipation. He knew that he had done nothing wrong. At least, he had done nothing seriously wrong. Still, he skipped his final class for the day and then spent the intervening time playing some video games to calm down his nerves. He wondered whether the two men were going to be nice or nasty to him. To him, they were just a bunch of old guys in charge of COU. He'd only seen the president once, and that was after a lacrosse game, when the team and the president posed for a picture. The president didn't even stay around long enough to meet each member. The dean of students was an entirely different matter. He hadn't met him personally, but from rumors, he'd heard that he was somewhat creepy. A regular Jigsaw. Even from a distance he looked creepy, and now he was scheduled to meet both of them as they decided his fate because of a ridiculous complaint.

Twenty minutes before the meeting, Ian grabbed a soda from his fridge and walked over to the president's office. As he climbed the steps of the building, he felt queasiness rise in his stomach. He knew that it wasn't the soda. His hand gripped the guardrail as he ascended to his possible doom. He strolled past a number of assistants as they ran from copiers to offices and back again. A man with a piping hot cup of coffee sauntered next to him as he walked down the hallway. The man said, "Student going to see the president, huh? It's a privilege, you know." Soon the coffee drinker was past him, heading toward an open office. "I don't think so," Ian said to himself. He then reached his destination, the president's office, entombed beyond a closed door. He put his ear against the door and heard soft conversation. He knocked, and a voice told him to enter. He entered.

"Mr. Mueller, how are you doing this afternoon?" Sam said.

"I'm fine—I guess," Ian said, his voice turning staccato. He walked over to the men, looking around at the stacks of papers and the countless books stowed in the shelves.

"Please have a seat," Sam said. Sam had positioned a seat before Sam's desk. There was also another chair parallel to Sam's chair and facing the positioned chair.

Ian noticed that the other man, Dean LeBlanc, was standing beside the other chair and smiling as Ian walked to the offered seat and sat.

"I'm glad that you could join us, Mr. Mueller," Tom said. "I wish that it was under better circumstances."

"Me too," Ian said.

"You obviously received our letter and understand that serious allegations have been leveled against you," Sam said.

Ian nodded.

"Although I understand the need for fun, especially during the holidays, I was disturbed when I received a report that a student had arrived at a gathering in stereotypical blackface attire. We at Central Ohio pride ourselves in making this an inclusive environment. If any of our students feel threatened because of ethnicity, gender, or sexual orientation, the university takes it seriously. Do you understand?"

Ian nodded again.

"First, what caused you to attend that gathering dressed in that manner?"

"It was just a joke. My roommate thought that it was okay. He's black, you know."

"That's irrelevant, Mr. Mueller," Tom said.

"You see, I'm a fan of *Miami Vice*, and there's this character on the show, and I wanted to portray him. It wasn't done in malice. I really like the character. Also, I didn't want to offend anybody. That wasn't my intent. I didn't even know that I offended anybody until I received that email from you Wednesday evening."

"Well, you did offend a number of individuals, according to the complaint that we received. This past Tuesday a Domnique Fisher and a D'ante Smalls stopped by my office, and they were livid at your actions."

"D'ante?"

"You know this D'ante?" Tom said.

"Yeah, I know him. He's arrogance personified and thinks that he's better than everybody."

"So there was an altercation between the two of you?" Sam said and leaned forward in interest.

"Nothing that he didn't start. But no, I didn't fight him. I restrained myself, and his friends restrained him."

"He said that you were the aggressor and that he was fearful from the time that he first observed you until the time of that altercation."

Ian laughed. "That's the biggest lie that I've ever heard. D'ante fearful? That's a joke. He's the aggressor and bully on this campus. He has this university wrapped around his fat finger."

Sam adjusted his glasses. "I assure you that he doesn't have either me or Mr. LeBlanc wrapped around his finger. We believe in hearing both sides before we come to a conclusion."

"But I'm telling you that's a complete fabrication. Yes, I did wear the costume, but nobody complained, and I was there for hours."

"Dominique Fisher says that she has witnesses that say that others were intimidated by your outfit," Tom said. "Can you refute that?"

"I don't know. As far as I know, she wasn't even at that party. I never saw her the entire night. Maybe she was upstairs. But I don't know how she can say such a thing without her personal observation." Ian was getting angry at the baseless accusations. He began to loosen his tie somewhat as he felt it tightening around his neck.

"Listen," Sam said, "we're facing a number of angry students. We don't want any nasty controversy. We promised that we would come to a swift resolution that would be beneficial for all parties. We thus just have one request."

"What's that?"

"Please write two letters apologizing for your actions that took place that night."

Ian shifted in his chair. "Why two letters?"

Tom leaned forward to address Ian. "One letter will be directed toward the university community as a whole. The other letter will be directed toward D'ante Smalls."

"That's outrageous!" Ian jumped out of his chair, got behind the back of it, and glared at the two men.

"Why do you say that, Mr. Mueller?" Tom said.

"I told you that I did nothing wrong against D'ante. It's unfair to have to apologize for something I didn't do. I don't mind writing the letter to the university community. I don't think that my actions were wrong, but some people might've received the wrong impression. I don't want to put the university in a bad light or anything like that. But I won't write that letter to D'ante. He doesn't deserve an apology letter. He's a punk liar. I'm the one that deserves an apology."

"Mr. Mueller, you're going to write both of those letters." Tom, with crossed arms, stared back at Ian.

Sam looked at the dean. "Tom, there's no need for confrontation with Mr. Mueller." He turned to Ian. "Please comply with the university's wishes. I beg you. I don't want any further consequences to fall on your head."

"What kind of consequences?"

"I'm afraid that certain privileges could be in the balance. I've talked with others in the administration and with the undergraduate honor council, and there's talk of possible suspension from the lacrosse team, among other lost privileges if there's failure to comply with this reasonable demand."

Ian sat back down in his seat. "I guess that I've no choice but to write those letters."

"That's right, Mr. Mueller."

"When's my deadline for turning in those letters?"

"You should turn them into the office no later than Tuesday

morning as most students and staff will be leaving for break that evening. Is that clear?"

"Sure." Ian looked past Sam out the window at the students walking the campus green.

"Is everything all right?" Sam noticed Ian's dejected look. "Nothing bad going on in your personal life that you wish to talk about?"

"Everything's fine." Ian shook his head. He looked at Sam Castle and Tom LeBlanc. "May I go now? I have some reading that I need to get to before I leave for break."

Sam moved his eyes from Tom to Ian. "You may leave. Just remember that the office needs those two letters by Tuesday at noon. Okay?"

Ian sheepishly nodded. He tightened his tie, told the two men to have a good day, and walked out of the office.

"That went better than I expected," Tom said. "I expected more ranting and raving from him."

"I kind of feel bad for him," Sam said. "He participated in a foolish action, but I believe that he's truly sorry. I hope that when he has written those two letters, this whole business is settled. Then we can look forward to the upcoming break. Tom, I need it."

"I hear you."

"I didn't tell you why Jane is no longer my assistant, did I?"

"No. What happened? I noticed that she was missing when I walked in here. I thought that maybe she took the day off or she went home early."

"You wouldn't believe this, but she came on to me. Here, in this office."

"What?"

"Yeah, that was my reaction when it happened. I was talking to her, and she just stood over me, leaned down, and then kissed me. I was taken aback."

"I would be too."

"I told her that I was still in love with Val, even after all that's happened."

"I guess she didn't take it too well."

"She didn't even put in her notice. She said that she'd finish her work for the day, but that would be it."

"Crazy."

"Yeah. I didn't even know that she felt that way about me. I knew that she admired me. But romantic feelings—didn't notice it."

"You must love Valerie."

"I do. I couldn't turn my back on her even with her current actions."

Tom nodded. He admired his friend's devotion; he just wished things worked out better for him. He deserved it.

"Come on," Sam said. "Let's get some more coffee before the pot is emptied."

* * *

That night Ian explained to Troy what had occurred during his summoning to the president's office. He mentioned how frustrated he had been when he tried to tell them the truth of the situation. He didn't know whether they believed him, but he knew that they were serious when they mentioned the possible consequences. He knew that he couldn't lose that scholarship, but he was still so mad about that second letter.

"Just write the stupid letter, man," Troy said. "I know that it'll be difficult to sit down and start typing, but just do it. Once next semester comes around, you'll probably forget all about this mess. I know that it'll hurt your pride, but if you don't write that letter, where do you think you're going end up? It won't be here next year."

"I think that you have a point. I just wanted to get my frustrations out to somebody. I tried calling Milly, but she had some theater stuff going on. I don't think that I'll get to it tonight. I need to ponder what I'm going to put down, but I'll try to work it out Sunday. He said the university wanted them by Tuesday."

"Listen, Ian, I know that this episode's been tough on you, but it can only get better for you. I know that you'll come out on top. And D'ante—just forget about that fool. Remember, what goes around, comes around. He'll get his one day. It might not be at college, but it'll happen."

"Thanks again. You always know how to cheer a brother up."

Troy laughed and returned to listening to Crowbar's "Self-Inflicted." Later he would recognize the irony in the title, but for now, he turned up the volume and lost himself in the world of sludge.

The weekend flew by, and fortunately for the majority of the students, most professors were merciful, recognizing that most students' minds were focused on feasting, and thus they assigned little work for that following Monday. That Sunday afternoon Ian had finished his first apology letter. He sealed it up, and it was ready for him to deliver. He, however, hesitated on the second. Finally, around ten that night, he sat himself down in front of his computer and started typing. He boosted his spirits with one, then another, and then another, and, finally, another serving of whiskey. He proofed the letter, and it appeared finished to him, so he sealed up that letter and went to bed. The next morning, before his class, he stopped by the main office and dropped off the letters. He put on his headphones, started whistling, and jogged to his class as he was running late.

Chapter 7

The Friday after Thanksgiving, Shazzam received a phone call. It was the most important phone call that he had received in months. While he listened patiently to what Dominique told him, he became agitated and giddy at the same breath. After the fifteen minute rant in his ear, he told her that the Black Arms had the BSO's back. He let her know that they would be down in Columbus by Sunday. He told her to arrange for the local news to cover the event. They would be marching on the president's office Monday. To him, it was disgraceful—the trials a black brother like D'ante had been through the past month. It was a collective punch in the gut of the Columbus black community and thus affected the entirety of Ohio's residents of African descent. He wished her a good night and told her to prepare for the protest on Monday.

"Listen, y'all," Shazzam said, "we've got a mission this upcoming weekend. Our sister Dominique has related to me a troubling situation at Central Ohio University. An individual has been harassing our beautiful brother D'ante Smalls—one of their star football players. The university gave this individual a chance to apologize to D'ante. He instead sent a letter that was a slap to D'ante's and our community's face. This won't be tolerated. What say you, my brothers?"

A loud cheer rang throughout the warehouse. One Black Arms member was even so excited that he pulled out his glock and shot the roof. The other members turned around and looked at the trigger-happy man. "What are you doing, nigga? You want the police down on us? Crazy fool." They continued to berate the man until Shazzam held up his hand for them to stop.

"Put that thing away, my brother." Shazzam turned his attention to the assembled militants. "We won't be allowed to bring our weapons on campus, but we'll still bring our anger as we march on that bastion of reactionary thought. I want all minds focused this evening and tomorrow on our mission. Our anger will turn us into a collective hammer that will smash the barriers down as we seek justice for D'ante. That's what I want. Also, cameras from the local news will be there, so I want all of you on your best behavior." He looked at one of his fellow militants off to the side. "Some of you should iron those uniforms before we leave for Columbus Sunday morning. I want to make a good impression. Is that understood, my African brothers?"

They shouted a collective yes and soon dispersed into smaller groups, talking eagerly about the upcoming protest.

Five minutes later Shazzam dialed an acquaintance in the East Side of Columbus, Reverend Dill Johnson.

"Is this Reverend Johnson?"

"Yes. Who is this?"

"Who do you think it is?"

"Oh, Steff—I mean, Shazzam Africa. I haven't heard from you in a while."

"Cut the small talk, Reverend. We've serious business that's going down."

"What kind of business?"

"Racial business."

"Huh?"

"From a source at Central Ohio, it's come to my attention that a grievous racial injustice has taken place. A student dressed in blackface and intimidated a star athlete, D'ante Smalls. You may have heard of the name."

"He's a strong linebacker for the Titans. I think that he gets his hair cut in the neighborhood."

"Well, the bigot in blackface was assigned to write a letter of apology to D'ante. He wrote a letter all right. One that was not an apology and restuck D'ante in the belly with a metaphorical knife. Obviously, this Ian Mueller learned nothing from his censure by the university. He needs to understand that our community won't be insulted. We won't be trifled with, even by a kid who has money."

"How do you know that he has money?"

"He plays lacrosse, damnit!"

"Oh."

"So are you going to meet us on the steps of the president's office this Monday?"

"I don't know. I've a number of plans for that day."

"What plans? You're a preacher. All your works ends Sunday afternoon. You better show up."

"I don't know if we should stir up so much controversy. I mean, are we sure that it was an insincere apology from this Ian person?"

"Yes, I'm sure. Dominique emailed the letter to me."

"Who?"

"It doesn't matter. What matters is that you show up and that we form a wall of support for D'ante and the African American community. It would be good if a spiritual advisor was there."

"I'm still wary of attending this event."

"Listen, you lascivious coon, I know all your secrets. What if I tell your congregation about that honey pot that you been dipping into after services? Don't think that I don't know. I've my sources in Columbus. If they found out, you'd be ruined. What would you do then? Preach on the corner of the street?"

"Shazzam, you don't have to go to name-calling and blackmailing."

"You're going to be at the president's office steps at eleven forty-five sharp! The protest begins at twelve. My men like to sleep late Mondays. We're likely going to be staying at the Comfort Inn." Shazzam paused. "Oh, and bring that obnoxious queer choir director with you. The news media will be there, and they probably want to see some more diversity. You understand? If you don't, I'll be roasting your nuts on an open fire by the time Christmas comes around. And with your extracurricular activities, I know that you would miss those."

"Yes, I'll be there. You said eleven forty-five—right?"

"Right, so don't be late. I know how everybody loves running on CPT, but it'll not cut it that day."

"Have a good night, Shazzam."

"Remember—African pride!" Shazzam shouted.

Reverend Johnson didn't say anything in response and hung up the phone.

Later, Dill called Maurice and told him about Shazzam's agitation.

Maurice was more than willing to attend the protest. Often he felt that he had missed a life of action and service. This upset him when he thought upon it. It was why he had chosen to accept the directorship of the black history event occurring in February. He had the preliminary meeting last weekend. He knew that Professor Brown, who was helping him, would be interested in the protest. From his brief conversation with him, he appeared to be a socially conscious individual. Maurice decided to call him tomorrow to see if he would be attending.

* * *

Troy and Ian returned from their homes the Sunday after Thanksgiving stuffed and filled—almost bloated. It had been awesome eating all around. They had enjoyed the association with their respective families. Although there were arguments around the table, all made up again before it was time to send people home. Troy himself was not looking forward to upcoming final exams, but he knew that he had prepared as much as he could. Ian, on the other hand, wasn't too worried. His worries had been focused on other issues, but those were now over. He looked ahead to a nearly one month long break. He didn't care whether it snowed or not—despite his avid snowboarding interest—just as long as his parents would ease up on the responsibilities.

That evening Ian met up with Milly for dinner at the cafeteria. He knew that she didn't like him romantically, but she was still a good sounding board. He asked her how her Thanksgiving was, what food she had had, and whether there were any arguments with family over dinner. She explained to him that her father still didn't want to talk about her theater work. She had tried to tell him about the part she had played in one of the fall productions, but he kept brushing her off. When walking away from her, he just kept asking how that would help her become a good doctor.

He said that she needed to focus on her biology and chemistry classes and not on playing make believe in costumes. She replied that she would never make a good doctor and that this forcing her down that career path was abuse, plain and simple. He then slapped her and said that he had had enough disrespect from her this year. It was becoming embarrassing to him in the community, and she needed to cut it out. She screamed at her father, packed her bags, and left for a high school friend's house, where she had stayed until she returned that Sunday afternoon.

"It seems like you had an eventful holiday," Ian said.

"I didn't want it to turn out that way, but we both just exploded."

"Have you called him since you returned to campus?"

"No. I'm still mad at him. I don't really think he's abusive, but he didn't have to go and slap me like that. That was so uncalled for. I told my mom about what happened. She was out shopping at the time. She said that my father had a point. How could my acting support becoming a doctor? I told her, as I had told my father, that I was tired of them pushing their dreams onto me. It's really unfair. She said that she loved me; however, my goals were the real dreams. If I put in the effort, she continued, I would then love to learn to practice medicine. I said whatever, and that's when I went to my friend's house to camp out."

"That's some crazy stuff."

"Yeah, but what's been going on with you? I heard that there was some fallout from Halloween night. You got into trouble?" Her eyes widened.

Ian shifted in his seat and took a sip of his drink. "It's a long story, but basically, D'ante—you know, the thuggish guy—told the university administration lies about me. He and Dominique created this whole bother about how I'm apparently racist and an antagonist to the black community because of my costume choice. So the president and the dean called me in and forced me to write two letters of apology—one to the university community and another to D'ante."

"You've already written the letters?"

"Yeah, I wrote them. When I was writing the second, the one to D'ante, I'll say that I was somewhat under the influence of Troy's Old Grand-Dad. I started writing a clear, sincere apology, but I wrote some snarky things at the end. To be honest, I don't even remember what I wrote. I sealed it up that night and dropped both letters off the next morning. Now that I think about it, it was stupid of me, but what can I do?"

"So you haven't heard from D'ante?" She rested her hand on her palm, looking curiously on.

"Nope. I figured that if he were still mad, I would've heard something before I left for break. Although I think that he's a petty individual, I don't believe that he would waste his and my time continuing with this nonsense. Because nonsense is what it is."

Milly shook her head. "You still should've written that letter sober. You didn't realize it, but it was probably filled with misspellings and grammatical errors."

Ian laughed. "Sorry, but I don't think that D'ante would know the difference? The guy's pretty dense, and I'm not talking about his massive bulk."

Milly giggled a little. "Still, if you hadn't worn that stupid costume, you wouldn't be in this world of mess."

"The costume wasn't stupid. Maybe a bit silly, but not stupid. I thought it was different."

"It was that, but when I was saying stupid, I meant that if you hadn't picked something controversial, then maybe there wouldn't have been this buildup of tension."

"I didn't think that it was that controversial. But that's beside the point. A lot of things are controversial. You don't just go throwing people under the bus every time there's controversy. I never even got a chance to defend myself. That's not right. Look at you, Milly. Your theater stuff is controversial with your parents. What if you abandoned your dreams because you decided that you just didn't want to court controversy with them anymore? Would that satisfy you?"

"That's different."

"Is it?" Ian crossed his arms and cocked his head to the side. "I just want to live my life. Same as everybody else. People claim that I'm stepping on their toes, while they trod on mine. Well, I'm going to fight that. It may make people uncomfortable, but I'm going to fight it."

"I guess there's truth in that saying that 'a man has to do what a man has to do.'"

Ian took another sip. "And a woman has to do what she has to do."

* * *

The next morning numerous people crowded onto and below the steps of the president's office. A cacophony wailed across the space. Banners, signboards, and flags hung limply due to the weather. A steady rain had fallen last night and had continued through the morning. Although the forecasters predicted a few dry spells throughout the area, overall it looked like it was going to be a wet day for the Central Ohio campus. Still, anger and determination flashed throughout the raindrops as news crews descended upon the location.

The Black Arms had driven to the campus from their hotel. The sight of a caravan of black cars had created a stir among the observing students. A few students wondered whether President Obama or the governor was visiting the campus. There was chatter among them until the doors opened and out stepped a crew of black men dressed in black uniforms and topped with black berets. The Black Arms looked around at the campus and at the gawking students. Some of the Black Arms smiled, while others grimaced. Shazzam gathered the members into a cluster. He told them to get the music ready. They were going to parade through the center of the campus until they reached the president's house. A member grabbed a portable stereo from the back of a vehicle and made sure it had working batteries in it. Shazzam directed the member to play the anthem of the Black Arms. The campus needed to see not only the visual manifestation of the Black Arms' power but the audio manifestation also. The member set the CD to "East 1999" and pressed play.

The Black Arms began a slow march toward the president's office. Shazzam was at the head of the column flanked by Bulk and Hulk. The column was three men wide and had thirteen rows, for a total of thirty-nine members. A look of determination flashed across Shazzam's face as they strolled onward. A few members, instead, flashed smiles as students pulled out their phones and took pictures of the procession. Others students were jamming as Bone Thugs-N-Harmony blasted out of the boom box when they passed by. Shazzam didn't care. He was on a mission for some pure social justice.

At the bottom of the office's steps, a crowd already waited for the proceedings to begin. Members of SDS, the BSO, the Campus Progressive Alliance, Young Democrats, the Environmental Protective League, Feminists for Choice, Allies of Feminism, Chicanos of COU, and the Humanist Society, among other groups, including some local area labor organizations, gathered in front of the building, braving the rainfall and making sure that their signs featured no misspellings or awkward grammar. A protest last fall had embarrassed some of the members of these groups as the news media report showed a few misspelled signs and banners. Comments in the newspapers questioned the education that the students had received at the university. Most of the members decried the comments as coming from a bunch of bigots, although they said among themselves that they needed to be watchful of their writing next time before they headed out.

When the Black Arms came into view of the other protestors, cheers and applause rang throughout the crowd. They immediately took a premier spot on the steps. Already on the steps waiting were Reverend Dill Johnson and Professor Herbert Brown. Dill was dressed in a three-piece baby blue suit with a matching handkerchief. Beside him was Maurice, who had on an equally striking suit. On the other flank of the reverend stood Professor Brown, whose attire was somewhat more demure. He had on a navy sports coat and some loose tan khakis with a matching tie. If he hadn't had such a serious expression on his face, an observer might have gotten the impression that he had just returned from a weekend regatta. They would have been wrong as Herbert couldn't swim and he was tired enough of the rainy circumstances under which they'd been drawn out.

"Good to see that you're early, Reverend," Shazzam said into the ear of Dill.

Dill didn't say anything; he looked straight forward, down into the frenzy of the crowd. He saw that quite a few of the protestors had brought umbrellas. He thought to himself, *What a good idea. I should've thought of that because the suit's probably going to have to go straight to the dry cleaner.* It was good that at least a canopy had been raised over the steps.

Shazzam walked up to the microphone and thrust out his arm, the symbol of the Black Arms. "My brothers and sisters and my fellow travelers on the road to justice—I'm privileged to be in the company of fellow minds, even on this drizzly day. I am, however, sad that we have to come together under such a distressing situation. We've been cheated of justice. Let my young sister explain."

Dominique and D'ante stepped forward to the microphone, and she began to speak.

"For the last four weeks, D'ante—a star linebacker and a respected student—has suffered." She scanned the crowd, which nodded in affirmation. "A bigot by the name of Ian Mueller has been allowed to run rampant upon this campus. First, he suffered little consequences for his actions, which intimidated the African American community. Then, what apology the university required of him he chose not to take seriously. He has chosen to spit into the collective faces of the minority communities of Central Ohio." Boos and grumbles rose from the assembled protestors. "Obviously, the university has chosen not to take seriously the feelings of people like D'ante, despite the reality that they are willing to use him as a slave for the profit of the university's athletic program. I want to read to you the remarks in this letter, and you'll become as enraged as I was by the disregard that Mr. Mueller had for the seriousness of his actions. Through the majority of the letter, it appears that this student is contrite, but at the end Ian turns it around and says that 'D'ante is a liar, a bully, and will come to nothing, and the only reason I'm writing this letter is because of the prissy sensibilities of a wannabe thug.' How dare he! How dare Ian try to claim the moral high ground as there is no denying what he had done. We've come here on these steps to demand justice from the university and President Castle and Dean LeBlanc. If they don't take seriously our demands, we won't hesitate to go to the highest authorities with our concerns. They'll receive a bigger media storm than that which they're receiving now."

D'ante stepped forward to the microphone with sad puppy dog eyes. He cleared his throat before softly saying, "I just want what every individual wants. To be treated as a man. To be treated as a real human being. It saddens me that we still have racial conflict at what is supposed to be one of Ohio's most diverse universities. It saddens me that the university doesn't take seriously cases of bigotry and intimidation. How can I play for the Titans with a full heart if I don't believe that they care for me as a real human being, instead of just a jersey and number? I believed in this university, but I don't know anymore. I believed in President Castle, but I don't know anymore. This rally is our last option for getting justice." D'ante stepped away from the microphone, and his eyes began to tear up.

Shazzam patted D'ante on the back and then walked to the microphone. "You've heard the young brother. This incident has nearly broken his spirits, but does anybody care, besides you fine folks who have rallied to this just cause? No. That's why I—Shazzam Africa of the Black Arms—have journeyed all the way from Cleveland in the cause of this upstanding man, D'ante Smalls." Shazzam turned around and looked up at the president's office window. "And so I turn my attention to you, President Castle, if you're up there. Will you seek justice for poor D'ante, just as you've sought riches and respect for yourself? If you have any decency, you will further censure that young man Ian. His attitudes have no place in this community, whether it's Central Ohio or the greater Columbus area. I urge you to find your courage in order to provide healing for this campus. Otherwise, there may be consequences further down the line and a reckoning that you'll not be able to hinder." Shazzam turned back around to the crowd, which broke into a grand applause and a deafening roar of acclamations for his stirring words.

Dill took his handkerchief and wiped the remaining droplets of rain from his face. He stepped forward. "My brothers and sisters, it is at times like these that we should look to the hands of the Almighty for strength. Listen, I didn't want to attend this rally. Not because I didn't care for the welfare of the students of Central Ohio. Oh no. I didn't want to come because I didn't want to face the issues that we all have had to face the past weeks. I wanted to believe that under a president of color, it was past time for marches and protestations for racial justice. I wanted to believe that we as citizens of this United States of America had come together as one united family. These past few weeks have shown that I was gravely mistaken. My reluctance to come today was due to the fact that I didn't want to face the cold, hard truth. I was a coward in that regard and a fool, but now I'm as devoted as ever to the cause of justice in regard to D'ante. We will move forward as a community and fight until every last member of our community is free." The applause rose up again, and Dill stared off with pursed lips into the gray clouds. "I know these are difficult times, but I want you to gird up your spirits. With that—let us return to a familiar song that we shall cry out in earnestness not only to President Castle but also to the university community as a whole. Maurice, lead us in 'We Shall Overcome.'"

The assembled protestors shouted out the familiar song. Dill, Herbert, Shazzam, and Maurice interlocked arms and swayed back and forth. The assembled crowd below the steps, excepting those still holding banners, signs, and flags, followed suit and interlocked arms. They sang out a song of freedom for D'ante and the insulted community of African American students. After they finished singing, Shazzam told the assembly that they would march around the campus garden thirteen times to show the strength of their support for D'ante. Thereafter the assembly left the steps and marched through the rainfall.

* * *

Ian was coming from class when he spotted the procession from a distance. His teammate Eric Hawkins had walked by the protestors, and when Eric saw his teammate, he sprinted toward him.

Reaching him, he said, "Hey, we better go a different way. Just trust me."

Looking at the marching crowd and back at Eric, he said, "What's going on with all that commotion ahead?"

Eric took Ian's arm and turned him around. "Come on, this way!"

"I still would like to know why we're in such a hurry to go in the opposite direction. Do you have something to show me or what?"

"I'm getting you out of here for your safety. That's what!"

Ian looked at Eric. "What are you talking about—my safety?"

Eric hurried into a quick step, pulling Ian along. "I was walking by that crowd over there. Apparently a rally about—no, against—you has been taking place. I heard some crazy stuff, man."

"What!" Ian was genuinely surprised.

"Yeah, man. I looked at some of those signs, and they were calling you the grand wizard or some other mess. One of the protestors said that they ought to teach you a lesson about being respectful. So you see why I had to get you out of there before they caught sight of you. Or you would've been in big trouble."

Ian looked back. "That entire crowd was about me?"

"Yeah. I was walking by quickly, so I had only a glimpse. But apparently there aren't just students marching around. Looks like there are some real outside agitators involved. Some of them look like some real bruisers. It was kind of scary."

"I bet it was." They continued to walk back, heading toward Ian's dorm.

"Tell me, man, why do you have that whole crew agitated at you?"

"I don't know."

"I know that you said that you got into trouble for that Halloween thing, but you told me that you wrote a letter of apology before you left for home."

"Yeah, I did."

"So why is that group still pissed at you?"

"I've only told Milly this, but when I was writing that second later to D'ante, I was partaking a bit of the bourbon. I wrote some things at the end. But I ended up dropping it off anyway. I guess that it did end up angering him. I didn't know because I hadn't heard anything before I left."

"You've gone and done it again, Ian."

"What?" Ian stopped walking. "I wasn't going to allow that thug to bully me around like he does with so many other students. I've been proclaimed the liar, when he's obviously spent the past weeks spreading falsehoods against me. I was willing to say sorry to the university, but I was not going to let D'ante get away with reputational murder."

"I understand you, but you have to know that you've really stepped into it. I won't be surprised if you get a message from the president or the dean."

"As long as Coach Leonard doesn't get on my case, I'll be fine."

Eric agreed and went his separate way, while Ian went back to his room to contemplate what he was going to do.

* * *

Sam rose from his chair and looked down on the campus gardens. He breathed a sigh of relief as he saw the crowd dispersing across the campus. *They stayed around long enough, despite the rain*, he thought. *I was afraid that they would storm the building and hold me hostage, or worse.*

"They're gone now," he said to Tom, who was sitting down at Jane's former desk.

"Thank God!" He jumped up and slinked over to Sam's desk, worried that the assembly would return for their heads.

"What am I going to do? You heard how angry they were. They were really baying for blood. If not Mr. Mueller, then ours."

"I know. I heard it all and got a glimpse of the marching. Some scary business—and I encourage the students to voice their concerns."

Sam loosened his tie and took a sip of his water. "I didn't know this Ian business would turn so serious. I thought that it was all over last week."

"Didn't you say that D'ante and Dominique sent you an email complaining about the tone of the apology letter?"

"Yes, but I just blew it off. I thought that they would forget it too. It's why I've been ignoring it these past few days. I guess that I was wrong." Sam shook his head.

"So what are you going to do?"

Sam looked down at his feet. He stood there in that position for about a minute. He lifted his head and walked around the room, contemplating. "I'm afraid that I'll have to pay a visit to Mr. Mueller this evening. I don't want to, but the reputation of this university is at stake. The board won't like it if events proceed anymore down this road of controversy."

"What are you going to tell him?" Tom turned his head upward.

"I'm afraid that this is now an honor council matter. I didn't want it to get to this point, but I'm afraid that I have no choice.

What do you think?"

"Sam, you have to do what you have to do. I mean, it's just one student."

"That's not the point. I've let things get out of control. I've never let things get out of control before. Well, maybe in my personal life, but never with the university. I've failed myself." Sam walked back to his desk and slumped into the chair.

"Don't be too hard on yourself. I know that life's been difficult for you recently, but you can't beat yourself up. You have to realize that sometimes life takes these little detours. That's what you have to be prepared for. Otherwise, you'll fret over matters that you can't stop."

"I know, I know. I just hate making difficult decisions like this. Sometimes—I wish that I could turn my authority over to someone else at these times."

"But you can't. You're the president. The university expects firm leadership, especially in matters like this. Listen, though, if you feel uncomfortable, I can go over to Mr. Mueller's room with you to—"

"No, that won't be necessary. I'll send an email out right now, telling him that I'll be visiting later."

"Good. That's the Sam that I know. I know that it'll be painful, but you have to think about what's best for the university."

"I guess that you're right."

* * *

That evening Troy and Ian received a knock on their door. While Troy didn't know who it was, Ian realized that his judgment time had arrived. He had received an email from the president an hour after his escape from the mob. He had read it over twice, knowing that the ax was about to fall on his neck. He had resigned himself to the meeting, praying that all would come out all right. He hadn't even eaten dinner as his stomach was queasy from the anticipation of the president's arrival. He spent the majority of the rest of the day sitting at the edge of his bed thinking. Then around seven forty-five, he heard the familiar voice.

"Mr. Mueller, may I come in?"

Ian didn't say anything, but he rose from his bed and began walking to the door.

"Who's that?" Troy said. It didn't sound like any voice that he recognized.

Ian opened the door and said, "Good evening, President Castle."

"May I enter and sit down?" Sam asked.

Ian stepped aside, and Sam walked into the dorm room, looking all around him at the various posters and electronic gadgets. Ian followed behind him and looked over at Troy, who was wondering why the president was in their room.

"Ian," Sam said. "Do you think your roommate would mind if we spoke privately for a few minutes?"

"No, I don't think so." Ian turned to Troy, who was reading a textbook and listening to his music. "Troy, would you mind heading down to the lobby for about ten to fifteen minutes? I have important business with President Castle. I really don't think that it will take too long." Ian looked over at Sam.

"No," Sam said. "It shouldn't be longer than ten minutes. If it is, you can go ahead and knock on the door to alert me. Okay?"

Troy looked from Ian to Sam and back again. "Okay, I guess."

He put the iPod in his pocket, gathered his papers and textbook, and exited the room.

"I'm sorry that I booted your friend from the room," said Sam, now relaxed in the chair in front of Ian's computer. "I just wanted to speak with you confidentially, being that it's such a serious subject. I know how friends can get riled up at what they feel are injustices."

Ian nodded in agreement.

"It's hard for me to discuss judicial matters such as this, but I'm required to do so. I'm afraid that due to your actions concerning that letter to Mr. Smalls, you're going to have to go before the honor council this Friday."

"What?" Ian said, shocked at the severity of the consequences. He knew that the president was coming over to censure him, but he thought that he was just going to receive a stern speech. "How am I going before the council? I didn't steal or cheat."

Sam shook his head once more. "No, you didn't do any of those things, but you told an untruth by your actions. You promised the university that you would write two letters."

"I did write those letters—in the time requested of me."

"Yes, but the letter written to D'ante was not written appropriately, according to the university's agreement. You promised an apology—something that you incompletely delivered to Mr. Smalls."

Ian jumped up from his bed. "I told you that I was not going on my knees for that lying troublemaker. I wasn't doing it. And I'm not going to do it."

"I'm sorry, but you leave the university no choice but to go through with these judicial proceedings. I didn't want it this way, but your attitude has been so belligerent that it has been distressing to all those involved. I don't know if you were there in the campus gardens, but your little stunt has created a media firestorm in the Columbus area. It's put the university in a bad light."

"That's all you care about, isn't it?"

"No. But it's the primary thing. That's why I'm head of this university.

Ian shrugged his shoulders. "So what am I supposed to do? What's going to happen to me?"

"That'll be up to you at the proceedings, but it'll also be in the hands of your peers. I urge you to make a good impression at the meeting, or there could be further serious consequences."

"What time will it be?"

"I informed the council this afternoon about a trial. They'll get back to me tomorrow afternoon with a confirmed time, but it'll likely be early evening."

"I guess that I'll be missing lacrosse practice then."

"Mr. Mueller, these proceedings could mean your athletic career. Please take them seriously." Sam stopped. "I should let you know that you've right to counsel during the proceedings. It can be either a faculty member or a student. Your choice."

"Mr. Castle, I think that I'll just be up there by myself. I don't think any counsel will help me any more than the truth will."

"Your choice, again." Sam rose from the chair and walked to the door. He turned around and looked at Ian pitifully. "I wish that this could've turned out differently." He opened the door and shut it behind him as he headed outside.

Troy walked past Sam as he returned to his room. He

wondered what the president and his friend had discussed. He had been thinking about it downstairs, so he had failed to keep focused on his reading assignment. Gripping his materials, he walked into his room and sat back down on his bed.

"What was all that about?" he inquired.

"You know that letter that I had to write to D'ante?"

"You wrote it, didn't you?"

"I said some things in there that I probably should've refrained from."

"Why didn't you tell me, man? I'm your good friend." Troy's hands were up in the air in disbelief.

"When I thought about it, I was embarrassed. Not because of the things that I said, but because I knew that you'd think that I was stupid or something."

"I think that it was a stupid action, but it's too late to change that now, isn't it?"

"You're right." Ian thrust his hands into his pockets. He turned his back to Troy and sighed deeply.

"So what did the president say?"

Ian turned around. "Troy, it's bad news. I'm being summoned in front of the honor council this Friday."

"Did he mention any possible punishments?"

"Nothing specific, but just that my athletic career could be in jeopardy."

Troy shook his head from side to side. "You've really fallen into it now."

Ian stepped forward, pleading. "But you know that this whole mess isn't my fault. Yes, I may have exacerbated it, but if it hadn't involved that fool D'ante, then I doubt it would have gotten this far. I know that's the truth."

"I believe you, man. I believe you. But do you think that the honor council will believe you? That's the question that you need to ask yourself, and from looking at it, you only have a few days before you'll find out."

"You're going to be there and help me, aren't you?"

"Of course I'm going to be there as a witness, but I don't think that it'll be just my testimony that'll save you from a judicial hanging."

"So it would be good to ask Milly, Rachael, and perhaps even Jay to be there?"

"I would if I were in your situation."

"I'm sorry that I have to involve you all in this.

"Don't worry. Just try to be relaxed by the time you enter that hearing room. We'll be waiting there for you."

"Thanks again. You're a good friend."

"I try to be. Now, let's order some pizza. I already ate, but it looks like you're starving like a refugee."

Chapter 8

That Friday Ian's honor council hearing was the talk of the campus. People who knew nothing of the October 31 incident now had opinions one way or another. Some claimed that he was guilty and that his initial punishment wasn't severe enough. They believed that Ian knew that he had gotten off easy, and that's why he felt entitled to spit into the face of the university. Other students believed that although Ian's original actions had been stupid, the university had punished him enough and any further action, and thus subsequent coverage, would lead to further ostracism of the college community. Most students didn't care which way the honor council ruled, but they found the controversy interesting enough to interrupt their dull lives.

In the afternoon Ian had been surfing online, and he had found numerous articles referencing him and the ongoing controversy at COU.

"Look at this, Troy! All these things these people have written about me. This pisses me off tremendously. These bloggers don't even know me, and they're calling me a bigot and a disgrace to university life. It's not true! Shouldn't they focus on something more important? I know that there are more important things in the world than my case. But all this energy is focused on me. It's ridiculous."

Troy bent over the chair and looked at the open internet tabs. "You shouldn't worry about these people. All that is just a bunch of obnoxious and pretentious blather. Here." Troy closed down the internet windows and walked back to his desk.

"I'm still worried about the hearing. Since I've never been before the chair and never even dealt personally with him—I don't know for a fact, but I've heard that he means business, especially with sensitive issues like these."

"Don't worry; we're going to give truthful and honest answers in your behalf. D'ante may be popular, but I know that the council will see through his lies. Come on. Cheer up a bit."

"I know that you wouldn't be cheerful with the prospect of facing sixteen peers—people who have your head under the guillotine."

"Knock it off with all that morbid talk. You probably just need something to eat, which is why your mind is all over the place."

"I'm good. I'll grab something to go from the cafeteria before I head for the University Center."

"I have to get to class. Afterward I'm going to meet up with the other two. So, I guess that I'll see you around seven. Try to take courage. Okay?"

"Yeah." Ian was left alone in the dorm room, counting down the time until he would meet his fate in meeting room B.

* * *

An hour before the hearing, Sam sat in his office—just staring out the window. He heard a knock on the door. He told the person to enter.

"Hello?"

"Hey, Tom."

"I thought that you had already left for home."

"No, I was just catching up on paperwork. Still been behind

since Jane left us."

"But it doesn't look like you're working. I saw you from outside just staring off in thought."

"I was thinking about that hearing tonight."

"You need to get that out of your head. It's basically done. You might as well say that it's already happened. I'm sorry."

"I feel that I put that young man into a really rough place. I still don't know if I did the right thing. The look on his face when I left the room—it still floats around in my head. I can't get it out."

"What were you going to do? The Black Arms are still over at that hotel. They said that they weren't leaving until the university delivered justice. They're a scary group. It's lucky that they're usually up in Cleveland. I'm just glad that they're haven't been any more marches around the university since Monday. I figured that it was the weather that's been keeping them at a distance. But I also believe that they're giving us a chance to rectify an awry situation."

"Really? Did anything need to be rectified?"

"Looking at all these reports, both in the papers and online, I'd have to say yes." Tom paused. "At least Mr. Mueller is getting a fair hearing. It's all he should really ask for in the first place."

"But Tom, how do we know that it's fair? We may not have received the entirety of the facts. Isn't that going against the university's motto?"

"There's a limitation to what anyone can know. We just have to live with that and make our decisions accordingly."

"I still don't know."

Tom sat down on a chair and spun around. "Didn't Herbert

have some concerns about Ian? He's in his class, right?"

"Yes. Herbert questioned some of the humor that Ian had displayed during one of his lectures. Ian hadn't initially said anything out loud. He had whispered something impolitic to a nearby student. Herbert noticed the intrusion into his teaching and asked Ian to explain himself. Ian hesitated, but then he went on to tell the statement or joke to the entire class. Some students giggled and then quickly hushed down, while others sat with mouths agape at what they perceived as the offensiveness of the remarks. Professor Brown, of course, was offended. He held him after class and explained to him that such things could never be said again in his presence."

"What happened next?"

"Nothing. All this occurred before the Halloween incident. Herbert pushed it to the back of his mind. He didn't report this incident until that occurred, and he believed that it was part of a larger pattern of ethnic insensitivity on campus. To an extent, I agreed with him."

"And now you're upset because this has escalated to the point of possible racial strife on campus, besides the smearing of the name of the university?"

"Yes."

"Well, I'm sorry, but the kid cooked his goose after all those chances. If someone wants to be that disruptive on this campus, we have no other choice but to censure him in whatever way is effective. If not, he could hinder the academic efforts of others."

"Do you really believe that's true?"

"Yes."

"I guess that the chips will have to fall where they will."

"You may not entirely believe D'ante, but you trust Herbert, don't you?"

"I wouldn't have stuck my neck out for him if I didn't."

"So what's a small time lacrosse player weighed up against a pioneering professor?"

"You make it sound economical. That's rather crass."

"It is. That's university life, and if you don't know this after all these years, then you better prepare to look for another university. And a few years later, look for another university. And this will go on and on, until you tire and look back on your life as a waste. You don't want that, do you?"

Sam shut his eyes tight then opened them, staring at his friend. "No."

"Good then. Why don't you head home? Pick up something to eat and relax a little. Take all this Ian and D'ante and letter business and forget about it until next week. Exams will start late next week, and after that we don't have to think about the university for nearly a month."

"You're wrong, Tom. I'm the president. I have to think about university always. Maybe it's why the rest of my life is collapsing."

* * *

Troy, Rachael, and Milly met at the cafeteria. They were hungry, but more than that they wanted to discuss the upcoming hearing.

"I know Ian," Milly said, "and I can't believe that it's come down to this. It's crazy when you think about it."

"True," Rachael said.

"Well, I told him to write that letter—properly," Troy said. "I don't like what's happening to him, but he could've prevented it.

If he had just let go of his ego for a few moments."

"But you forget that he's going up against an even bigger ego—D'ante," Rachael said.

"I know." Troy ate a fry. "I just meant that he would've been better off if he had swallowed his pride. I know the alcohol had an effect, but still he had to have realized what he had written the following morning. And then to send it? I'm sorry, but that's crazy. I understand the anger at D'ante. The guy is the biggest douche I've seen. But he has a scholarship, and now that's on the line. And I'm upset about other things too."

"Like what?" Rachael said.

"How come Milly was the only one who knew about this letter business? I'm supposed to be his best friend. It's like he thought that I didn't care. I do care. Otherwise I wouldn't be talking about it with you two."

"Maybe he thought you'd react too judgmentally," Milly said. "I mean—if you listen to yourself right now, you do sound heated. I'm not saying that you don't have a right to be, being that he's your friend, but he probably didn't want to face that after all you said prior to the letter writing."

"I believed that I had his best interests in mind," he said. "I still do. I've never been in a position like the one he is in. Oh, maybe some minor trouble in middle school, but nothing serious. Still, I knew that if he didn't play by their rules, the university would wallop him. And it looks like the walloping will continue later on tonight."

"We still can say good things about Ian at the hearing," Milly said.

Troy shook his head. "Maybe it'll matter; maybe it won't.

You've got a good heart, but I don't think that you really understand matters like these. With your father, Milly, you may have disagreements—fierce disagreements—but I still don't think that he's out for your blood. He wants what's best for you. You probably disagree, but there can be no doubt that the intent is well-meaning. In Ian's case, it's different. All the bloodthirsty involved, for whatever reason, have found a victim, and they've prepared a sacrifice. Like I said, they all have different reasons for going after him, but it's much easier than dealing with whatever issues they have. When I think on it a little, I don't believe that it has much to do with Ian. He's just conveniently there."

"My, oh my, Troy," Rachael said. "You've developed into a little cynic lately—I don't think that all is that bad. We aren't even in the meeting room yet, so we don't know how events will turn out."

"I wish that I had your positive feeling. I did at one point, but when I look at things from a distance, it stinks."

Milly patted Troy on the hand. "I believe that I know how you feel. But you have to have hope that people will see the truth. You have to, or you're just going to look at situations and despair."

"We would be sitting here talking about our upcoming break plans and not Ian's trial if people saw reality." He sternly looked at Milly, who withdrew her hand.

"Listen, I just think that everybody needs to get some food into their bellies, and then everybody's attitude will improve," Rachael said. "Troy—you've just been nibbling on those French fries."

Troy glanced and smirked in her direction. "How like a Jewish mother of you to be so concerned."

Rachael, grinning, took a fry from his tray and playfully threw it at him. "I should report you to the dean for those remarks."

"I'm just playing around." Troy returned the smile.

"Yeah, but it was just playing around that got Ian into trouble," Milly said.

After her comment the table fell silent. They then discussed which of their upcoming finals they expected to be the most difficult and what times they were planning to leave for home when they had finished.

* * *

It was a quarter to seven, and Ian had just left one of the cafeterias. He hadn't put too much food in his takeaway bag—just enough so that he wouldn't collapse in front of the honor council. He had just finished eating his sandwich when he arrived at the University Center's front doors. He noticed that not many people were standing around. The few people loitering in the hallway likely didn't even realize why Ian was there. They stepped aside as he strolled past. He noticed a trash can, into which he deposited the remnants of his dinner. He noticed that his stomach gurgled, and he wished it to stop. People were going to focus enough attention on him that night. He tracked his way upstairs until he arrived at the dreaded room B. He drew in his breath and entered.

He observed everything around him. He noticed that students packed the gallery. Even though he knew that the hearing was big news on campus, he hadn't expected so many students to skip their evening activities just to watch a judicial proceeding. As he walked to the defendant's seating, he noticed that Troy, Milly, Rachael, and Jay were sitting together among the other students. He saw his professor, Herbert Brown, and he wondered why he was here. Because he was noticing the individuals to his flanks, he forgot that the honor council would be waiting up ahead for him, so that when he looked straight forward, the sight of the serious-looking sixteen caught him off guard, and his eyes widened somewhat. He quickly sat, but the council immediately called him to attention.

"Everybody, please rise," the chief council member said. Everybody, including the nervous Ian, rose. "The council has convened to hear the case of Mr. Ian Mueller, who has been accused of violating the principles of the honor code and the community standards of conduct. How does the defendant plead?"

Ian looked up at the council, then over to the plaintiff's section, where he saw D'ante smirking, and then back at the gallery. He didn't respond.

"Mr. Mueller, what is your plea?"

Ian fumbled a bit with his words. "I…I guess not guilty."

"You guess?" The honor council member leaned forward.

"Yes, I plead not guilty."

"All right then, all may be seated now." All butts hit the seats with a loud pow.

"We'd like to hear first from the accuser. Dante, will you please step forward to the bench."

As the lumbering linebacker stepped forward, he said, "The name's D'ante."

"Huh?" the council member said.

"I said that the name's D'ante." He glared at the council members.

"Here in these papers before us, we have Dante. Just like the poet?"

"Yo, I ain't named after no poet. You probably got my name wrong up in there. It's spelled 'd,' then there's an apostrophe, then 'ant,' pronounced like 'aunt,' then 'e,' pronounced like 'e.' Okay?"

"Okay, Mr. D'ante Smalls," the council member said, jotting some notes down on the papers. "Do you solemnly swear or affirm that you will tell the truth, the whole truth, and nothing but the truth?"

"Yeah."

"All right, go on and tell us about the incident that took place on October thirty-first and the aftermath."

"Sure. I was at that party at Jay's. I came in strolling with my crew. Then I saw Ian with that blackface getup. It pissed me off, but I showed restraint. I came over to him, but he started getting aggressive. I still showed restraint. Maybe my friends held me back some, but I soon walked away. And stayed away from the rest of the night. I haven't really seen him until tonight. I'm almost getting sick looking at him. I'm sorry."

"Go on, Mr. Smalls."

"Well, I complained to the president and the dean. Finally, got a response. They had Ian write a couple of letters of apology. Well, I got my letter, and I was shocked. I knew that he didn't like me, but I thought that he'd be the bigger man, and I'd just get a decent letter—but no! He just had to behave antagonistic. That's why I'm accusing Ian with violating the honor code. He promised the university to write that letter. He wrote a letter, but he didn't deliver what he promised. I just want some respect. I've come to feel that students of color can't get no respect at this university. That's really all I have to say. Okay?"

"Okay, Mr. Smalls. We have the letter before us. You can sit down. If we have any more questions, we'll call you back to the bench."

D'ante sat down. He had a sad, lost facial expression. He looked back at the gallery, and then he turned around and laid his head down on the desk.

"Mr. Smalls, can you please sit up during the proceedings. I understand that you may be tired from your football practice, but we assure you that these proceedings will not take the entirety of the night."

"Sure, no problem." D'ante sat up and nodded to the council.

"Good," the council member said. "Now if we may continue—we would like to have Ms. Dominique Fisher come before the bench."

Dominique wended through the gallery audience. She adjusted her hair and her clothes as she stepped up to the bench. She turned to Ian and glared at him but turned around when one of the council members called her to attention.

"Ms. Fisher, do you solemnly swear or affirm that you will tell the truth, the whole truth, and nothing but the truth?"

"Yes."

"Ms. Fisher, are you familiar with the defendant?"

"Not personally. I know that he's a friend of Troy Thomas's. I also spotted him around campus when he was a freshman. I'm currently a junior."

"Ms. Fisher, you're president of the BSO?"

"Yes—I've been proud to lead the organization. My goal has been increasing membership this year. From what has transpired, I now really understand the necessity of doing so."

"Okay. So you haven't had any serious run-ins with the defendant?"

"No, I've just heard some things that are questionable. From what I've heard, he doesn't care about the sensitivities of other students, or even the faculty members. It was only a matter of time before he would steep so low as to engage in the racial harassment that occurred on that night and since."

"Ms. Fisher, are you intimidated by Mr. Mueller?"

"No, I just find it pitiable that in these supposedly enlightened times that such a student believes that he has the right to engage in such conduct. I thought that this university had banished such attitudes to the past. Apparently not. I'm not surprised, though, that Ian isn't progressive. He likes that show *Miami Vice*."

"Okay, Ms. Fisher, you can step back to the gallery."

She again flipped her hair and glared at Ian. She made some sounds when she walked by and headed back to her seat.

"The honor council would like to next call Professor Herbert Brown before the bench."

He strolled to the bench and agreed to conduct himself honestly during the questioning.

"Professor Brown, Ian Mueller is in your class, right?"

"That's correct. The class is Transmigrations of Cult and Cultural Practices of Marginalized Ethnicities in the Americas."

"Have you had any problems with him? Do you consider him a good student?"

"I think that he's a bit of a cutup in class at times. Many young men are at that age. When I think on it, I know that he could do better in my class. He's not failing, and I believe that he knows the material, but at times I don't think he takes seriously the information that I'm trying to impart—if you understand what I'm saying."

"Go on."

"One day, Mr. Mueller was joking with the student next to him. Now, don't misunderstand me. I understand that young people play around. I did. It was obvious, though, that Mr. Mueller was not paying me the slightest mind. I get that some of the text can get monotonous—that's why I try to liven the atmosphere of the classroom, but he was showing me and the rest of the class complete disregard. When I caught sight of him, I was embarrassed for him. I asked what was funny. At first he declined to tell me, so I asked him again—and to tell the entire class. He then said the joke, if you could call it that, and the majority of the class was appalled. I was too, but I mildly told him that wasn't appropriate for this community, but if he was going to continue with such humor, to do it on his own time and not on the class's and my time. He agreed, apologized, and said that it wouldn't happen again."

"And did it happen again?"

"No."

"When did this event occur?"

"I'm trying to remember. Because I didn't report it, I don't have an exact date down, but I believe that it was in early October."

"So, it was definitely before the October thirty-first incident."

"Yes." Herbert paused and looked upward and then returned his gaze to the council. "Now that I think on it, I believe that I should've reported the comment. I might've saved us much trouble. I just thought that what came from his mouth was ignorance. I didn't realize that maybe I was dealing with a stone-cold bigot. I want to apologize to D'ante for my actions, which may have encouraged Ian to continue on his reckless course. I'm sorry."

"That will be enough, Professor. You may leave the bench."

"Thanks."

"Will Mr. Jason Conrad step up to the bench?"

Jay went to the front and affirmed his honesty.

"Mr. Conrad, how long have you known the defendant?"

Jay paused, trying to calculate the months and days. He squinted, and he looked upward.

"Mr. Conrad, we don't need an exact date. Just an estimated time or event would be sufficient."

"I think that I first met Ian last term. It was early spring. One of his lacrosse teammates brought him and his friend Troy to my house for a party."

"Was there underage drinking taking place? I mean to say, did Ian and his associates indulge in any alcohol being served?"

Jay laughed. "Of course they did. It's college life. And Ian can be a wild one sometimes. Don't get me wrong, I think that he's a good person, though."

"Has Ian attended any more of your gatherings, and if he has, has he indulged in the alcohol?"

"Yes, he's been to a number of my parties and 'indulged,' as you put it."

"So, Mr. Conrad, he attended your costume party on the thirty-first?"

"That'll be a yes."

"How much alcohol do you believe that Ian partook of on that night?"

"I really couldn't say. I talked to him some that evening, but you see, he wasn't really conjoined to my hip. I saw a beer in his hand, but after that I went and conversed with some of my other guests. My job as host isn't really to babysit people. They just come and go. I figure that my job is to facilitate a means for entertainment—if you get my drift."

"Please don't develop an attitude, Mr. Conrad. Otherwise the council could cite you for contempt of these proceedings. We just want straightforward answers. Nothing else. You're fortunate that we don't consider your admitted facilitating of underage drinking, do you understand us?"

"Sure, I don't want to get in trouble. You can continue on."

"We will continue on when we are ready. Now, did you notice any antagonistic behavior from Ian to D'ante?"

"No. He told me he had a confrontation with him. But from what he told me, it sounded like D'ante might have been the aggressor. I don't know for sure, but I know Ian, and I don't think he's that type of person to start fights."

"But there was no fight?"

"That's correct. Cooler heads prevailed. I know that Ian isn't really fond of Mr. Smalls. However, I know that evening nobody brought a violent action against D'ante. After that confrontation, the two went their separate ways for the rest of the night."

"Mr. Conrad, were you offended by Ian's costume?"

"I wouldn't have worn it, but I can't say that I was personally offended. I don't know about anybody else, though. Most of our minds the booze overshadowed. So you'd have to ask every single person that attended. That would be a lot of questioning." Jay grinned at the chief council member.

"I don't believe that will be necessary. You may return to your seat."

Jay was standing in position, somewhat dazed, until the council member said again for him to return to the gallery.

"We would like to call forth Rachael Buxbaum."

She wiggled her way past the row of students. After a small delay, she was standing before the council. She swore to the truth of her next statements.

"Ms. Buxbaum, you've known the defendant for how long?"

"We're in a class together this semester. That's where I first saw him, but I didn't know him personally at that point. Later, my friend Milly, who's in the same class, introduced him to me in the cafeteria."

"Do you find Mr. Mueller to be a charming individual?"

A quizzical look overtook her face. "What do you mean by that question?"

"I mean, do you find him to be pleasant? The reason why we're asking this question is that his accusers make it sound like he's aggressive—not very nice. Although in your statement you claim to be his friend, we want to know how you really feel about Mr. Mueller. Okay?"

"I think that he's an okay guy. Maybe sometimes he can be a bit vulgar. But aren't most guys, occasionally?"

Laughter sprung up in the gallery.

The council member leaned forward, focusing into Rachael's eyes. "Vulgar? In what way?"

"Look at me, council member. Even if I was all the way back at the entrance of the room, you could tell that I have quite a bosom. Thus at times Ian would make comments. They weren't really rude comments. I've received those before. But they were comments. I don't think that makes Ian a bad guy. Just a guy."

"Ms. Buxbaum, do you believe that a similar lack of restraint led Ian to make his costume choice that night and subsequently to write that letter to D'ante?"

"No. I think that Ian thought that his costume would be entertaining. Maybe he didn't think about repercussions. But I don't believe that it was done maliciously. He's not a malicious person. I haven't seen it in him at all."

"One final question, Ms. Buxbaum. Were you offended by Ian Mueller's costume choice, even in your initial reaction?"

"No. I was taken aback, but I wasn't personally offended. I'll say that the makeup surprised me at first. Maybe I'm not the one to ask about being offended, being that I'm not black. I don't know how others felt when he walked into the party. I didn't see anybody else taking offense at his costume, not even D'ante. However, I don't know what they felt on the inside. Like Jay said, you'd have to ask everyone that attended."

"Thank you for your cooperation, Ms. Buxbaum. We would now like to hear from your friend Ms. Milly Kwon. All right?"

Milly already knew that the honor council would summon her next. She passed Rachael, glanced at her from the corner of her eye, and situated herself at the bench.

"Ms. Kwon, is it true that you came into contact with Mr.

Mueller, as in Ms. Buxbaum's narrative?"

"Yes."

"Furthermore, is there any closer relationship between you and the defendant than there is between the defendant and Ms. Buxbaum?"

Milly glanced at Ian and then looked at the the council members. "Yes—I mean no. It's no."

"You seem somewhat confused, Ms. Kwon. Explain yourself."

"I know that Ian liked me. You know—as more than a friend. That's why he came up to me that day in the cafeteria. Like Rachael said, we had seen him in our class. He usually sat behind us. I didn't really talk to him at that point. Not that I was unfriendly, but I just didn't have anything to say to him. He still seemed nice. So that's why I didn't turn around and walk away when he started to approach me. I wanted to give him a chance?"

"You say, 'Give him a chance.' Did you find out something about him that caused you to hesitate?"

"I'm sorry, council member, but these questions are getting kind of personal. I don't know how they're relevant to the proceedings."

"Ms. Kwon, please answer the question. You don't have to go into explicit details of your personal life, but we need to know whether you came across any character flaws that may pertain to this case."

"Character flaws?"

"You said that you were going to give him a chance. Were you seeking to date him?"

"No."

"Because you saw something that you didn't like in his

personality?"

"Yes—I mean no." She shook her head side to side, exhausted from the questioning. "Ian is crazy at times. I don't mean that he's wicked or bad or that he has mental issues. I mean that sometimes he just lets words fall from his mouth. Sometimes he thinks and sometimes he doesn't. In a way I admire that disposition. I'm not that type of person. If I were, I'd probably not have to work so hard with my acting, but that's another issue. I just don't think that I could have someone like that in my life right now. As a friend, yes. Romantic interest, no. I might be able to handle it when I've matured some more, but not when my life is in such a flux."

"Has Mr. Mueller ever said anything that was offensive to you, even if it was in a joking manner?"

"Has he said anything to me? No. I'll say, and I hope that this doesn't get him into trouble, that he does like telling quite a number of ethnic jokes. As you all probably know, I'm Korean. Well, he told a Korean joke one night. I wasn't offended. If my parents had heard, they might've become offended. I couldn't tell you for sure since I didn't tell them it. But I wasn't offended. And if you're going to punish Ian for telling a couple of jokes, you should be ashamed of yourselves—"

"Ms. Kwon! We're not punishing anyone for telling jokes, but we are examining the character of your friend. If a person builds a pattern in his life, then we must look at the pattern and compare it with the end point. The end point was an ugly letter that a member of this community should've never written. We're here to see whether such an individual should remain at this university."

"But it's not fair!"

"Please, Ms. Kwon. You're becoming excited. If you will—please remove yourself from the room so that you may cool down."

"Now you're kicking me out!"

"No, we are not. Your current actions are removing you from our presence."

Milly stomped out of the room and let the door slam behind her.

"Now that that's over, let us call the final witness before the bench. Mr. Troy Thomas, please step forward."

Troy walked to the bench. Although he had anticipated this moment, he still couldn't believe that it had arrived. He was wondering what his friend was thinking during the hearing. He looked over at Ian, who was staring at one of the the council members. He affirmed his honesty before the council and tried to settle his emotions before he spoke.

"Mr. Thomas, how long have you known the defendant?"

"We met during freshman orientation. So it was back in August of 2010."

"Did you always get along with Mr. Mueller? How did you find him to be?"

"We get along most of the time. Obviously, there are going to be disagreements between people. Like entertainment choice or food that you enjoy. But that's normal and bound to occur. I don't remember any big arguments. There might have been some, but I don't remember—and how I find him to be? I think that he's one cool cat. I wouldn't hang out with him if I didn't think so. Sometimes he has a temper, but I get a temper too when I feel that I've been mistreated. Like Milly said, he can be somewhat crazy at times, but I think that this just makes him a more interesting guy. You understand?"

"I see, Mr. Thomas. Now, have you ever felt that Ian acted bigoted toward an individual?"

"He's best friends with me. I'm black. I've never felt anything negative from him."

"I mean, have you ever heard him talk negatively about an individual because of some personal characteristic? This could be anything."

Troy paused, not wanting to incriminate either Ian or himself. "I mean, he's said that a girl was chunky or something like that. But as far as I could tell, that might've been a positive. He's been pretty open concerning the girls to which he is attracted. Even if he wasn't attracted to somebody, I don't think that he'd be mean about it. He might joke around, but that's different from meanness."

"That means that you've never heard a racial or ethnic comment from his mouth?"

"What do you mean by that question?"

"Mr. Thomas, the question has been stated simply. Have you ever heard a remark that could be construed as offensive?"

"Does that include humor?"

"Yes, that may include humor."

"As the young women said before, he likes to tell ethnic one-liners. But I don't think that makes him racist. I can tell a few, and I don't see myself as a bigot. He just likes to make people laugh. Furthermore, that's not the only humor he's into. He likes other things."

"Now, let's get to this past Halloween night. When you first saw Mr. Mueller dressed in his costume and makeup, how did you feel?"

"I didn't know who he was until he told me. The Noogman. I still think that it's a funny name."

"But you obviously noticed him wearing blackface. Did it upset you?"

"He told me that it was brownface. I don't think that he was mocking black people. It was just part of the costume."

"But you must've had some initial feeling when you saw this Noogman outfit. Were you taken aback? Please, Mr. Thomas, answer truthfully."

Troy looked over to Ian. He looked down at the floor before pausing to reply. "A little."

"So you were offended by Ian?"

"It wasn't like that at all. I was wondering what some of the other students would think. I know Ian, but they might not know him. They could've mistaken his intentions."

"That's why we're here, Mr. Thomas. Individuals have accused your friend Ian of deliberately offending and intimidating a fellow member of this community—not only this action but also failing to rectify the situation properly once informed by university officials."

"But it didn't go down like that. As my friends said, we didn't see any intimidation on the part of Ian. I'll admit that I questioned him about the costume, but once Ian makes up his mind, he goes ahead with his business. It's hard to stop him."

"So are you saying that Ian Mueller is so egotistical that he would disregard the opinions of those that he calls his friends?"

"It's nothing like that at all. Honest."

"That's what it sounds like, and if he would disregard the judgment of an individual that he would call a friend, how are we of the honor council to believe that he acted in good faith toward an individual that, according to his own written and spoken words, he does not care for?"

"You're making him out to be a bad guy. Ian's not a bad guy. He misspeaks at times. He may do stupid things. But I do stupid things. We're not even twenty yet. He's not this monster that you're trying to twist him into."

"What about the letter? When he told you that he was required to write an apology letter, didn't you stress the importance to him?"

"Yes, but you don't get it. Ian told me that there wasn't any incident with D'ante. He's my friend, and I believe him. Why should he write a letter if the basis for that letter is a lie?"

"That would be because the university administration required it of him."

"Ian was willing to apologize to the university for the disturbance that his actions caused the community, but he couldn't admit to doing something that he knew that he didn't do. That would be going against the university motto, *fidelitas propter verum,* and that would be an honor code violation in itself."

"We're only going by your words."

"I still think that you're twisting them."

"You're welcome to that belief, but as we have limited time, we need to move on. So if you would, please return to your seat. Thank you. Now we would finally like to hear from the defendant himself. Please come before the bench."

While Troy mumbled and left for his seat, Ian went before the council and swore that his testimony was also truthful.

"Mr. Mueller, we don't need to go over much as it would be redundant. The facts are evident from both the physical evidence and the sworn testimony of your peers. You wore that costume, and then you disregarded the instructions of the president and the dean. But you have a chance to explain yourself now if you wish."

Ian cleared his throat. "All of that's true, council members. But you have to hear me out. I believe that I would have been breaking the honor code if I had written that letter as instructed—full of contriteness. I still affirm that I neither intentionally nor unintentionally antagonized D'ante Smalls. It's correct that I really do not care for him, but it's not because of his color or his ethnicity. I do not like him because he's a liar and the worst braggart. He's dishonest, and thus he should be defending himself. I could not affirm his dishonesty as truth, and that's why I added those comments to the second letter. I apologize that these proceedings have disturbed the tranquility of the university community. I apologize that my friends have had to use their free time on a Friday night to defend me against these defamatory allegations. But I still cannot apologize for the second letter. I may have said in it untactful words, and thus that was my mistake, but the sentiments within are truthful, and I can't disavow the truth."

There was commotion in the gallery after Ian's firm words. The chief council member banged his gavel and told the audience to quiet down.

"If this is your final statement, then the council is willing to accept it."

"Yes, it is. It's all that I have to say."

"This, then, closes the verdict hearing. We shall deliberate, and then we'll rule on the defendant's innocence or guilt." The council left the bench and exited to convene in a private location.

Fifteen minutes later the council returned to the bench.

"We of the honor council find the defendant, Mr. Ian Mueller, guilty of breaking the spirit of the honor code and the code of community standards."

Ian hung his head down and closed his eyes tight. He shook his head, mumbling something to himself.

"We shall now begin the sanctions hearing," the council member said. "Since the facts have been established, and likely not much more evidence can be brought forth, we're willing to move on to sanctions deliberation. However, if Mr. Mueller would like to bring forward any witnesses, new or prior, he's allowed to do so at this time."

Ian shook his head no.

"If Mr. Mueller would desire to speak on his own behalf to present any mitigating circumstances that the council may weigh, he's encouraged to do so at this point."

Ian shook his head no.

"Then the sanctions hearing is over and the council will deliberate to decide the consequences that Mr. Mueller will receive." The honor council exited again.

They returned twenty minutes later with grim faces. They settled into their seats, while the chief member shuffled some papers in front of him. Ian waited patiently.

"Mr. Mueller, we've come to an agreement concerning your punishment in regards to these proceedings. The council has decided that for the remainder of the 2011 to 2012 university term, you will be suspended from the Central Ohio lacrosse team. If you've behaved well during this period, then you may be restored to the team the following school year."

"But this is not fair!" Ian cried out.

"I'm sorry, Mr. Mueller, but the council has already come to its decision, a decision that we believe to be just and temperate. Now you may exit the proceedings and return to whatever activity you had planned for the rest of the night. Thank you all, witnesses and audience, for your cooperation with these proceedings."

With that, the hearing concluded.

"I can't believe it," Troy said. "They're really removing him from the team. What about his scholarship?"

"I know, I know," Rachael said. "I knew that they would be serious, but I was thinking hours of community service. Something like that."

"I know that he's feeling horrible right now. I would be. I still can't believe it."

"Do you think that we should go talk to him?" she inquired.

"He probably wants to be left alone to his thoughts. I know how he is. I'll go back to my dorm later, so why don't we go out right now. It'll give him time to think matters out."

Rachael called Milly to find out where she had headed off to, and then the two glum friends exited meeting room B.

* * *

Troy returned to his dorm room around ten-thirty. Although filled with the sugary goodness of a double-scoop waffle cone, he had zero energy, and he felt like flopping down onto his bed and falling asleep immediately. As he entered he noticed that the lights weren't on. He thought that maybe Ian, exhausted from the hearing, had already gone to sleep. Then, when Troy walked to his bed, he felt an object hit him in his back.

"What the hell?" Troy said. "What's going on?" Troy went back and turned on the light switch. He saw Ian standing with a fierce look on his face.

"That's for the testimony that you gave at those proceedings." Ian glared at Troy.

"What are you talking about, man? I went up there and told the truth. I'm sorry that they didn't believe me."

"What you told got me kicked off the team. Now how am I going to pay for college without my scholarship? Huh?"

"Again, what are you talking about? I said that you're a good guy. Sometimes impulsive, but a good guy. I told the council the truth—that I didn't see any aggression or antagonism on your part at the party and that I know that you didn't write that second letter maliciously."

"You said that you were offended by the costume."

"No, I didn't. I said that the costume took me aback. There's a difference."

"What's the difference?"

"The difference is that even though I know you to be a crazy kind of guy, I didn't expect you to have on that makeup. Not that I was personally offended. I just couldn't believe that even you wouldn't think of the possible consequences down the line."

"So you think that I'm stupid?"

"No, I just don't think that you take into consideration other people. It doesn't meant that you're wicked, but it just means that even if you have the right to do something, but it's unwise, you just push ahead. Sometimes, this can be admirable. Other times, like this time, it leads to unwanted consequences."

"So why didn't you warn me about the letter?"

"What do you mean by 'warn you about the letter'? I told you to write the damn thing. I didn't know you would add a bunch of stuff in it. Listen, D'ante may have deserved the earful that you gave him in it. But you should've known that there would be serious consequences. Even if you were intoxicated, you should've known better. You were already beat when you went to the party in that silly costume and D'ante saw you. I'm sorry, but I did my best. Rachael did her best. Jay and Milly did their best. It just wasn't good enough. Again, I'm sorry."

"I just want to go to sleep. I really don't want to talk about it anymore. Okay?"

"Okay then, go to sleep! I don't really like the way you're speaking to me anyway. I told the truth. I went to bat for you. I'm sorry that it didn't work out. Maybe we can find a way to get a loan—"

"I'm going to sleep." Ian got under his covers without changing his clothes. Fifteen minutes later he was asleep.

Troy fell asleep a half hour later.

The next morning Troy awoke and told Ian that he needed to head to the library and study for a few hours for his final exams, which would occur during the next two weeks. He said that he didn't know when he would be back but to give him a call if he needed anything. Ian said all right, and Troy headed out.

When Troy returned in the afternoon, he noticed that all of

Ian's belongings were gone. He looked over at the stripped bed, and he found a note. In it Ian said, "I'm sorry, but I don't believe that I can stay here with you anymore. For the short time that I have at Central Ohio, I'm now staying over at Eric's dorm. While I know that you tried your best to help me at the hearing, for some reason I'm still angry at you. I know that it sounds unreasonable. It is, but that's the way I feel right now. I wish you the best on your exams and in the rest of your college endeavors. Goodbye. Ian."

Troy couldn't believe it. Ian really was gone. Likely he would never see him again, especially if he didn't return to the university next fall. Troy dropped his book bag and sat down on the edge of Ian's bed with the note still clutched in his hand. *Damn this university*, he thought. He sat for ten minutes before he decided to call Rachael.

Chapter 9

The drive to Hamilton County after exams was not the pain that Troy thought it was going to be. The previous day, after his last exam, he had packed the majority of his belongings into his car. It had rained early that morning, but it had cleared up by the afternoon. He was pleased that he wouldn't have to be drenched while he carried items out to his car. Although the sky remained overcast for the rest of the day, it remained dry. He, however, woke up to drizzle outside his dorm room that Thursday. Although he was glad that it wasn't a downpour, he wished that the weather would clear up completely by the time he left COU. It was depressing, especially looking across the room and seeing the empty space that once contained Ian and his belongings. Troy grumbled, ate a light breakfast, and he was soon out of the Columbus area.

The hour and a half journey down I-71 was relaxing despite the weather conditions. Hearing the light rain smack against his roof was actually soothing to Troy, as his thoughts shifted from the present back to the previous semester's events. He was also pleased that he had left midmorning as there was little traffic on the interstate. He didn't have to worry about as many aggressive or reckless drivers as he thought that he would. He focused on the nearly four weeks of time off from school. He needed to refocus his mind somewhere else. Before packing he had chosen his classes for the upcoming semester. He had chosen one class that didn't appear to be too interesting, but it fit his schedule. He didn't even realize, when he clicked to add the class to his schedule, the name of the professor. When he went back later that day to confirm that everything had gone through, he noticed that the professor teaching the class was Herbert Brown, the same man who had helped railroad his friend out of the university. He immediately felt like removing the class from his schedule, but then he realized that his entire schedule would become screwed up; he would've ended up having to drop this interesting class on the Civil War. He thus decided to suck it up and keep Brown's class on his schedule.

When he arrived home, the house was empty. His parents were still at work, and his sister, working down in Dallas, wouldn't arrive until a few days before Christmas. He moved his bags inside the house and plopped onto the couch after preparing a bowl of cereal. He waded through the morass of the television, stopping at one channel, then moving on. This continued until his mother returned from work.

She asked how his finals had gone, what grades he thought he was going to receive, and if anything new had come up in his life. He mumbled some nondescript answers, and she said that she would leave him alone until he recharged and could give better answers. He mumbled something again. She told him that his father should be home around six-thirty. He said that was fine.

When his father came home, his father said hello and went through the routine of questions that parents ask their children. Troy went through the routine of answers, which would be a loose term for his response to his father. His father saw that not all was right, but he didn't press things further at the time. He realized that his son must be tired, and so he told him after dinner that even though he was home on break that he should try to sleep more regularly than he did at the university. What's the purpose of a rest from working if you're not getting any rest? Troy agreed with his father, but he didn't fall asleep until about one-thirty in the morning.

For the next week, Troy didn't engage with many people. He stayed inside and listened to music, read a book, and occasionally turned on the television. His mother thought that he must be sick. She asked him, but he denied it. He just wanted people to leave him alone. She said okay and left him to sulk in his room. His father had to work late most days, so there was little contact between them, but he always asked if he was doing okay when he returned home and walked by Troy's room. Troy always replied with the same mumbling "yeah."

That Friday Troy headed to Boone County to pick up his sister at the airport. She had flown in from Dallas and was staying through the weekend. He had never been really close to his sister. She was nine years older than he was and settled in a professional career. Growing up, they hadn't discussed much together, and even when they got together during breaks, they drifted in different directions. When he pulled up to the curb, he noticed that she wasn't carrying much luggage. He was glad.

She put her bags in the car's trunk and slid into the passenger front seat. Troy drove off for home.

"How're you doing, baby bro?"

"Fine, I guess. How was the flight? Not too bumpy?"

"No, it was good. How's Mom and Dad?"

"You didn't speak with them on the phone?"

"Not recently. They just left a message that you were going to come and pick me up—and you've arrived. But looking at you for just these couple of minutes, you appear to be kind of down. Anything that you'd like to talk about? I'm all ears for the next three days. I didn't even bring my laptop with me."

"I think that I'm still fine."

"Okay." His sister transitioned in thought. "I hope Mom makes that pie tomorrow evening."

"I'm sure that she will. She always has."

"Well, I haven't been eating much lately. Work has really put its claws into me this past month. It would be good to get a good home-cooked meal before I return to that rat race."

"I get you, sis."

"So how has college been treating you? Anything exciting? I hope that you're doing well in your classes. I don't want to have to come up there and make sure that you're studying."

"College has been okay. A friend of mine had to leave. I don't know whether it's going to be permanent or not, but the current situation is depressing."

"I'm sorry to hear about that. I don't know whether you want to go into any details or—"

"I really don't. The entire business was sordid. It's making me angry just to think about it. So if you will—just change the subject."

"That's all right. How about we just listen to some music as we drive back to the house?"

Troy turned on the radio, but he allowed his sister to choose the station. The drive back to their parents' house was quiet except for the music coming from the radio.

While his sister and his parents spent much of the holiday in joyous reverie, Troy brooded from that Friday evening through that Sunday night. He would say hello to his parents and sister when they walked into a room, but other than that the conversation was minimal. Then that Monday, the day when his sister was to return to Dallas, Troy approached his sister and sat down on the couch beside her.

"Hey, Troy, nice to see you. Except for Christmas dinner, you've been keeping your distance. What's bothering you?" She put down the book that she had been engrossed in and sat up.

"Nothing much, Veronica. I just had a question. I don't know why I've been thinking upon it the past couple of hours."

"What's the question?"

"It's kind of silly, but I was wondering, how would you feel if I went out with a white girl?"

"Like dating?"

"Yeah, like dating."

"I don't know. I've never thought of it before. I mean, I've never really thought of you dating at all before. When you entered high school, I was already out in the career world. You might've told me about a couple of high school girls that you went to the movies with, but I didn't get any details or anything like that."

"Those weren't really serious."

"And this is?"

"I think so. I don't really know. I don't think that we're really dating. At least, nothing official."

"What's the young woman's name?"

"Her name is Rachael. She's nice. Attractive too. She's also Jewish."

"You're a regular Richard Wright, huh?"

"Huh?"

"Do you like her because she's different, or do you like her just because you like her?"

"Maybe it's a little bit of both. She's easy to be around and pleasant. When that situation was going down with my friend, I could call her up, and she'd listen. Then she'd tell me something, and I would take it into account. I don't know if that's a romantic relationship, but I know that's a friendship. I don't know if I would allow it to develop into something else. I don't even know if she's willing to take it toward that direction. She's got plenty of goals, and I don't even know if I would be a part of them."

"Are you afraid that unwanted attention would fall on you if you started going out with this Rachael?"

"I don't want to say yes, but it's part of my fears." Troy jumped up from the couch before he continued. "It's hard to explain. I'm not trying to go off on a tangent, but consider music. I like listening to all different genres of music. But I've been afraid before to show that. For instance, back in high school, I once was listening to a CD, and this guy came up to me, asking me what I was listening to. I lied to him. I told him that I was listening to some rap album. Now, I don't mind rap. I've a number of songs on my iPod, but I wasn't listening to rap at that time. Why did I lie? I didn't want the other guy to see me as some oddball. So I hid what I liked. That's why I'm asking your opinion about me dating Rachael. You're my sister, and you're a dedicated professional woman. If you were to have a problem, then I'd know what I was getting into."

"Listen, Troy. I can't lie. If you brought Rachael home on a holiday weekend, like this one, I might feel uncomfortable at first. I might wonder why my baby bro is with her, whether he's truly in love with her or the idea of her. But my opinion doesn't really matter. And if my opinion doesn't really matter, then why should the opinions of others, who might just have other issues in their lives? I don't think that's just a black-and-white issue, nor do I think that it just revolves around romance. You have to live your life. You can take other people's opinions into account, but you can't dwell on it; otherwise, you'll be at a standstill—not going one way or the other."

"As I said before, I'm not sure that there is even a romantic connection. I just wanted the opinion of someone else. I've been going through a lot. Different controversies. I don't know what to think—even though at times I believe that I should know. I'll be twenty next month, out of the teenage years."

"Troy, you still have time to grow. I'm almost out of my twenties, and I didn't learn that until a couple of years ago. Just don't take yourself too seriously yet. You have a lifetime left to do so. And when you do take yourself seriously, do it sparingly, otherwise you won't be laughing at yourself, but others will be laughing at you."

"You make a lot of sense. I don't know why I didn't listen to you more often."

"Perhaps because you were still in elementary school and more interested in cartoons."

Troy laughed and gave his sister a hug. He was glad that he could engage in a real heart-to-heart—more of a mind-to-mind—with her before he drove her back to the airport.

* * *

The weekend following the last exams of the fall semester, Sam Castle received a telephone call. It was his wife, whom he hadn't heard from in weeks. She told him that the relationship with Katashi had disintegrated. One day Katashi had said to her face that not only was she old but also that he wanted to move in a different artistic direction. For the first couple of days after the blow up, Valerie sulked in bed while Katashi packed all of his belongings and moved back to his parents' house. After looking at the emptied house, as well as some past paintings that she had kept in her closet, she decided that she needed to make amends with her husband. She called him that weekend and arranged to come home to Columbus sometime before Christmas, after she had wrapped up her final gallery dates. Sam was so pleased that he cried out, "Jane, you were wrong! Where are you now with your predictions?"

The Wednesday afternoon before Christmas, Valerie flew in from Tokyo. She took a cab home to surprise her husband. When she knocked on the door, Sam knew exactly who it was. Before she stepped inside, he gave her a sweeping hug. He noticed tears fall on his shoulders, and he told her to come inside the house. Dark clouds overcast the sky, and it seemed like the rainfall might start again.

She begged his forgiveness for what had transpired overseas. He said that he was still upset and frustrated over her affair but that he forgave her. He mentioned that maybe he had not been the husband that he thought he was and that's why she had strayed. She said that she still didn't know why she had engaged in such behavior but that it was over. Although the patrons were willing to continue the gallery through next year, she decided that she needed to be home with her husband. Distance had already done enough damage to their relationship, she explained to the patrons. They didn't really understand. She said, "Oh well," and thus she returned to the Midwest from the Far East.

That evening Sam told her about the controversial events surrounding the university and Ian.

"Honey, I don't know what I was supposed to do," he said.

"You did what you had to. You shouldn't have any regrets," she said.

"I don't know if I've allowed myself to be bullied around. I found Ian Mueller's course of action atrocious, but I still don't like the way things unraveled. Those outside agitators really set the campus on its head."

"When did they leave?"

"When the honor council's decision reached Tom's desk, they somehow found out. Although the Black Arms talked about filing a civil suit against Ian on behalf of D'ante and Dominique, apparently Reverend Johnson talked them out of it. He said that there had been enough punishment. Now was the time for healing in the community. Shazzam grumbled a little at the perceived weakness of Johnson, but he ended up driving back to Cleveland with his men. He did, however, say that he would be back down in Columbus if there were any more troubles. I hope not. His presence intimidated a number of the students."

"It seems that you've been definitely going through a great deal since I've been gone."

"And that's the primary reason that I've been upset. I needed you during these trials, and I had nobody."

"I'm here now."

Sam got up from his chair, turned around, and looked at his wife. "Yeah, you're here now—but how do I know that you'll be here tomorrow or the day after? I trusted you when you went away, and look where that trust left me. A cuckold to a Japanese man. How embarrassing. It's a good thing that only a few people know, otherwise I'd feel like attempting hari-kari."

"Don't say such things. I couldn't bear to lose you, Sam!"

"Really? Then what was that about concerning the emotional connection with Katashi? Before couple of weeks ago, I didn't even know if you were returning to the country. You like playing with emotions. Always have. But I still love you. I don't know why, but I do. There are some people who say that you take advantage of my love."

"Who says that? Who?"

"I'm not mentioning names, but they have said things to me."

"But I'm your wife. We've been together for a decade."

"That must've not meant much when you were shacking up with that Katashi fellow."

"But you said that you forgave me. I can't bear it if you'll always hold this transgression over my head. I might as well move on in my life."

"I didn't say that I wouldn't forgive you, but these pains that you've given me will take time to mend. I still do love you, but right now, my mind will always go to Tokyo when you reach out and touch me. I can't help it. I may have been distant, but it's your actions that have strained this relationship. I'm sorry if we're both going to have to suffer a little until all things are worked out."

"I'm willing to take that suffering," she begged.

"Me too, which is why I'm willing to work with you despite all that you've done."

After this discussion Sam and Valerie became more pleasant with each other. Despite underlying tension, they begin to enjoy each other's company. Although images of the virile Katashi flashed through his brain when she leaned forward to kiss him, he began to try to ignore those visions.

As the winter break closed, Sam's thoughts returned to the university. He knew that he had to balance his love for his wife and his love for Central Ohio, or he would end up with nothing, as he almost had these past few months.

* * *

Following the departure of Veronica, Troy became much more open with his father. Although there still wasn't much small talk, they seemed to enjoy each other's company more than before Christmas. One day his father decided to take a day off from work, and they went to go see a matinee. Following the movie, they sat down at the kitchen table and talked.

"It feels good to get away from the job for a while. You'll understand that once you get out in the workforce."

"Dad, I know that I haven't been really talkative since I came back from college. It's not like you haven't tried to draw me out, but I've just been really down. I haven't wanted to talk about it, though."

Mr. Thomas sipped on a lukewarm cup of coffee. "Do you feel like discussing it now?"

"I'm not sure, but I guess that I'll have to force myself. I only have a week before I return to campus." His hands, which were on the table, slipped into his pockets.

"What's it about, son?" He took another sip.

"I told you about my good friend Ian—how he was no longer attending Central Ohio. Well, I didn't really explain why."

"Go on."

"We went to this party on Halloween. It was a costume party. To keep the story short, you see, he went dressed as this character. And part of the costume was that he was wearing blackface. Well, it wasn't really blackface. It had more of a brown tinge to it. There was some sort of blowback afterward, and the end result was that he lost his scholarship and thus can no longer afford COU."

"Do you want to know what I think, is that it?"

"I don't know. Maybe?"

"First, it was probably stupid of your friend to come dressed with that makeup on his face."

"I told him that."

"But I don't believe that a person should throw out his friends for one mistake."

"The thing is that I wasn't even offended by his actions. Other people were creating the whole hullabaloo, which seemed to keep getting more and more out of control. I wanted to stop it, but I couldn't."

"You feel that you let your friend down?"

"I know that I did, but it's more than that. I feel like I'm a coward." Troy hung his head down.

"Why do you say that you're a coward, Troy?"

"It's because I've been a coward before. I just didn't realize it at the time."

"When?"

"I remember that when I was seven there was this incident at the playground. I had befriended this little Asian boy. I think that he was Vietnamese. We were playing down at the bottom of the slide in the sand. He was friendly, so I thought, *Here's a good pal for me to spend the afternoon at the playground with.* Mom had brought me to the park alone. Anyways, while we're playing, this other kid comes flying down the slide. I noticed that he was sliding, so I jumped out of the way, but my Asian pal was still busy digging in the sand. The sliding boy thus knocked him down as he flew off the slide. The sliding kid didn't say anything to the Asian kid, but he walked over to me and said, 'Those Chinky eyes must've blocked his vision. He needs to get those eyes fixed.' I didn't want to appear disagreeable, especially since the sliding kid seemed to be tough, so I nodded my head in agreement. It was just a reflex movement of my head."

"Troy, you were seven. You didn't know any better."

"No, I knew that I should've spoken up and defended that Vietnamese kid, but I didn't. I knew that I had done something wrong when I felt uncomfortable playing with the kid for the rest of the afternoon. Even though the kid didn't hear the other kid's remark, I felt that somehow the Asian kid knew that I was a fair-weather friend. I barely said anything to him for the rest of the afternoon. I didn't even ask Mom to ask for his mom's phone number so that we could get together again."

"That was nearly thirteen years ago. I'm sure that kid doesn't even remember you."

"That's the point, Dad. Thirteen years later—and I'm that same person, the person who's afraid to truly defend a friend because he's worried about what other strangers think. I'm a coward."

"No you're not, Troy. You're a young man with a good head on your shoulders. You're my son. Maybe you could've helped out Ian somewhat more. I don't know. I don't know all the details, but it sounds like that you did your best. You weren't quiet when asked to speak up in defense of your friend. Sometimes you're just put in a predicament and the finality is never what you would desire. It's unavoidable. But how you act through that predicament—that shows what sort of man you are."

"I still feel bad. About both situations."

"Even though I don't think that you did any intentional wrongs, maybe those feelings aren't such a bad thing. At least it shows that you have a conscience. A number of people can barely hold on to that."

"Dad? Another thing."

"Okay?" Mr. Thomas had finished his coffee, and he pushed the mug to the side.

"Were you ever in the Black Arms?"

"Black Arms? That's a rather random question. You mean like a militant group?"

"I guess so."

Mr. Thomas paused and pursed his lips. "No, not really. My brother—your Uncle Charles—was in the Black Panthers for less than a year. I went to some of the meetings with him, but I was only eleven."

"Did you get anything out of it?"

"Oh yes—free pancakes." Mr. Thomas laughed.

"Huh?"

"The main reason my brother went was the food. He was

interested in their message too. However, at the time, my mother had a hard time providing enough food for us. So when she heard that the community center, which was run by a number of Black Panthers, was providing free breakfast, she sent us over there during the weekends."

"But did you get anything out of it besides the breakfast?"

"You mean like a philosophy? No. Neither did your Uncle Charles. It's why he didn't stay that long. Listen, some of those people might have meant well, but ultimately it was as much dress up as that Halloween party you attended. Marching around in a getup might give you some excitement for a short while, but do you really think that it'll give you contentment? I didn't see any contentment in their eyes. Anger, yes. Contentment, no. I just don't think that you can build much on negativity. At least nothing that'll last."

"I think that I'm feeling somewhat better. I don't know yet, Dad. But I just needed to talk some of these things out that had been building inside."

"I'm here for you, son. Not just right now, while you're in my house, but when you go back to college, and even when you leave our home for good."

"Thanks again."

"No problem. I'm going to do some work outside, but if you need me, just yell. I think that your mom should be returning in a little. Why don't we surprise her by ordering some pizza?"

"That's not really much of a surprise."

Chapter 10

Early February brought a sledgehammer of severe weather against Columbus. When the students had returned to campus in January, they had received alternate blasts of snow and rain. January usually is dreary, but that January was bleak, especially with the heavy fog that sifted through the metropolitan area. The one positive thing about the harsh weather was that it forced students to stay inside and study. It was still early in the semester, and the eagerness to do well in their classes still showed on their faces. Troy was one of those students, and he was especially glad that he had been able to get into that Civil War class. A couple of weeks into the semester, his professor informed him that there was going to be a student panel the weekend of Lincoln's birthday. In honor of the upcoming sesquicentennial of the Emancipation Proclamation and Black History Month, the university was hosting a debate between three students on Lincoln's legacy. The student representatives were Scott Stevens of the Scholars for Liberty, Tim Wallace of the BSO, and David Michaels of the College Republicans. Troy asked Rachael if she wanted to go to the debate with him. She declined. She wasn't that big on history, especially not nineteenth century U.S. history. Anyways, she, Milly, and another student were having a girls' night out that Friday. Troy agreed that the night out would likely be more fun than the debate. She, however, promised to come to the black history program at East High

School later in the month.

Troy arrived at the auditorium a little after the debate had begun. No one looked at him when he entered, and he quickly found a seat. He noticed that everybody was paying rapt attention to the stage; an animated discussion was occurring.

"Listen!" Scott said. "Mr. Tim Wallace is right. Lincoln was a racist. It's all in his speeches and writings. Plain as day. For instance, he wanted to send African Americans back to Africa after they had been set free. He believed that from the start of his political career until Booth assassinated him. I mean, he was a member of the American Colonization Society. They didn't want any blacks running around in America."

"First," Michaels said, "let me mention the point that we can agree on. Lincoln was a member of the American Colonization Society. Many notables such as Henry Clay, Daniel Webster, and James Monroe were members at one time or another. It can be debated, however, whether Lincoln changed his views on colonization. Some historians say that he did, while others disagree. However, unlike many other whites at the time, Republican or Democrat, Northern or Southern, he never spoke of blacks as being physically or mentally inferior. While some declared that they were lazy and only slavery encouraged them to work, Lincoln disagreed and said that they had great potential as free men. He also never implied that blacks were naturally immoral or licentious, unlike a number of pamphlets floating around at the same time."

"So then why did he continue in his colonization scheme as long as he did if he wasn't a bigot? Tell me that, David," Scott said.

"I don't know Lincoln's mind or heart. Maybe he voiced the sentiments of his political mentor, Clay, who saw that colonization was preferable to plain emancipation because of what he saw as the unconquerable prejudice of the majority of free white people toward blacks at that time. Lincoln, though, had many black personal friends, such as Frederick Douglass, Jameson Jenkins, and William De Fleurville."

"There you go with the 'my best friends are black' argument."

"And let us then compare that with the other leader of the other states at the time, Mr. Jefferson Davis. Yes, people may have viewed him as a lax slave owner, teaching his slaves to read, as well as allowing them to dispense judgment among the other slaves, but you can't take away the comments that he made at the start of the Civil War. Let me see, according to my readings, in January 1861 he said his state had seceded because the state had heard proclaimed a theory that all men were created free and equal, and this created a basis for the attack on slavery, and that the Declaration of Independence was being invoked to maintain the idea of equality of the races. Now let's go to the vice president, Stephens, who said that slavery was the immediate cause of the rebellion and that protecting that slavery was the cornerstone of the new Confederate government. These aren't my words. These are words from the actors on the scene back then."

"Well, it doesn't matter. Lincoln was a tyrant. The ultimate dictator. He wanted complete federal control over the states." Scott slammed his fist down on the table, splashing some water out of his cup.

"What about the Fugitive Slave Act and other federal protections of slavery? What about the Dred Scott decision?

Weren't these federal aggrandizements over the free states?"

"Still, Lincoln was an ironfisted dictator not only over the South but also over his own citizens. There's the suspension of habeas corpus."

"Which is allowed in the Constitution during times of rebellion. Moreover, the Confederacy suspended rights on a greater basis. Before Lincoln even called out troops to suppress the rebellion, the Confederacy had a newspaper correspondent arrested near Fort Sumter. It's estimated that there were nearly four thousand political prisoners in the CSA."

"That's not true! That's not true!" Scott stamped his feet, while Tim looked askance at the young man.

"Not only that," David continued. "Southern citizens were required by law to use a passport system for domestic travel. Before the war only free and enslaved blacks were required to have such passbooks. Many individuals at the time claimed that such a requirement strained commercial trade and helped lead to the collapse of the Confederacy. And you can't forget that Richmond was under martial law at the time."

"But the South was just resisting the socialism that the North was imposing on it. Look at the tariff situation."

"If any region was supportive of socialism during the Civil War and the antebellum period, it was the states that comprised the Confederacy. A prominent thinker of the period, George Fitzhugh, said that a slave-based economy was more moral than the industrial economy of the Northern states. He said that the antebellum Southern economy was the original Marxist community and that as such the 'benefits' of slavery should be spread beyond blacks to whites as well. The state and local

Confederate governments adopted such viewpoints and preached anticapitalism in antagonism toward the North."

"But what about the stomping of dissent under Lincoln?" Scott stomped his feet in accord.

"It's true that there were restrictions of civil liberties, such as with the newspapers. That was unfortunate. But a similar situation occurred down south. Numerous warrantless seizures, searches, and arrests of civilians occurred from the start of the conflict. Many civilians by the end of the war felt life in the Confederacy was more restrictive than it had been in the antebellum South."

"And do you agree that the inflationary greenback policy in the Unites States was good?" Scott pointed his finger at David in an accusatory manner.

"I don't think that it's a good economic policy from a long-term standpoint, but it was necessary for the wartime economy. But as you've likely read from your sources, the Confederacy printed paper to the levels seen in post–Great War Germany and present-day Zimbabwe. Even if they had won their independence, it was unlikely that they would've gone back to stable gold-backed currency, which the United States did a decade after the war ended."

"Listen, the only reason why the North was able to triumph was because it had that noxious bureaucracy that ran the government instead of Congress. They had all the power."

David just shook his head. "Many citizens of the Confederacy complained similarly about their government. There are estimates that by the height of the Civil War there were nearly seventy thousand civil servants in Richmond alone. They complained that

Davis and the bureaucracy were running roughshod over the legislative responsibilities of the congress and the individual rights of the citizens. Also, going back to that racist Lincoln assertion, during the 1864 campaign, he was accused of being for miscegenation. During his debates with Douglas, he had stated that he was against intermarriage, but he then jokingly replied to the 1864 accusation that if such marriages created good Union families, how could he be against it? So changing circumstances do move individuals to change their attitudes and positions."

Scott jumped out of his seat and faced David. "I've had enough of your rhetoric praising that gorilla Lincoln. You're besmirching the South with all your talk. It's all false. You better take what you've said back or else."

David looked up at him. "Or else what? I'm just stating facts that can be found in primary source documents. If you want to look at them yourself—"

"I don't want to touch your Yankee propaganda, you liar!"

"Although I do have Union soldier ancestors, my family history is Kentuckian. Hardly Yankee. Anyways, this was just supposed to be a friendly debate concerning the sesquicentennial. There shouldn't be any hard feelings." He raised his hands up.

"You get up out of that seat now!" Scott grabbed David's hands and tried pulling him up.

"Get your hands off of me, you delusional thug!" David said, resisting Scott but still trying to remain seated.

Troy looked around, and he noticed a commotion to his right. He saw that a security guard was rushing to the platform.

The guard yelled, "Get your hands off of him, sir!"

Scott failed to let go of David, who was now sprawled upon

the floor. The guard continued to sprint toward the struggle. Suddenly, the guard was upon the two oblivious antagonists.

Within a brief moment, Scott was screaming, "My eyes!" He kicked and squirmed on the floor as the pepper spray blast continued to soak into his eyes and flesh.

Tim jumped off the stage and ran toward the audience seats. Troy thought, *I should've brought some popcorn for this. Even Rachael would've sat through the debate to watch this brawl.*

"Help! Help!" Scott said. "I can't see. I'm blind. Police brutality!"

"Can you please get that person out of here?" David said to the guard. He picked himself off the floor and went back to the table. To the audience, he said, "I'm sorry, folks, that you had to see that violence on the part of a fellow student. Unfortunately, his actions have ended the debate. I'm sorry that it ended earlier than planned, but we have lemonade and cookies in the lobby if anybody desires. Thank you for taking your time out to join us tonight."

Troy got up from his seat. He looked back and saw that the guard was still struggling with Scott. He let out a grin and walked toward the exit doors.

* * *

A week and a half later, Troy met with Rachael and Lola after class at the library. Although he had thought about Rachael, he hadn't spoken with her since prior to the debate. He knew that she had been engaging in some community service work at the beginning of the semester, but she hadn't discussed any details with him. Although they discussed it during their meeting, this wasn't why she had met up with Troy.

"Long time no see nor hear," Rachael said.

"It hasn't been that long," Troy said.

"Considering the circumstances, yes."

"That's true."

Lola was busy scribbling notes from a textbook and didn't look up during this exchange.

"How was that debate?"

"The Civil War thing?"

"Yeah."

"Oh, you should have been there. You might've overheard. It was very spirited. This guy, David Michaels, really embarrassed the two other students. I couldn't believe that Scott lunged out at him, though. They had to get a security guard. Why do you ask?"

"I just picked up the latest issue of the school paper. Look here." She handed him the paper.

"That's crazy that this happened so fast," Troy said, glancing again at the title.

"From what I read and what you told me, Scott Stevens seems to be an unhinged character. I'm not surprised that he left his leadership position."

"Yeah, looking at this article, it says that the members were embarrassed that he even showed up to debate that Lincoln topic. Apparently, he was spending all his time focusing on these Civil War issues, and they felt that he was neglecting other libertarian concerns." Troy silently read a couple of paragraphs. "Actually, the reason he left was that he recently found out from his family that his ancestor had fought for a Tennessee volunteer regiment. As a Union soldier. He was so embarrassed, given his past rebel flag waving, that he felt that he could no longer stay in the spotlight as president. I rather feel bad for him. He seems to be a mixed-up individual."

"Anyways, I'm not here to speak with you about Civil War history or the Scholars for Liberty. I wanted to discuss this tutoring that I have started this semester. It's for second graders."

"What about it?" Troy cocked his head.

"Do you think that I'm spreading myself too thin?"

"I don't know. Have you been able to keep up in your classes? That would be the principal concern."

"I warned you not to overdo it," Lola said, poking her head up from her scribbling. "Even though you have good intentions, devoting yourself to too many extracurricular activities will end up taking a toll. I know this girl, and her hair started falling out after her schedule stressed her out so much. You've lovely hair, chica. You don't want it all to clog up the drain."

"I think that I can handle myself. It's only a couple of hours a week."

"But aren't you doing that medical volunteer work too?" Troy asked. "I mean—helping people is good, but how much help can you give if you burn yourself out?"

"I think that I see where you're going."

"Listen—the last thing that I want to do is discourage someone from helping another person. You're better than me in that regard. I haven't really done any community service since high school. Yes, I know that sounds bad. But sometimes you have to relax; otherwise, you'll be no good when you want to do something good."

"I didn't know that someone could so persuasively make a virtue out of laziness." Rachael laughed.

"It's not laziness. It's common sense. Stretch yourself too much, and you'll snap. Why do you think that we have all these neurotics around this campus? Because they don't listen to their minds or their bodies. They think that if they pile on the activities that they'll make a difference in their lives and others'. They might to a certain extent, but then they'll collapse in on themselves. And what will happen to the people who need help? They'll collapse because they'll have no help."

"To a certain extent, Troy's right. You're a good person, Rachael. But I've seen people tire of their good deeds if they forget to look after their own health. Saying no to some activities may appear to be selfish, but do you really want to give people a half-assed job?"

"You have to make up your own mind," Troy said. "But I don't want to see you burn out of this college. I've already lost one friend, and I don't want to lose another."

"I'm not going to burn out, but you guys are giving me a lot to think about. I'm not saying that I'm going to stop the tutoring, but I'll see how it's affecting me and my other activities over the next couple of weeks."

"That's the reasonable Rachael that we've come to love," Troy said.

"Speaking of being reasonable, how's that class with Professor Brown?" Lola said. "I heard that you had a rough start."

"Of course I did. He's the one who testified against Ian. He's so full of himself that he didn't even recognize me until he called out my name during first day roll call."

"I heard that he was absentminded," Rachael said.

"I heard that his wife was one hot Latina," Lola said.

"I think that she's Brazilian, at least according to Ian, but that's beside the point. The guy is a pompous windbag, and despite the accolades that he's acquired along the way, I think that he's a phony."

"I'm sorry," Rachael said, "but it looks like that you're going to have to deal with him for another three months, unless you drop the class."

"That's not an option. I need the credits."

"When's that talent show that he assigned your class to go to?"

"Why?"

"Because I said that I was interested in attending." Rachael smiled.

"Knowing Brown, it's likely to be ridiculous."

"Still, I want to go. It'll be an experience."

"Some experiences—if it can be helped—are best left alone."

"Still, when's the date?"

"It's this Friday."

"Good thing that I didn't have any plans."

"I have plans," Lola said. "Milly decided to reconcile with me. I don't know why we were at odds. I never really had a problem with her. I think that we're just going to go shopping, though. It looks like I'm going to have to get some new underwear. So then that just leaves you two for a hot date. Ha!"

Troy looked at Lola as strange.

"Oh, you're probably wondering why I mentioned underwear. It's rather embarrassing to say, but you know that last fall a number of students had their unmentionables stolen from their rooms. The president notified us by email that likely there was a pervert running loose on campus. Well, I thought that it was all over, but around the second week of this semester, my clothes ended up going missing again. I think that the pervert is back again. I think that I'm going to have to write another letter to the president." She shook her head.

"That's some freaky business. I hope that it gets resolved soon. But going back to the upcoming event, I don't think that it's really a date, unless Rachael wants it to be." He looked over to her.

Rachael shrugged her shoulders. "We'll see. Just don't get your hopes up for any good night kisses or anything like that. I may not even feel like giving you a hug." She laughed.

"That's okay. I'm just glad that I'll have a fellow traveler to suffer through some potential pretentiousness."

"What are friends for?"

"I don't know if I'm a good enough friend. I'd think that friends wouldn't let friends attend a ridiculous spectacle, but then I'm more of the sadistic type."

"And I guess that I'm more of the masochistic type."

"Come on, guys," Lola said. "Let's leave all this talk to the dungeons and French history."

"You're right," Troy said. "I have to return to my assigned reading anyway. I'll be in the computer lab. And if I don't see you before, then I'll see you on Friday." He pointed at Rachael and then left the two young women at the table.

* * *

Troy drove over to Rachael's dorm. Where his car was standing was a no parking zone, but it didn't matter as Rachael was already downstairs waiting for him. She got into the car, and they drove off, heading to East High School.

Rachael looked amazing to Troy. She was wearing a stunning black dress. Although her hair had been down for the past couple of months, that night she had her hair up in a Grecian goddess style. The style went well with her naturally wavy/curly hair. Her nails were painted dark red, but her lips just had a glimmer of gloss.

"You're dressed fancy for a high school talent show," he said.

"I always try to look presentable, but I'm not trying to show off. I just want to exhibit something to which the kids of Columbus East High could aspire."

"Still, you look really nice."

"Thanks. Although you're not dressed in a tuxedo, that blazer and tie look good on you too. My father would say that you're *farputzt* too."

"Thanks, I think."

"Don't worry. It's Yiddish for 'dressed up nicely.'"

"Oh, thanks then." He smiled to himself. "So let's get this show on the road, or, more accurately, get on the road to the show. Ha!"

Troy and Rachael sped off eastward toward their destination.

Troy thought that he would have difficulty finding parking spots, which were situated around the back of the school, but there were still many vacant spaces. He pulled into a space on the left side of the building and turned off his engine.

"So we've made it," he said. "Glad that there wasn't much traffic going through downtown."

"I know. Usually it's packed on Friday nights."

"Come on, then. Let's find a seat. I think they're going to start in about fifteen minutes."

So the two of them strode around to the front and entered. Although the two of them had never been to the school before, they easily found the auditorium by following the sounds of conversation that they heard from the school's lobby. They entered the auditorium and quickly found seats that were neither too close to the stage nor too far away.

"This is so exciting," Rachael said. "I haven't been to a high school production since I was in high school. I didn't even go to many when I was in school. I was too busy hitting the books, you know?"

Troy nodded and looked around at the audience. Although at first the audience seemed sparse, a number of people began trickling in behind them. He noticed a large number of young people seated, likely high school students. He also spotted the majority of his classmates from Professor Brown's class. He saw a fewer number still of adults waiting patiently for the program to begin. They could've been parents or not. He wasn't sure.

"Where's Brown?" Rachael said. "You know—since he's in charge of this production."

Troy looked around. "He's likely backstage making last minute adjustments. You know that he isn't the only non–high school official that's involved in the show."

"He isn't?"

"No, he's been working with this choir director from a local church. I haven't seen the guy, but I heard that he was at that protest for D'ante as well. From the people who saw him, I heard that he was pretty gay."

"Troy!" She looked at him in shock.

"I'm not saying anything about that in a judgmental way—I just heard that he was flamboyant in a funny way. So chill a little. I think that the program is about to start anyway."

Troy didn't notice who he was, but a few seats over was a man dressed in a sharp bright blue pinstripe suit. It was Reverend Dill Johnson, who was still riding high after his courageous stand during the Ian-D'ante controversy, at least according to the East Columbus community. He folded his hands into his lap, and he appeared to stare straight ahead, although one could not tell since he had on a fine pair of shades. However, when the school principal walked on stage to the microphone to announce the start of the black history program, he took off his sunglasses and returned them to his pocket.

"Welcome, students and guests, to our Black History Extravaganza this evening. We have many exciting performers for you. To those who don't know me, my name is Principal Henry Baldwin of our illustrious high school, Columbus East. Since late fall our students have been preparing their pieces for you. Black History Month is a time when we as a community can come together and reflect on the past, the present, and the future of our people. We've come a long way from the time we were snatched from the shores of the motherland, through the struggles of slavery and segregation, unto the time where a black man resides in the highest office of the land, not as a servant but as president. Yes, we've come a long way, but we still have many roads to travel. These students tonight are traveling some of these roads, hopefully to their hopes and dreams. Many have endured struggles as well. Things such as poverty, parentless households, gang intimidation, as well as the proliferation of drugs in the community. These students are survivors. Although people could call them heroes, they do not wish to be called that. They want people to know them only as survivors of a society that can and has beaten them down. As you look on and listen to their art pieces, I want you to reflect on that. Yes—not just enjoy their pieces but also reflect on their lives and your lives."

"I wonder how much longer he will go on with these preliminaries," Troy whispered into Rachael's ear.

As Troy turned his attention back to the stage, Professor Brown and Maurice, both wearing prismatic dashikis and mudcloth kente kufi caps, stepped from behind the curtains to the microphone.

"I would like you in the audience to give a round of applause to the codirectors of this evening's events," Henry said and stepped aside for Herbert.

"I would like to thank you all for coming to the event," Herbert said. "Looking out at the filled seats, I see the grand appreciation that you have for the work of these youths. I know that they appreciate you appreciating them. Although I enjoy my work as a professor, I've really enjoyed working with these performers from the East Columbus neighborhood. They've taught me much—that I should be grateful for the blessings that I've received. Being cloistered away in academia, one forgets that at times, but I don't think that I can forget that anymore. I don't think that I can say anymore, but thank you again for letting me have this experience in working with these brilliant young people."

"I have the privilege of working in music and performances with the Oh Lord, Give Us Strength Baptist Church down the street," Maurice said. "Sometimes when you're engaged in the same activity week in, week out, you take for granted the gifts that you've been given. First, I see my boss out there. Hey, Reverend Johnson!" Maurice waved to the preacher, who rose, bowed, and quickly sat down. "Now back to speaking about gifts. I had failed earlier to appreciate the beauty of young people as they expressed themselves through their various art forms. I now know the gift of seeing the world through youth. Even as a youth, I failed to see life through that viewpoint. Seeing life as a youth is both frightening and thrilling at the same time. While I helped these students to grow artistically and emotionally, they helped me to grow as well, as a person. I will forever cherish that experience."

Come on! thought Troy. He looked around and noticed that many of the audience members felt the same. While a few gave their rapt attention to the preprogram speeches, others were messing around on their cell phones, dozing off, and whispering into the ears of their neighbors.

"Now we give you the start of our program," the principal said. "Again, the students have worked hard, so please treat their parts with the dignity that they deserve. Thank you." At that, the three walked back behind the curtains.

Troy looked at Rachael, who was staring straight ahead, wondering what would come next. He looked down at the program and noticed that intro music would be next. Thirty seconds later it started. *My God!* he thought. *They're playing the opening music to The Lion King. I guess that they had to start with some dramatic African-style score, but couldn't they've picked something a little less cliché?*

The audience loved it, with many of the younger attendees singing along about "the circle of life." It almost could've been about their lives, if they were animated beasts of the movie screen.

Afterward a young man walked up to the microphone. He was dressed in a dashiki, like the codirectors, but his attire wasn't very colorful. His garb was just black with drippings of brown and gray. He had in his hand a folded piece of paper, which he unfolded after clearing his throat.

Troy again looked at his program. It said that next up was Jamal Piggot, who was going to read a poem. *I wonder if it will be any good*, he thought.

"My blackness does not define me. It tells the world what they see. But do they envision the true me? They may see shades of darkness coming to them as in a fairy tale, but it does not define me. Maybe my heart is black, or maybe it's not. Or maybe it's both when viewed from different angles, but does the color or noncolor define me as a young man? I say no. When I wear my clothes the way that I want them worn, does that define me? When music is played the way I want it played, does that define me? It may tell the world, here is black as blackness defined, but is true blackness defined the way the world wants it and has it defined? Perhaps I define blackness as being beyond all colors and thus chained to no colors; has the definition changed, or have I redefined myself? What if black upon white and white upon black were not inverses of each other, but the same items seen though redefined eyes? Tell me, if I choose to wear these black clothes, have I moved beyond color? Yes. And no. For having embraced this black color, I have in effect embraced all colors, including white, which is the absence of color. Thus I'm colored and noncolored, a person of color, and a person without color, nonwhite and white, black and nonblack, and all the spectrum in between. That mystery defines me. The internal blackness with the external blackness is combined and divided to create a person where blackness matters, but it doesn't matter. That mystery defines me. If I choose to embrace the blackness, maybe it will choose to neglect me, and if I reject the blackness, maybe it will claw after me. These are the mysteries of the spectrum. But should I let it define me? Let definition be a word. And let black be a word. And let them define themselves separately so as to find the truth within and without of blackness."

Jamal stepped away from the microphone to thunderous applause. Troy only tapped his fingertips together. He didn't even know if poor Jamal deserved that recognition. He looked around at his fellow audience members, and he wondered if they even understood the message of the work, if it had a defined message.

The next acts that stepped up on the stage were generic. They were either solo or group rap acts. The only variety that many in the audience could discern was the flow speed. Some were fast, and some were slow. Most were of a moderate pace. The topics did have range, somewhat. Both Troy and Rachael, however, wondered how much teenagers from East Columbus knew about Bentleys and Cristal. They probably couldn't even get into the Axis or Fahrenheit nightclubs. Troy looked over to the reverend and noticed him bopping his head to the rhythms of the jams. He wondered if he was even paying attention to some of the questionable lyrics.

Before the final performance, there was another round of

spoken word poetry. Troy couldn't believe it at first, but they were as confounding and baffling as Jamal's earlier piece, if not more so. Everybody walked off the stage with either a smile or frown that said, "Here are my words and deeply felt thoughts; you can take it or leave it." Troy believed that most of the audience left them there when they exited the auditorium.

Maurice and Professor Brown returned to the stage after these prose poems. Troy thought that maybe the night's events were over, but he looked again at the program and realized that there was one last performance.

"Friends, we have one last treat for you," Brown said. "Maurice and I have personally worked with this group. We expect that you will enjoy the performance of theirs. Most people know that people of African descent express themselves through movement, especially dance. We and the dancers that you're about to see have developed choreography and a musical program that we believe tells the story of our people and our struggles from the Old World to the New World. We have constructed it for your enjoyment and education. Please let the music and the visuals flow over you. I present to you the East Columbus High Motherland Dancers."

The codirectors went back behind the curtains, while the two dozen female dancers came flooding out. As they prepared to start their routine, the intro music played. It was Paul Hardcastle's "Introduction." It really got both the dancers and the audience into the right frame of mind.

Troy looked at the stage in shock and turned his head toward Rachael. "Can you believe what they're wearing?" he said. What outfits they wore left little to the imagination. Dressed in black, red, green, and gold low-cut unitards, they exhibited more cleavage and camel toe than a beach in late July.

"I know," she replied. "It's rather risqué for a high school production. I think back to that costume I wore, but I probably wouldn't even wear these. I would be afraid that I would pop out somewhere."

"I know." Troy turned his head to the right, not wanting to look at this high school display. He noticed that the reverend had leaned forward, his mouth almost salivating at the show.

Troy tapped Rachael on the shoulder. "He's enjoying it." He pointed his thumb in Johnson's direction. Rachael rolled her eyes.

Soon the dancing truly revved up with the next song on the program, Hardcastle's "King Tut." Under the bright lights, the dancers were tutting, bopping, bouncing, strutting, and shaking in choreographed rhythm. A narrative from Professor Brown started booming over the music: "From the days of Ancient Egypt, our Nubian princesses have told their stories through the slinky, seductive motions of supple bodies. The hot sun that warmed the skin and hearts of those back in ancient times still heats our fevered blood today. Listen to the rhythm. Let it take hold and transport you back to those times." Troy thought that visual spectacle was probably transporting the men in the audience to somewhere less noble in mind.

The dancers kept their groove on when the music switched to Hardcastle's "Rainforest" (the original version, of course). Brown's voice again rose like the Wizard of Oz: "Slavery took them from their African homelands and transported them across the Atlantic to the New World, from South America to North America. Although their spoken languages were lost, they didn't lose that primal language within all of us. See them gyrate their chains off. See them gyrate their bodies to freedom." The dancers definitely gyrated.

Following that display, the final music and dance sequence started. Mitch Murder's "Inner City Chronicles" played in the background. "Many of our brothers and sisters, some of those among us, have to deal with the struggles of inner city life," the Brown voice said. "Let us never forget those that we have lost. Perhaps their examples can point us in the right direction, toward a brighter future. We can only hope for change." With that breasts and butts shook to a violent conclusion, and the dance sequence and the program ended with applause, whistles, and catcalls. The reverend, among other individuals in the auditorium, was up on his feet, hollering for an encore. Troy and Rachael sat there for a moment, stunned, as the principal, Professor Brown, and Maurice returned to the stage to give their closing comments.

Walking out of the school to his car, Troy asked Rachael, "How did you find the program?"

She was silent for a moment. "It was different. What about you?"

They got into the car. "I might later come up with a number of descriptions, but 'different,' like you said, will have to do for now. It's the best that I can say."

And they drove westward back to Ohio Central.

* * *

"Thanks for letting me make up for that weird experience at Columbus East," Troy said. "I don't know what I was thinking when I allowed you to come with me."

Rachael got in Troy's car and bucked up. "It was a spectacle. I could say that. And that dancing. I like dancing but that was…"

"I know what you're going to say. A bit too much."

"Yeah, if I wanted to watch jiggling like that, I would just look in the mirror."

Troy didn't say anything further on that topic. "How was your spring break? I forgot to ask before you left, but did you go on any exciting community service adventures?"

She laughed. "No, I actually played semihooky. I went down to Miami and stayed with Lola. I followed your advice and became lazy for a short while. Nothing but sand and surf."

"Good. How did you feel afterward? Guilty?"

"Actually, no. I felt rather refreshed, so afterward I've felt more willing to get my nose to the grindstone, so to speak."

"I'm glad that you gave yourself time to relax."

"What about you? Did you just go home to Cincinnati?"

"Actually, I just stayed in Columbus. The dorms, of course, closed, but Jay allowed me to stay at his place. I didn't do much because I was somewhat depressed."

"Why?"

"You know, I was just thinking about Ian and his situation. I thought that maybe he would call me by now to give me some updates. I read on Facebook that he was thinking of going to a different school next fall. They might want him to play for their team. But I don't even get anymore Facebook updates—one day I went online, and I saw that I was unfriended."

"I'm sorry to hear that."

"Yeah, me too."

"Hey, maybe Ian will come around. You just have to give it some time. He's probably still hurting over the university's decision. I would be hurt."

"I get what you are saying."

"But Troy, let's turn our attention to something more positive. Where are you planning to take me this evening? I know that you said that you wanted to keep it a surprise, but can't you tell me now?" She laughed. "I hope you aren't kidnapping me—that I would have to protest."

He smiled. "No, I'm not kidnapping you, but I still want to keep it a surprise. Okay?"

"Okay, I guess."

Troy drove through the city until he reached downtown.

Rachael spoke up. "I think that I know where we're going."

"Where?"

"The Museum of Art."

"I guess that wasn't much of a surprise, was it? You're probably like, *Oh boy, a museum*."

"No it's fine. I've been there before. When my parents brought me for freshmen orientation."

"I myself wasn't much of an art person before this year. I enjoyed some stuff, but I didn't really sit down and reflect on things. This past year has given me much to reflect on. I've been to the Museum of Art twice since the start of this semester. I've really enjoyed the time to just look and think about the pictures." He briefly looked at her and then refocused his eyes on the road.

She nodded and acknowledged him and then went to take a sip of her water.

They arrived at the museum parking lot around seven, and they then briskly walked into the building.

"You know why I chose a Thursday evening to come here?'

Troy said.

"Why? Discount for students?"

"No, that's every day. I chose tonight because it's the day they're open the latest. Normally, they would be closed right now, but this gives us time to walk around and look and talk."

Troy stepped up to the counter and purchased Rachael's admission ticket. They began strolling around the galleries.

Rachael spoke up after a few minutes. "Did you know that my family has art pieces around our home? They're not as famous as what we're looking at, but my father likes to collect things."

"Do you appreciate them?"

"What?"

"The art pieces. Do you appreciate them? It's a simple question."

Rachael had a puzzled expression and she turned her face toward him. "I don't know. I never really thought about it. They were just there, either hung on the wall or placed in the dining room."

Troy waved his finger. "You see—"

"See what?"

"Nothing."

"What do you mean 'nothing'? I think that you are implying that because my father has a little bit of money, I don't appreciate the art as much as someone without easy access."

"It has nothing to do with money, Rachael." He shook his head. "What I'm trying to get across is that because the pieces are in your presence day in, day out, you may not acknowledge them. Of course, at your house, you may walk by a painting and know that it's a painting, but you might forget that the painting isn't just a painting. There are a personality and ideas behind the work that created it. It's not just a canvas. Listen, I'm not saying that you or your father are the type of person who just has something because it fits the surroundings and it looks pretty. I'm saying that when you don't have something, anything, in your grasp, you often fail to appreciate it. This goes whatever your social class. I didn't mean to offend you—if I happened to—with what I said. I probably should've been more tactful in trying to explain myself."

"No, it's all right. I think that I see what you're talking about. And to answer your question, I haven't appreciated those pieces in my house. Part of it is because I'm not much of an art girl, but I could also agree with your argument. To me, the pieces are just there, or they've come from out of nowhere. I guess that we all could look closer than just the surface in some matter or another. Not just in art appreciation.

Troy nodded, and they continued down the gallery.

"Do you have a favorite piece here?" Rachael said. "You mentioned that you've been here multiple times. There has to be something that keeps drawing you back."

"Actually, we're coming up to one of the pieces right now. Look over there."

Rachael looked over to her right.

"This portrait was done by Emerson Burkhart. He was a local painter. The model that he painted here was also an artist—Roman Johnson."

"I've never heard of them before."

"Yeah, but you can still see the gift that Burkhart possessed. He wasn't a genius. No, but he was gifted at what he did. He marched to his own beat. You see, at the time everybody was going wild about abstract art, but Burkhart here stuck to his guns and painted realistic portraits such as these. It didn't make him really famous beyond Columbus, but he kept his integrity by continuing to paint the way that he wanted to paint. I like to look into those eyes of Johnson's and think about what he was thinking about while Burkhart painted him. Then I try to think about Burkhart, what he was thinking about at the time. This was the height of his career. He had to know that he wasn't going to become any more famous, but he kept doing what he loved—no, what he needed to do."

"Seems like you've spent a lot of time thinking about this, Troy."

"Primarily I enjoy the way he caught a moment in the life of a real human being. I find that amazing. But I also wonder about the men themselves—how they lived and thought, how that made them who they were."

"I do think that it's a thought-provoking portrait. Just standing here, I could probably become entranced by it."

Troy pointed her in a different direction. "I want to show you something else. This one you might recognize from television or one of your textbooks. Come on."

They walked down the gallery, admiring the other twentieth-century American paintings, until they came across *Morning Sun*.

"Hey, I remember that one. I mean that I've seen it here when I first visited. But like you said, I first saw this in one of my high school textbooks. It's rather depressing, even more so than that portrait of Roman."

"It's supposed to be. Look at the woman's eyes. Black. And

unlike the portrait, this woman is just staring off into the distance. It's unsettling, but I like that, in a way. Why? Because no matter how many people we surround ourselves with, sometimes we feel just like that woman in the picture: alone and wondering if everybody else feels the same too. The painter and the subject were Manhattan-based, but it applies to any city, including Columbus. No, it applies to wherever you live. We're all disconnected from each other to some extent. Some people try to reach out, but most people are like that woman, sitting on their beds, hoping and praying for something different but going through the motions and not changing a thing about their lives. You know, Rachael, I don't want to be that person."

"I don't think that anybody does, but a lot of people just end up falling into a rut."

"I guess that's why self-examination and contemplation are good from time to time. You think that it halts your journey, but it actually keeps you going on the path that you choose."

"Troy, you know that you're an interesting guy?"

"Thanks, but I want to show you some other pieces before they close. I believe that we have another half hour."

Chapter 11

Sam slammed the phone down again. He had been receiving mysterious phone calls weekly at his house since mid-March, and it was now the penultimate week of classes. He couldn't trace who was calling him. Either the number came up blocked, or if a number showed on the caller ID, it went to a random or disconnected number. Moreover, the voice differed during each call. The first couple of times, he didn't tell Valerie, but by the third week, he had to tell someone. It had become creepy and suspicious.

"That annoying voice was on the line again," he said to Valerie, who was sitting down in an armchair, reading the newspaper and having her morning coffee.

"What did they say this time?"

He turned around and walked over to her. "It was a gruff, rather noble voice today. Latin again, as well. It said, '*Magni dominator poli. Tam lentus audis scelera, tam lentus vides?*'"

"What does that mean?" She put down the paper and looked up at him, puzzled.

"It means that the individual believes that an injustice has been done him or her."

"Honey, maybe it's just a prank. It's the end of the year. You know how the students are. They're restless and ready to go home. The seniors are about to get their degrees. It's probably just that. I'll tell you what. Once commencement is over, the phone calls will stop. Trust me." She got up and gave him a lingering embrace.

He backed away a little but touched her shoulder. "I just don't want anything to happen to you. There are some dangerous people out there. Dealing with all I've had to this year has really shown me that. Crazy people all around. Just think of that pervert running wild on the campus. It's even made me a little crazy."

"No sweetheart, you're not crazy." She brushed his cheek. "But I was thinking to myself, who do you think would be calling all this time?"

"I don't know. I've got a lot of enemies it seems." He paused while he walked around the living room, deep in thought. "I don't want it to be, but I'm thinking that it might be, Ian."

"The kid that left the school because he lost his scholarship?"

"Yeah, him. I'm going to give his parents a call to see what he's been up to. I don't want to prejudge anybody, but these calls have to stop. It's turned into pure harassment. It's making me lose my mind."

"Don't worry, Sam. We'll get this solved ASAP. Just think that in less than three weeks, the spring term will be over. We can then think about the vacation that we've wanted to plan. How's that sound?"

"Sounds great, Val. Sounds great." He left the living room and went to his study, where he stayed until dinner.

* * *

"You won't believe what just happened, Rachael!" Troy said; he had just come from class.

"What? You seem so excited." She brushed her hair while Lola looked on the two from her corner of the room.

"I didn't know that I had it in me, but I do."

"Have what in you?"

Troy scratched his chin. "I went and told Professor Brown off."

"You did what?" She stared at Troy in disbelief.

"I had been pondering the conversations that we've been having, and I just couldn't take it anymore. I told him that although I enjoyed a few things that he had taught over the semester, I believed that he was doing a disservice to me and my fellow students. I said that his academic research might be innovative, but what lasting value did it have? And that it seemed rather prurient too. I said that it might be difficult to hear your work described as a waste, but I could no longer sit there and take in the nonsense and feeble opinion that he spouted as truth and reality. I couldn't do it."

"What did he do then? Did he yell at you to get out of his class?"

"Actually, no. He sternly but softly told me to sit down. He said that he wanted no more outbursts but that I intrigued him. Never before had he had a student with such balls to denounce him in front of a class. He disagreed with my sentiments, but said that I was entitled to them even if he viewed them as fallacious."

"So after class did he tell you off?"

"No," Troy said laughingly. "He actually invited me to dine with him and his wife this upcoming Thursday. The penultimate day of classes."

"What did you say? I'm intrigued."

"Surprisingly, I said yes. I don't know why."

"Maybe you just want to articulate better what you said in

class."

"Perhaps. Or likely I just wasn't thinking straight."

"That's okay. Where are you planning on going?"

"He said a place called HiddenOak. It's relatively new, but I haven't checked the menu online."

"HiddenOak?" Lola lifted her head up from her textbook. "That place is rather expensive, especially for a college student."

"Oh, I think that I can scrounge some money together. It's the end of the year anyway. I should go ahead and splurge."

"Did he say that you could bring along a guest?" Rachael asked

"He didn't mention anything, but I don't know why you can't join me. Believe me, I don't want to be alone with the Browns, even though I've already made a commitment."

"If it's any trouble, then I can pay for my meal. I mean if it's already expensive, it'll be doubly expensive if I tag along."

Troy held his hand up. "Just a minute. I'm still riding a masculine high on Professor Brown's 'I've got balls' comments; don't you go busting them now. This can be our second official date, so I'll pay."

"What do you mean, second date?" She showed a sly grin.

"Well, what do you think the trip to the museum was?"

"I'm just kidding, Troy Thomas. And yes, you can pay for me. I'd again be honored to join you on one of your little adventures."

"Again, it'll be Thursday. I'll call you to tell you the exact time that I'll be picking you up."

"I'm telling you, Troy," Lola said, "it'll be expensive. You'll be shelling out the bucks that night."

"Don't worry; I'll be prepared." Troy thought of something

and laughed. "By the way, how—or should I say where—is your underwear?"

"Oh, shut up!" She threw a box of tissues at him.

"She lost another pair last week," Rachael said. "But she can't be too angry because Marie lost two pairs as well." Rachael turned to Lola. "At least in a few weeks, you won't have to deal with the pervert running around."

"Yeah, whatever." Lola went back to her textbook.

Troy opened the door, but before he exited he said, "If I don't see you before, I'll see you Thursday night."

"It's a date."

"Yep, it's a date." Troy exited and left the girls to their studying.

* * *

"What did your father say about you going to LA for that internship?" Rachael said.

Milly adjusted her skirt and then took a sip of her coffee. "He basically told me that if I was going out there, then I was on my own financially."

"You mean that he's cutting you off."

"Not exactly. He's eased up a bit since spring break. He just told me that he wasn't providing me with any additional money. I would even have to pay for my plane ticket, but that doesn't matter as the internship covers my travel expenses. He'll still pay for my school when I return to Ohio in late August."

"If you return. If you get a big movie role, then I believe that you'll be saying to your pops, 'Bye,' or, in your case, '*Ahn-nyeong-hee-gyea-se-yo.*'"

"Yeah right; it's just an internship. I don't even think that I'll be in front of the camera. I'll probably be just the coffee girl." Milly lifted up her cup. "Good thing I'm getting practice now."

"I hope that all will turn out right for you. I want to see you on the big screen one day."

"Or on the small screen or Broadway. I just want to act and prove to my father that it's a respectable profession. You know—that I won't lose my mind and act crazy in Hollywood. I think that this internship will help him change his thinking a little."

"Are you well prepared for your finals?"

"As well as a person with little interest in the sciences can be. Yeah, if I do well on my finals, I'll make it through with at least Bs in my biology and chemistry classes. My father is probably hoping for As, but he was likely only going to get those if I had interest in the material. But let me switch up the topic a bit. How are you and Troy doing?"

"We haven't really gone anywhere since the art museum. Just meeting up for lunch a couple of times in the cafeteria. He's, however, invited me to dinner at HiddenOak."

"How romantic! And expensive!"

"It's expensive. I've checked the menu. For the romantic part, I'll go halfway. It's not just going to be me and Troy. Professor Brown and his wife invited Troy, and I'm kind of tagging along for the ride."

"Oh. I'm sure that you'll still have a good time. I heard that the food is delicious. I wasn't able to go, but my parents went when they were in town."

"I just hope that there is no terrific argument like the one that occurred in his class. I know that both Troy and Brown can be opinionated."

"Don't worry, Rachael. Just enjoy yourself. You'll have a lovely dinner, and then the following day will be Blowout, the last day of classes. I'm looking forward to Friday myself. I may even surprise Lola and drink a little—being responsible, of course." Milly chuckled to herself.

* * *

Troy and Rachael arrived at HiddenOak around seven-fifteen. Professor Brown had told Troy that he had made reservations for seven-thirty. During that conversation Troy told his professor that he wanted to bring along a lady friend. Brown said that he had made reservations for three but that a quick call to the restaurant should be the only necessary thing for adjustments. Troy and Rachael walked into the establishment, looking around for the professor and his wife. Troy mentioned to the host that they had reservations under the name of Brown. She directed them to the dining room, and the two sat down at the white tablecloth setting.

"Mr. Thomas, good that you could join us this evening. This is my wife, Sophia."

Troy introduced himself to her and then introduced Rachael to Sophia. Herbert had remembered Rachael from the hearing.

The waiter came up and asked the group for their drink orders. They gave them.

"I believe that we can also start ourselves off with some appetizers," Herbert said. "What would you like?" He looked over at Troy.

Troy looked over at Rachael for her answer. She didn't say anything.

"I'm fine with just my tea, for now," Troy said. Rachael also declined to order appetizers. Herbert and Sophia decided to split a half dozen fried oysters.

"So Mr. Thomas, you disagree with my research, do you? What are your specific reasons, besides bourgeois prejudice? Huh?" He had an oyster while he waited for Troy's answer.

"I just think that your conclusions are incorrect. Not everything can be boiled down to prejudice. Yes, problems still exist in this country, but problems exist in every country. The players across the globe might change, but it's still a human society problem, not just a problem of one group or one country. I think that you forget that sometimes in your lectures."

Herbert wiped his mouth. "Mr. Thomas, I think you may be spending too much time with elements that have been twisting your thinking." He glanced over at Rachael, which Troy noticed.

"What does that mean? Just because I have some friends who are paler, I shouldn't take into account their opinions? First, this is my analysis. Not Rachael's or Ian's. Or anybody else's." Troy hesitated. "I don't want to bring your wife into this, but that's rich anyway, coming from a man whose wife is blonde and paler than most of my friends, including Rachael sitting here."

Herbert cleared his throat. "My wife is a person of color."

"Who says? The government? And which government? Why should it matter anyway? All this year and years before it, I've heard people like you in school and on television speak about unity and coming together. How can you say and believe it when your actions repeatedly do the opposite? I don't doubt that you believe in your research and its supposed value to humankind, but have you ever reflected on whether you've shamboozled yourself?"

"Listen here. I'll converse with you, and I'll debate you, but

I'm not going to be lectured by some sophomore with a superficial understanding of these matters. I'm a valued member of the academic community. My accolades in numerous humanities and scientific journals support this assertion." His face turned smug, and he violently crossed his arms.

"Maybe that's the problem, Professor."

Both Rachael and Sophia looked on the confrontation with nervousness. Rachael didn't say a word, but Sophia told her husband to watch his temper.

Troy continued. "Speaking of mysteries, what about that incident that occurred at Brown University. Somebody asked you about it in class, but you've kept it all such a big secret. What are you hiding from us?"

"That wasn't my fault!" Herbert slammed his palm down. Some of the other diners turned and looked at their table. "The student didn't believe."

"Believe what, Professor?"

"One day, I told my class the Yoruba story of 'The People Who Could Fly.' You've probably heard of it. The enslaved Africans relearned their heritage and language. A wise old man taught magic words that gave the gift of flight. They spoke those words, and they escaped to freedom and back to Africa. A student came up to me after class, expressing his desire to know those words. I told him. I then explained that they would only work if he had faith in their power. He swore to me that he did. A week later he opened the window during class and jumped. He dropped like a rock."

"Of course he did. It was just a story. A tale that that gave those people back then hopes, but fantasy nonetheless."

"No!" Herbert slammed his hand down again. "It's truth. He just didn't believe, like you don't believe. We African peoples have magic coursing through our skin and blood. Just look at Michael Jordan…"

"I'm sorry to say this in front of your wife, but you're more delusional than I thought." Troy shook his head in disbelief.

"You may say that, Mr. Thomas, but one day you'll see. And doubt will tremble and fall before reality." Herbert waved his finger at both Troy and Rachael

When the main courses arrived, they ate in near silence. Although the food was excellent, the previous conversation had left a bad taste in Troy's mouth. An uncomfortable fog hovered over the table and halted any further conversation between Troy and Herbert. After they paid the checks, the couples headed outside to their cars.

"Mr. Thomas, I haven't told anybody else yet, not even the president, but I'll be taking a semester off from the university," Herbert said as Troy and Rachael began walking to the car. "Do you know why?"

Troy just looked at him.

"I've been chosen to help out with the president's reelection campaign in Ohio. How does that sound?"

"It suits you, Professor Brown."

"Is that all that you can say?" Herbert had his arm around his wife's waist.

"Yes." Troy walked Rachael back to his car and left the perplexed Herbert and Sophia standing in the parking lot.

* * *

Blowout arrived as it does every year—in an explosion of

excitement. It was the last day of classes for the school year. Students threw their notes up in the air and then quickly gathered them up to prepare for their upcoming exams. In class both students and professors drank. Most didn't cause great disturbances, but one year a class had become so rowdy that the desks and chairs in the classroom had been utterly destroyed. The administration didn't like that at all. In some cases, the students skipped class entirely. Generally they don't miss much as the professors are exhausted by the end of the year, and if the students haven't gotten the material down pat, it's too late to do anything about it at that point.

Rachael, Lola, and Milly returned to the Spanish House after their last classes. Rachael and Milly were sober, but Lola was mildly intoxicated. They held her up as they walked upstairs.

"You know, you guys are really funny," Lola slurred out. "Even you, stick-up-your-butt Milly. You're some of the best friends that a girl could have."

Milly gave a weak smile but continued to hold her as they made their way to the girls' room.

At the door Milly noticed something. "Did you guys forget to lock up before you left?"

"Why?" Lola said.

"Um, the door is unlocked." Before entering, she pressed her ear up against the door. "I think that there is somebody in there. Should we go in?" Milly looked over at Lola, whose facial expressions began to change.

Lola roared, "Of course we should go in! It's my room! And there better not be anybody in there!" She moved Milly's hand away from the knob and thrust the door open.

There was somebody in there. A man sprawled out. And in the midst of dumped dirty laundry, he had Lola's panties over the top of his face.

"Oh my God!" Rachael said. "It's the pervert." She and Milly just stood there in shock, while Lola slumped to the floor and began to crawl to the almost-oblivious man.

"Who's there?" the man said. "I know that there's somebody here!"

Lola, standing over the man, yanked the undergarment off his face and began screaming. "You dirty dog! How could you? You're the pervert that's been yanking all of my stuff. I should've known it was you all along when I caught you upstairs during that party."

Tom, who was also reeking of alcohol, cowered under the blows that Lola delivered onto his body. He meekly cried out, "Please stop. Stop. I can explain the situation. I can explain."

"How can you explain?" Lola continued. "We all three saw you sprawled out with them on your face. You'll explain all right. Explain to the administration. The administration—you are part of the administration!"

Tom crawled away, but the three young women followed him around the room. Lola had an especially fierce look.

"Please stop; I can explain." He continued to scramble backward. "I know that I have a problem. It's not my fault. Please don't turn me in. I may lose my job."

"I'm sorry, Dean LeBlanc, but we're going to have to call the police," Rachael said. "You may have issues, but you're going to have to work them out with some professional help. Besides this incident here, you seem to be a nice man, but you've violated the students' trust by your trespassing and item pilfering."

"I'm sorry that I'm a sick man. I can't help it. I'm sorry." He turned his head and began weeping in a corner of the room.

Milly asked a pertinent question. "How did you get into the students' rooms? The lock wasn't broken." The other young women looked at Tom, still cowering and weeping, to see if he would answer.

"I know that it was wrong, but I stole and copied one of the maid's keys. I was desperate. I have such a love for the Latina students." He struggled to rise.

"You're right, Dean LeBlanc," said Lola. "You're a sick man." She looked away from him in disgust.

He lifted up his hand in protest. "Please, please, don't tell my wife. I don't know what she'll say."

Rachael stepped forward. "I don't know what she'll say either. We're not going to tell Mrs. LeBlanc, but she's going to know as soon as the rest of the university finds out."

He dropped back into a ball and continued to cry while Rachael grabbed her cell phone from her purse and dialed the campus police.

* * *

Sam reclined in his chair with his hands folded behind his head. He looked at the clock and saw that it was a little after eight. He then looked again at the copy of the police report. He couldn't believe it. His good friend Tom was the rampaging pervert. He thought, *You think that you know people, but how many persons have buried secrets like that? You wonder sometimes.*

Sam picked up the phone and dialed his wife.

"Honey, I'm sorry that I couldn't make it for dinner. I'll warm it up when I come home. I know that you went out of your way to prepare something nice for me, being that it's the last day of classes. Something unfortunate came up. It's actually very upsetting, but I'll talk to you about it when I get home. You said what? That creepy caller called again about two hours ago? Okay. I'll be leaving the office in about fifteen minutes. I just have to finish up with some leftover paperwork. I love you too. See you in a little." He hung up the phone, heard the office door open, and noticed a presence.

"Sam, I see that you're still here," a campus police officer said.

"Yeah, I'm just making some finishing touches to these documents. Crazy day, huh?"

"Yeah. Dealing with the drunken antics of the kids and then that Tom business." He halted. "You probably don't want to talk about it, do you?"

"Not really."

"Okay. I'm going out to get myself something to eat. You want something?"

"No, I'm good. My wife made dinner, and she wouldn't want me to spoil my appetite." He smiled at the officer.

"All right, Sam. I should be back in about fifteen minutes." The officer stopped and craned his neck past Sam. "Good Lord! What is that?"

Sam turned around and noticed that two of the academic buildings across the campus gardens were in flames. He could see people rushing out of the buildings and away from the spreading fire.

"You stay here," the officer said. "I'm sure that they already did, but I'm going to make sure that the fire department has been called. There could be people still in those buildings." The officer ran out of the room and down the stairs, rushing over to the radiant conflagration.

Sam sat back down in his chair and looked out the window. He thought that maybe he should walk across the gardens to see if he could offer any help. He realized that he might just get in the way, and so he sat back down. He was about to pick up the telephone when he heard a crash behind him and a slight whizzing noise.

"What's going on now!" he said. He turned around and saw that the glass was broken. He got up from his chair and noticed an arrow sticking into the carpet. He went over and noticed that there was an attached note. He read it: "And since there's no justice in earth nor hell / We will solicit heaven and move the gods / To send down justice for our wrongs." "Who did this?" he said, walking back toward the broken window. He looked down and saw a familiar face.

An elderly bearded man, dressed in a toga, topped with an Olympic wreath, dropped his bow and picked up a javelin.

"George! What the hell are you doing?"

He yelled up to Sam, "I've come to claim your life! You purloined mine."

"You're crazy, George. Put that weapon down. There's been a lot going on today. You see those buildings on fire over there."

George turned around and then back toward Sam. "Who do you think set the snare for the fall?"

"Dear God! You've committed arson and now you're out for me."

"True, Sam. Vengeance is in my heart; death, in my hand." George raised the javelin even higher. "Blood and revenge are hammering in my head."

"I know that you took that early retirement very hard. I'm sorry. It was a difficult choice for me, but I had to do it. It was basically beyond my control."

George paced back and forth on the grounds below. He looked upward. "You could've stopped it, Sam. You know how the system works. Foolish Samuel! Did you not perceive that the board is but a wilderness of beasts? You could've fought for me, but you threw me into the pits of shade. I curse your name."

"Listen to reason. We can get you some help. I know of a good doctor."

"It's too late for me. Too late for you as well. You smell that fire. It rises underneath your feet."

Sam could smell something awful. He left the window and made his way down the hall to the stairs. He jumped back. The ground floor baked with heat. It wasn't completely ablaze, so he ran downstairs and fled to the front door. He took a cloth and tried opening the door. It wouldn't budge. Something was blocking it from the outside. He pounded on the door and yelled, but only the crazed former professor was in the vicinity, so there was no response. By this time the smoke had become so heavy that he knew that he couldn't stay there. He looked to the back but noticed that it was no longer an exit. The fire apparently had been set back there first, and the area was completely engulfed. He ran back upstairs and into his office.

"You crazed fool!" he yelled out to George. "What have you done? You've left me here to die." Although he had closed the door behind him, smoke began pouring through the cracks. He knew that in a few minutes the fire would be seeking him out in the office.

"You will pay for your sins in fire and ash!" George screamed.

Sam hesitated. He looked down at George and back at the approaching fire. He couldn't take the smoke or heat any longer, so he took a chair and bashed through the rest of the glass. He closed his eyes and hurtled himself to the ground floor.

There was a crunch. "Dear God!" Sam cried out, clutching his leg. He writhed in pain along the pavement.

George, with his javelin poised, stood over the broken president. "Is not my sorrow deep, having no bottom? Then be my passions bottomless with them." He was about to strike when Sam raised his hand and yelled out, "Stop!"

"Stop!" also came from another person running toward the situation.

George turned and looked at a sprinting figure, but he then redirected his attention on Sam. "Die, die, Sam Castle and your shame with you, and with your shame, my, George Grave's, sorrow dies!" He lifted the javelin again, but he then heard the crack of gunfire. He looked at his chest. Then he heard another and fell to the ground, still clutching the javelin.

"Sam, Sam, you're all right?" the campus officer said.

"Do I look all right? My foot is broken, and a madman almost murdered me. This on top of the day's previous events. I think that I'm just dandy." He tried to get up, but he slumped back, his body aching.

"I'll call for the medics to come over here ASAP. Don't worry. Hang in there."

"I'm not going to die. I just need a vacation after all this."

Ten minutes later the EMTs arrived and put Sam onto a stretcher.

"Get a hold of my wife, if you will. Here's her number." He scribbled the number on a scrap of paper that he had in his pocket. He turned to the officer and the EMTs. "I guess that I won't be having that dinner after all." He groaned, and they put him into the ambulance, which was soon speeding off for the hospital.

* * *

The following morning the campus arose from the chaos. Students passing by the burnt presidential office and academic buildings looked on with wonder as they walked to the cafeterias or headed out to study for the upcoming exams.

Before heading over to get breakfast, Troy walked to Rachael's room. He knocked, and she opened the door.

"Where's Lola?" he asked. "I didn't think that she was normally up this early on Saturday mornings."

"She's at the library. She really wants to do well on her exams since next year will be her last."

"I see."

"You heard about that former professor and President Castle and then Dean LeBlanc? Crazy stuff."

"Yeah, I saw the flames from a distance while walking back to my dorm. Thank God there were only a few people in the buildings and they made it out safely. The fires really did a number on those buildings. And I then saw the information concerning the dean's arrest this morning, before I left. Lots of stuff went down. I still can't believe that somebody was shot and killed on campus. Obviously, the guy was crazy. I went and saw the remaining splatter on the ground. I got chills."

"Graves definitely lost it. I don't like what he did, but I sort of feel bad for him—like the dean.

"You feel bad for the dean? Why?"

"We were the ones that actually caught him. They probably mentioned in the news report that the police found him in a student's room. That was here. We found him knee-deep in Lola's things."

"No kidding."

"Definitely not kidding. It was terrifying and pitiful at the same time. I hope that his relationship with his wife isn't too damaged, although she is probably embarrassed to hear that her husband was nose deep in the student dirty laundry during the school year. If I were married to him, I would be too."

"Do you know what's going to happen to him? I mean, career-wise?"

"Nope. I just pray that he gets the help that he needs. It's likely, though, that he's not coming back here. I definitely don't think that the board of trustees would allow it. It'd cause too much outrage—not just here but on the outside as well."

"Have you found out about President Castle?"

"He's being treated at the hospital—a broken leg from that fall. Luckier than he could've been with that javelin business. But he'll survive."

"Do you think he'll make it to commencement?"

"Probably. You know him. He'll never miss a program. Even if he has to hobble up there to give that speech, he'll be there. And the seniors will be there cheering him on."

"Yeah." Troy rubbed his cheek.

"I didn't tell you, but Milly is being allowed to go to an internship in Hollywood. It's unpaid, so she'll have to find some other work while there, but it appears to be a nice stepping-stone into the business."

"Good for her. Did her father relent, or is she just pressing on despite his opposition?"

"It's a little of both. I told her that if somehow she got a good-paying role out there, she probably wouldn't want to return."

"Well, with all that's gone down this school year, she has experience dealing with craziness. I know that I do." His mind went back to all the school term's previous shenanigans and the characters involved. He closed his eyes and shook his head.

"Speaking of crazy individuals, have you had further contact with Professor Brown? I know that dinner was just a couple of days ago, but you were in class yesterday, weren't you?"

"No. Yesterday morning he sent an email and canceled the final class. Said that there wasn't anything more to be taught for the semester. Since the final exam is going to be a take-home essay, I don't think we'll be seeing each other for a while."

"Especially if he is getting involved in politics."

"Yeah."

"I myself can't wait for school to be done. Guess what, though?"

"What?" Troy was intrigued as Rachael had a giant grin.

"I'm going on a medical volunteer tour this summer to Nicaragua."

"That's great, but I already knew about that."

"But that's not the thing. I persuaded Lola to join me. She was hesitant at first, but she then thought about it. She said to herself, *Why not?* Nicaragua has beaches on which she could tan. Moreover, she could get to know the roots of her father's side better. So, we've decided to fly out there in June."

"How long are you staying?"

"I don't know exactly, but at least four to six weeks. I don't want to just drop in and then leave."

"I understand. But are you leaving any time during summer for me?"

She laughed. "I think that I can work something out."

"Okay." He smiled.

She continued, "So, do you also have special plans before you return to the madhouse known as Central Ohio?"

"Not really. I think that I might stop by Ian's house. He hasn't yet returned my emails, but I'm sure that he'll come around. Maybe the surprise visit will get to him, and he'll open his door."

"There's possibilities."

"I guess that effort is all that one can have sometimes. That's one thing that I've found out lately."

She stirred in her seat. "Are you hungry?" She got up from her chair. "I'm starving."

"I was going to go to the cafeteria, but why don't we go out somewhere?" He motioned with his arm.

"Sounds good to me. Can I choose where?"

"Sure, but I'll drive."

"You always do."

They briefly embraced and exited the room.

ABOUT THE AUTHOR

Christopher Fried (1985-) lives in Richmond, Va. His poetry collection *All Aboard the Timesphere* was published in 2013. He is a contributor to *NewRetroWave*.

www.ingramcontent.com/pod-product-compliance
Lightning Source LLC
Chambersburg PA
CBHW021109110726
47900CB00007B/2105